MURDER AS A FINE ART

For
Alexis Grace
and
Lliam

MURDER AS A FINE ART

John Ballem

A Castle Street Mystery

THE DUNDURN GROUP
TORONTO · OXFORD

Editor: Marc Côté
Copy-Editor: Natalie Barrington
Design: Bruna Brunelli
Printer: Webcom

Canadian Cataloguing in Publication Data

Ballem, John
Murder as a fine art

"A Castle Street Mystery."
ISBN 1-55002-385-3

I. Title.

PS8553.A45M87 2002   C813'.54   C2001-904037-7   PR9199.3.B36M87 2002

1 2 3 4 5   06 05 04 03 02

THE CANADA COUNCIL FOR THE ARTS SINCE 1957 | LE CONSEIL DES ARTS DU CANADA DEPUIS 1957

Canada

ONTARIO ARTS COUNCIL
CONSEIL DES ARTS DE L'ONTARIO

We acknowledge the support of the **Canada Council for the Arts** and the **Ontario Arts Council** for our publishing program. We also acknowledge the financial support of the **Government of Canada** through the **Book Publishing Industry Development Program** and **The Association for the Export of Canadian Books**, and the **Government of Ontario** through the **Ontario Book Publishers Tax Credit** program.

Care has been taken to trace the ownership of copyright material used in this book. The author and the publisher welcome any information enabling them to rectify any references or credit in subsequent editions.

J. Kirk Howard, President

All the characters in this book are fictitious.
Any resemblance to actual people is purely coincidental.

Printed and bound in Canada.
Printed on recycled paper.

Dundurn Press
8 Market Street
Suite 200
Toronto, Ontario, Canada
M5E 1M6

Dundurn Press
73 Lime Walk
Headington, Oxford,
England
OX3 7AD

Dundurn Press
2250 Military Road
Tonawanda NY
U.S.A. 14150

MURDER AS A FINE ART

"... behold a pale horse, and its rider's name was Death ..."

Revelation 6

prologue

High in the Canadian Rockies is a place like no other — eight rustic studios set in the midst of a dense forest of lodge pole pines. Artists, writers, painters, and composers from all over the world flock to this mountain retreat to work on their art in individual studios, free from the distractions of the outside world.

The resort town of Banff, slightly more than an hour's drive from the city of Calgary, is located in the beautiful Bow River Valley at an altitude of 4,500 feet. Surrounded by the towering and jagged peaks of Mount Rundle, Sulphur Mountain, Cascade Mountain, and Mount Norquay, it is an irresistible lure for tourists, skiers, and mountaineers. Although the town itself is small, with a permanent population of only 7,000, it is by far the largest settlement in the Banff National Park, a 2,300 square mile nature preserve. The small number of permanent residents is dwarfed by the five million visitors who stream through the park gates every year.

Overlooking the town of Banff, and facing the massive rock ramparts of Mount Rundle, the Banff Centre of Fine Arts is one of Canada's most important cultural institutions, providing instruction and training to aspiring artists in their various disciplines. Under the umbrella of the Banff Centre is the Leighton Artist Colony, which caters only to established artists with a proven track record, and offers no instruction, but rather an opportunity to work undisturbed in a setting of inspiring beauty.

As a writer, I have had the benefit of several stays in the colony, and know full well just how creative an environment it is. It is also a closed world, where you are thrown into the company, for weeks or months, of fellow artists from many different countries and cultures. Ideas flow freely at mealtimes and at get togethers in the lounge. In fact, this exchange of ideas and experiences is one of the great benefits of colony life. Nor, let it be said, do these exchanges always remain on the philosophical level. The artists come to the colony on their own, and find themselves in one of the world's most romantic settings and in the company of attractive and creative companions. It is not surprising that relationships spring up, to flower and usually to die, when the lovers' stay is over.

Add to this the fact that the artists are established, well known, and come to the colony with large reputations and, in many cases, even larger egos. It's a heady mix—one that sets the stage for murder.

chapter one

Alan Montrose was sprawled headfirst on the concrete steps below the stairwell landing. A narrow trail of blood ran from his nostrils down his right cheek. Blocked by a dense, tangled eyebrow, it filled his eye socket and was spreading across his forehead. Blood seeped from his ears and dripped onto the concrete.

Laura Janeway's hand flew to her mouth to hold back the gorge rising in her throat. She swallowed hard, the sound loud in the bare concrete stairwell. The sickening angle of his head told her that Montrose was beyond help. Nevertheless, she forced herself to feel for a pulse, pushing back the sleeve of his dressing gown to expose his wrist. His skin was still unpleasantly warm to the touch and she was aware of the rank stench of alcohol. Finding no sign of life, Laura sat back on her haunches and looked up at the top landing. The railing was dangerously low, coming barely above her knees. For some time she had been meaning to mention it to Kevin, but had never gotten around to it.

Kevin would have to be notified. Stepping carefully over Montrose's lifeless body, she climbed the stairs to the landing and opened the door to the hallway of the sixth floor that housed the members of Leighton Artist Colony. Once in her room, she glanced at the clock on her bedside table. Twelve-thirty. Kevin would be in bed asleep, but that hardly mattered. The phone rang four times before Kevin Lavoie picked it up. "Jesus!" he swore softly after Laura told him about finding the body. "We don't need that!" As the artist colony's coordinator the burden of dealing with all the details surrounding the death of a member would fall on him. "I'll get dressed and come right over," he told Laura, asking her to make sure that nothing was disturbed.

Laura went into her bathroom and splashed cold water on her face. Squaring her shoulders, she went back to the stairwell. Taking a firm grip on the metal railing, she leaned over and stared down at the body sprawled on the steps below. Montrose had either been in bed or had been preparing for bed. His portly body was dressed in pyjamas and a paisley silk dressing gown. What in the world had brought him out here to meet his death? Some of the initial shock had worn off, but that head lolling helplessly to one side made her wince. She sat down on the top step and stared straight ahead at the blank concrete wall as she waited for Kevin.

She didn't have long to wait. Kevin lived in a nearby duplex provided by the Banff Centre and he joined her in less than fifteen minutes. His blond hair was thinning, and he wore a perpetually harried expression that went with coping with the artistic temperaments that came and went in the colony. Laura was fond of him.

"He's been drinking," Kevin said as he bent over the body. He sounded relieved as though he had found a defence to any claim that might be brought against the Centre. "Not that there's anything unusual about that."

"The police will have to be informed," said Laura.

Kevin looked as if he would have liked to protest, then sighed, and said, "You're right, of course." He patted his pocket. "I'll use the pay phone at the end of the hall."

"10-11." Corporal Karen Lindstrom replaced the microphone in its clip and told the driver to proceed to Lloyd Hall at the Banff Centre, but not to turn on the siren or the flashing lights. Minutes later, the corporal's terse "10-7" told the dispatcher that they had arrived at the scene.

Lavoie greeted the Mountie like an old friend. He seemed relieved that she was the one who had responded to the call. After introducing her to Laura, who was struck by the policewoman's Nordic good looks, he gave a nervous little laugh and, with a suggestive sniffing of the air, said that it shouldn't take much detective work to figure out what had happened. The corporal's expression was noncommittal as she pulled a video camera from a carrying case and began to film the scene. The young constable with her, who looked as if he was not long off a Saskatchewan farm, was securing the area with yellow crime scene tape.

Kevin Lavoie flinched when the Mountie focused her camera on the low railing. Then she switched it off and climbed up to the landing to look down at the corpse. Gazing around at the bare concrete walls she said, "There's nothing here he could grab on to."

Turning around, she carefully backed up against the railing. "The deceased looks to be a little bit taller than I am," she said, almost as if talking to herself. "It would have been quite easy for him to topple backwards and land on his head. Was he a heavy drinker?"

"I understand he got sloshed every night," replied Lavoie. Laura confirmed this with a reluctant nod.

"The circumstances seem consistent with an accident." The corporal seemed to be choosing her words with care. "However, the body can't be moved until the medical examiner gives the okay. He should be here before too long. While we're waiting, maybe I could get a brief statement from each of you."

"I don't have anything to contribute," Kevin told her. "I was in bed when Laura called. I got dressed and rushed over. Now, if you'll excuse me, I have to tell the president about this unfortunate accident." The Mountie nodded permission and Lavoie hurried away.

"Correct me if I'm wrong, Ms. Janeway, but I get the impression that you're not as convinced as Mr. Lavoie that we're dealing with an accidental death."

Laura looked at her thoughtfully before replying. With her blond hair neatly tucked under her cap, ice blue eyes, and clear skin glowing with good health, Corporal Lindstrom looked as though she could pose for a recruiting poster. "What troubles me," Laura said finally," is what Alan was doing out here in the stairwell at this time of night. Or at any time, for that matter. He never used the stairs. You've seen how overweight he was. And where was he going in his pyjamas and dressing gown?"

"Anything else?" The corporal was looking at Laura keenly. "For instance, how did the deceased get along with the other members of the colony?"

Laura hesitated before saying, "You'll find out about this sooner or later. Alan Montrose was suing Jeremy Switzer, a New York playwright, for libel. There was a nasty scene between them at dinner tonight."

"Libel? That's pretty serious. Is your room on this floor? We can talk there if you like."

Laura nodded, thinking to herself that the policewoman seemed to have more than a passing knowledge of the Banff Centre. Corporal Lindstrom told the constable to let them know when the medical examiner arrived.

Laura's room, like all the others on campus, was spartan in its simplicity, but she had added little touches — a vase of freshly cut flowers, a few photographs, and stacks of illustrated art books — that gave it a homey, lived-in look. With Laura's permission, Corporal Lindstrom switched on her tape recorder and placed it on the narrow built-in desk.

"Everybody in the colony knows the story," Laura began, "but it really came to a head tonight. Montrose fancies — fancied — himself a gourmet and, as usual, he had fortified himself against the Banff Centre cuisine with several stiff drinks in his room and brought a bottle of red wine to the table. In many ways, he was a pompous ass and the drinks didn't make him any better. Or any more tactful. Montrose is — was, rather — a professor of English at Mount Hedley, a small college in Illinois. He wrote marginally successful plays on the side. Jeremy also writes plays. Appallingly bad plays. Jeremy is a dilettante, a professional art colonist who flits from one art colony to another. I have often thought that his plays are just an excuse to go on living the colony life. But Montrose took *his* plays very seriously, just like he took himself. About a year ago, poor Jeremy wrote an article for a literary magazine accusing Montrose of plagiarism, claiming that the plot of his latest play, *The Hostile Act*, had been lifted *holus-bolus* from the doctoral thesis of one of Montrose's graduate students. It caused quite a sensation. Montrose issued a furious denial, and Jeremy unwisely pressured the student into launching a court action against Montrose for plagiarizing his work. The case fell apart in the courtroom when Montrose was able to prove that he had been working on the play long before the student enrolled in his class."

"And the shit hit the fan."

"I couldn't have put it better myself," said Laura after a startled pause. "And then it turned out the student's claim had been motivated largely by revenge because Montrose had intervened and prevented him from obtaining an academic post. Ever since he arrived here last month, Montrose has been taunting Jeremy, and tonight he announced that his attorneys had commenced an action against Jeremy in California, where he lives when he's not at an artist colony. The magazine and the student are also being sued, but Jeremy knows he's the real target. The student is judgment proof because he's broke, and the magazine limps along from one financial crisis to another. You know how it is with those literary magazines."

"No, I don't. But you will tell me."

"They couldn't even afford the premium for libel insurance. Poor old Jeremy is out there all by himself, twisting in the wind. He basically lives on a family inheritance, that's what enables him to live the colony life. The lawsuit could wipe him out. His attorneys are trying to settle, but Jeremy knows Montrose would never settle. He wanted vindication and revenge in the full glare of a public trial."

"Jeremy Switzer seems to have confided a great deal to you."

Laura shrugged. "We've known each other for years. We both like to come here to Banff whenever we can. Besides," she added somewhat ruefully, "I seem to be the kind of person that people like to tell their troubles to."

"I think it would be useful to have a talk with this Mr. Switzer. Is he on this floor?"

"Two doors down the hall. I'll show you."

The Mountie knocked on Jeremy's door, softly at first so as not to disturb the other residents, then more forcefully. But there was no answer.

"He could be in his studio."

"At this hour?"

Laura grinned. "This place operates on a twenty-four hour basis."

The young constable came down the hall to tell them the medical examiner had arrived. The corporal turned to Laura. "Look, I hate to impose any further on you, but could I ask you to go down to the colony with Constable Peplinski," she paused to introduce them, the Mountie touching the peak of his cap in an informal salute, "and see if Mr. Switzer is in his studio?"

As they stepped outside into the cold night air and began walking down the cinder path that led to the artist colony's studios, Laura learned that her intuitive guess had been correct — he was a farm boy. Constable Peplinski had grown up on a farm a few miles north of Moose Jaw, Saskatchewan. Banff was his first posting since graduating from the RCMP Depot in Regina, he informed Laura as they walked past the deserted music huts toward the little footbridge that separated the colony from the rest of the Centre.

The Banff Centre for the Arts was a large, university-type institution, which offered post-graduate courses and instruction in music, painting, writing, dance, and drama. The famous "campus in the clouds" was located on Tunnel Mountain in the Canadian Rockies, overlooking the resort town of Banff, and attracted students from all over the world. The Leighton Artist Colony was an exciting offshoot of the Centre. It consisted of eight individual studios deep in a pine forest on the eastern edge of the campus. It was designed to be a working retreat for professional artists with a proven track record — a chance for them to escape the demands of everyday life and concentrate on their art, whether it be writing, painting, or composing music. Each artist was assigned one of the studios for the duration of his or her stay, which could be up to three months. The artists lived in the Centre's residence, and took their meals with the students and staff, but did not take courses or attend lectures. They were there to *create*.

"That's the Hemingway Studio," said Laura after they had crested the footbridge and approached the first building, a round hut with shingled sides.

"I've read some of Ernest Hemingway."

Laura smiled in the shadows cast by the single light burning outside the round, shingled studio. "I know why you would think that. But it's not the case here. The studios, there are eight of them out here in the woods, are named after the architects who designed them. Peter Hemingway was an Edmonton architect."

Laura wasn't surprised to see that the lights were on in the boat studio. Erika was putting in brutally long hours in her determination to finish her book before her time in the colony was up.

"That boat looks kinda out of place way up here in the mountains."

"Parks Canada thought so too," Laura replied. "They claimed it was out of keeping with the mountain setting and fought like mad to keep it out. But they were overruled. The Centre has a lot of clout in this town."

"How did they get it in here with all the trees?"

"Lowered it in by helicopter." Laura pointed out a wooden frame building at the edge of the path. It was barely visible in the darkness. "That's my studio."

"Were you there tonight?"

"Yes. I painted until eleven or so, then relaxed in the whirlpool and took a swim. And then ... well, you know what happened after that."

"Do you always use the stairs instead of the elevators?"

"Most of the time. I do it for the exercise."

Jeremy's studio, a round tepee-like structure, built of logs and designed by the celebrated Canadian architect Douglas Cardinal was at the far end of the cinder path that circled the colony. It was dark, as Laura expected it to be. It wasn't Jeremy's style to toil late into the night. However, there were times when he would sit in his studio at night, sipping wine and listening to classical music.

Now that they knew Switzer wasn't in his studio, Peplinski was in a hurry to get back to the scene of the crime. He picked up the pace and they soon left the colony behind them. As they rounded the music huts and stepped onto the parking lot, they saw an ambulance parked by the side entrance of Lloyd Hall. Because of the slope in the ground, the parking lot was level with the third floor. Out of consideration for the sleeping residents, the ambulance's lights were turned off.

Peplinski left Laura at the door of her room, thanked her for her help, and disappeared through the stairwell door. Laura stood for a moment looking up and down the hallway. All the doors on the floor remained shut. The fire door that led to the stairwell effectively sealed off all sound from that direction, and if any of the artists happened to hear footsteps in the hallway, they would have ignored them. They were experts at minding their own business.

Or they would have simply assumed it was Marek Dabrowski on his nightly treks to Isabelle Ross's room.

chapter two

Laura's sleep was interrupted by vivid and frightening dreams. She would wake up and then drift back to sleep again, only to fall into another mini-nightmare. In the morning the only one she could remember was a bulging eye spouting blood while its owner leered malevolently at her. In the bizarre way of dreams, the leering head was crowned with a top hat.

Soaping herself in the shower, Laura felt the incurve of her waist and smiled. Thanks to the Centre's bland cuisine, she had lost five pounds since her arrival. She had weighed herself yesterday at the pool, and 135 pounds at five-foot-eight was just where she liked to be. Stepping out of the shower, she scrubbed herself vigorously as if trying to cleanse herself of last night's gruesome discovery. Montrose had not endeared himself to her or to anyone else in the three weeks he had spent at the colony. She hated the way he had tormented Jeremy over the impending lawsuit, but in his own unpleasant way he had been enjoying life and didn't deserve to have it snatched away. No one did. Life was too precious and fragile a gift.

After towelling herself dry, she slipped into a terrycloth bathrobe, picked up the hair dryer and walked over to the window that overlooked the woods where the studios were located against the background of a snow-clad Mount Rundle. Richard Madrin was returning from his morning run. In his early forties, Madrin was fit and very good-looking. His handsome features were saved from being too preppie by the quizzical gleam of intelligent good humour in his grey-green eyes. And, so far as Laura knew, he was unattached. The break-up of his long-term relationship with a famous female television newscaster had been widely written up in entertainment and television guide magazines a few months ago. Laura was attracted to him, there was no denying that. But she had no intention of letting another man control her life. Her ex-husband was also an attractive man, but he had turned into a control freak as soon as they came back from their Caribbean honeymoon. He insisted on managing the household finances himself, refused to let her have a bank account, let alone a credit card, discouraged her from driving a car, and alienated her friends. In retrospect, Laura wondered why she had put up with it for five frustrating years. But she had been young — only nineteen — and unsure of how to assert herself against his self-confident and domineering personality.

It had been art that finally freed her. Driven by an irresistible urge to paint, she had found the courage to defy him and enrol in an art college. When her paintings began to sell, she left him and later filed for divorce. Laura smiled at the memory of the scandalized look on the judge's face when she said she wasn't asking for any of the marital property or any financial support. All she wanted was to be *free*.

Although it was pretty clear that Richard Madrin was interested, he had not made any advances. He would have heard the rumour — a rumour she had planted herself — that she had a lover back home in the Denver. There was no such person, but being taken for a "monogamous single" left her gloriously free to pursue her art without the distraction of dealing with would-be lovers.

Turning away from the window, she began to dress, her firm resolve to remain unattached and independent somewhat shaken by the fact that Richard Madrin was an attractive and intelligent man who didn't come across as someone who was into control. On the contrary, he was easygoing and laid back. He could well afford to be laid back, since he had made himself independently wealthy by flipping office buildings. And his books, which he wrote as a sideline, were beginning to sell extremely well. Sideline or not, he took his writing seriously and was rumoured to have retained a public relations firm to keep his name and his books in the public eye. He couldn't control the book reviewers though, and some of the "serious" critics took delight in putting down his thrillers. But none of them were a patch on Henry Norrington, Laura thought as she let herself out of her room.

With her usual interest in people she liked and in what they were doing, Laura, after getting to know Richard, had gone to some trouble to familiarize herself with his books. The Centre's library didn't carry fiction, but she had bought the two that were still in print at The Banff Book & Art Den on Banff Avenue, and by phoning several second-hand bookstores in Calgary, located one which had three of his out-of-print books. The bookseller was cooperative and agreed to package the books and put them on the Banff shuttle bus. He also promised to look for *Mission to Mykonos*, the only one she was missing, and send it to her.

Richard's books were not the kind Laura would normally read, but she found them, if not earthshaking, at least entertaining and surprisingly informative about places and events. They certainly didn't deserve to be savaged the way Henry tore into them in the reviews he wrote for the Associated Press newspapers. These thoughts occupied Laura on the short walk to the Banquet Hall in the basement of Donald Cameron Hall.

The Banquet Hall was buzzing with the news about Alan Montrose. Kevin Lavoie had made the announcement to the members of the colony and the Centre's graduate art students. He emphasized that it had been an accident and, while unfortunate, shouldn't be allowed to interfere with their studies or their art.

Laura joined the other colonists at the table where they usually sat. As always, John Smith sat at a table by himself, downing one large glass of orange juice after another. Today the tall, gaunt performance artist was dressed head-to-toe in black, complete with a bowler hat set squarely on his head. His face was smeared with white greasepaint. Reminded by his hat of her too-vivid nightmare, Laura gave a slight inward shudder.

Kevin Lavoie was passing among the tables, answering questions about the fatality and assuring everyone once again that it had been an accident. As he approached their table, Henry Norrington declared, "Of course it was an accident. I've told you before that that low railing is an accident waiting to happen."

"It already has," interjected John Smith from his nearby table.

Ignoring the interruption, Norrington went on, "You really should do something about it, Kevin."

"We're looking into it," Lavoie assured him, knowing full well that months would pass before anything would be done about it. Fixing it now would amount to an admission of fault on the part of the Centre.

All conversation at the table ceased when Jeremy Switzer joined them. "How come everyone looks so glum?" he asked blithely as he sat down, carefully arranging his breakfast tray in front of him.

"Alan Montrose was killed last night," Laura told him.

"What? What do you mean 'killed'? How did it happen?"

"He fell down the stairwell on the sixth floor."

"I'll be damned!" Jeremy's fingers were combing his beard. He cleared his throat and looked around the table. "Well, as you all know, there wasn't any love lost between Alan and me, but I'm sorry he's dead."

"It was an unfortunate *accident*," Lavoie said soothingly.

"Murder will out," John Smith chanted in his flat monotone as he put down his napkin and stalked out.

"John Smith always hopes for the worst," remarked Laura.

"He had been drinking, I assume?" asked Richard Madrin as, freshly showered and shaved after his run, he sat down next to Laura. He had heard about Montrose from a student he met on his way to breakfast.

Lavoie nodded glumly. "He reeked of the stuff. At first I was relieved because it could absolve the Centre from any liability, but then I realized it could backfire on us. As we all know only too well the provincial government is hell bent to make even deeper budget cuts, and we're a prime target. Montrose falling down the stairs dead drunk in the middle of the night is going to give them some great ammunition. A lot of politicians think of artists as parasites living high on public funds and this will only confirm it."

As he replied to Madrin's question, Lavoie's tone was deferential. The wealthy speculator in commercial real estate was a potential donor to the Centre, which depended on private donations to supplement the steadily shrinking public funding.

Erika Dekter got to her feet. "It may sound callous, but I've got work to do." Erika was only five-foot-two and there wasn't an ounce of fat on her diminutive frame, but she had an appetite out of proportion to her size. The breakfast she had just finished included fruit juice, three fried eggs, bacon, sausage, and several slices of toast. Erika was slightly hyper and had the metabolism to go with it. Her creative energy must burn up a lot of calories too, Laura thought. The two women had become fast friends during their stay in the colony.

"I'll go with you," Laura said and drained the last of her coffee. As they climbed the Banquet Hall staircase to the ground floor, she said, "Isabelle looked absolutely devastated, I didn't realize she and Montrose were close."

"It wasn't because of Montrose," replied Erika dryly. "Isabelle's family is coming to visit her."

"Oh no!" breathed Laura. Visits from "outside" were regarded as disruptive influences and were not encouraged. But this went far beyond that. Isabelle Ross and Marek Dabrowski had been carrying on an intense love affair for weeks. A *coup de foudre* was the way Henry Norrington, in his own pedantic fashion, had described the first meeting between the pianist and the dark-haired composer. Everyone on the sixth floor of Lloyd Hall was aware of Marek's nightly excursions down the hall to Isabelle's room. The attitude of the other artists toward the star-struck lovers was non-judgemental and even protective. It was the sort of thing that was almost inevitable in the hothouse atmosphere of the colony.

"She'll have to put her rings back on," Laura murmured. "You said her 'family'. What family does she have?"

"Her husband. He's a doctor. And a young daughter."

On the way out Erika picked up the box lunch she had ordered. They walked the short distance to Lloyd Hall and remained chatting together for a few moments on the front steps. Erika was going directly to her studio, while Laura was going to take a break in her room to sort out her thoughts and mentally prepare herself to resume painting. "How's the book coming?" asked Laura. "You're certainly putting in some incredibly long hours."

"I can't seem to stay away from it. A couple more chapters and I'll have finished the first draft." Erika was about to say something more, but broke off as John Smith suddenly appeared before them. Doffing his bowler, his painted face devoid of expression, he executed a more than passable tap dance, ending it with a low bow.

Laura clapped her hands, while Erika remained stony-faced.

"That's very good, John Smith," said Laura, using, as he insisted upon, his full name. She very much doubted it was the name he had been christened with; it was the kind of stripped-down name performance artists often choose for themselves. John Smith produced two pink carnations, seemingly out of the air, presented them with a flourish, and skipped away, whistling to himself.

Laura fingered her carnation. It was plastic. Typical of John Smith. With him, you never knew what was real and what was false.

"I bet I'll find him hanging around my studio," Erika muttered. "He's beginning to seriously annoy me."

"He certainly has fixated on you. I'd like to think that he's harmless, but I'm not at all sure he is."

"I'll go along with it for now," said Erika as she began to walk away. "But if it keeps up, I'll tell him where to get off."

"Which would probably be just fine with John Smith," said Laura. "It would add a note of tension to his 'art'. That's the problem in dealing with performance artists. They stand everything on its head."

If only Geoff were here, thought Erika as he headed for the colony. He would know how to handle John Smith. But Geoffrey Hamilton was history, she reminded herself sternly. She would have to deal with John Smith on her own.

As the Banquet Hall emptied, Kevin Lavoie made his way up to the small office in the administration building that had been assigned to Corporal Lindstrom for the purposes of her investigation. From past experience he had some reason to hope she could be prevailed upon to handle the investigation into Montrose's death with discretion. She had been gratifyingly discreet about that bizarre business of the poison pen letters and the bearded poet. But the Mountie quickly disabused Lavoie of the notion that an investigation into a death under suspicious circumstances could be handled in the same low-key fashion.

"We're dealing with a possible homicide here, not a gay lovers' tiff," she said. "You might as well brace yourself to deal with the media."

Lavoie found out how right she was as soon as he returned to his own office. His secretary informed him that both a newspaper and a television reporter were downstairs in the reception area, requesting an interview.

"I'm told you wish to see me." Jeremy Switzer stood in the open doorway.

Corporal Lindstrom looked up and closed her notebook. "Thank you for coming, Mr. Switzer."

"I didn't realize I had a choice," he murmured as he sat down on a chair facing her across the desk.

She responded with a wintry smile and took a moment to size him up. Laura Janeway had described him as a professional art colonist and he certainly looked the part. He was wearing a thick woollen sweater over an open-necked denim shirt and faded blue jeans. His thinning brown hair was tied back in a sparse ponytail, and the lower half of his face was covered with a salt-and-pepper beard. He seemed blithely unconcerned as he waited for her to speak.

"You know, I'm investigating the death of Mr. Montrose?"

"Yes. But I don't know why," Jeremy said with a shrug. "Montrose topples over a railing and breaks his neck. End of lesson."

"No one seems to know what he would be doing on the landing at that time of night. Apparently he never used the stairs."

Jeremy snorted. "The old fart was probably so pissed he didn't know where he was."

"I understand he was suing you for libel?"

"So you've heard about that load of crap." As always, when the lawsuit was mentioned, Jeremy was defiant, but the Mountie saw his fingers tugging at his beard, as if to distract his thoughts by the self-inflicted discomfort.

"You weren't in your room last night. At least not at the time it happened."

"No, I wasn't." Although it was hard to tell with his beard, Jeremy seemed to be smirking. "I was in a much more romantic place."

"And where was that?" Karen picked up her pen.

"Oh, I can't tell you that! It wouldn't be fair. My lover has a reputation to protect."

"You're saying you were with someone last night?"

"It was heavenly. The start of a wonderful new relationship."

"With who?"

"I'm not prepared to tell you. The age of chivalry may be dead, but some of us still have a code of honour." Jeremy frowned. "You're acting as if this was a murder. Lavoie said it was an accident."

"It's a death under unexplained circumstances. It's our duty to investigate such cases and part of that investigation is to interview people who knew the deceased and to establish their whereabouts at the relevant time."

"I'll tell you this much, Corporal," Jeremy said, leaning back in his chair. "I have an iron-clad alibi. If push comes to shove, I'll trot it out. But not until then. Okay?"

"Definitely not okay, Mr. Switzer. I could charge you with withholding evidence. But since the investigation is still in its preliminary stages, I'll just put you down as an uncooperative witness."

"I'm doing my best to be helpful," Jeremy said with a pout. "Don't waste your time on me, Corporal. I can prove I was nowhere near the residence last night any time I have to."

While Corporal Lindstrom was having her unsatisfactory interview with Jeremy, Laura was on her way to her studio. Snow drifted gently down through the lodge pole pines as she walked along the path. Her steps slowed as she approached the large music hut that housed the elegant Baldwin concert grand. Isabelle Ross was playing Rakhmaninov's Second Piano Concerto with savage intensity. Laura had never heard her play Rakhmaninov before. Very likely this was Isabelle's way of venting her feelings at the prospect of leaving her new lover's ardent arms for those of her husband.

As she continued along the path, she heard the deep, soulful strains of a cello seeping through the thick walls of one of the tiny wooden huts where the music students practiced. That would be Veronica Phillips, the graduate music student who was so openly and hopelessly infatuated with Marek Dabrowski. Laura had seen this sort of thing happen before at the Centre. In fact, she had been here two years ago when, to the shock of the entire community, a young ballet dancer — a "bun head" as they were called — threw herself off the sixth-floor deck because of her unrequited love for a principal dancer, who she never lived to know was gay and thus beyond her reach. Someone like Veronica, Laura thought, had probably been studying music since she was four or five years old. She comes here with this sheltered background of being immersed in music, with playing the cello the focus of her entire life, and meets the man who wrote the music she had played and loved since she was a child. Someone who was darkly handsome in the intense way the public thinks composers are supposed to look. But, unfortunately for Veronica, Marek is head-over-heels in love with someone else. So the student suffers silently as she sees them doing everything together — taking long walks through the woods, attending concerts — all the wonderful, fun things lovers do. To make it worse, she can't escape from them, not in the closed world of the Centre.

As always, Laura paused for a reflective moment on the footbridge. There were times when life at the Centre outdid the soapiest soap opera, but with the symbolic act of crossing the little bridge she knew she could temporarily leave all distractions behind and concentrate on her art. She laughed with delight as the falling snowflakes landed on her upturned face; one fat flake spiking itself on her eyelashes, blurring her vision. Refreshed, she crossed the bridge and decided to walk all the way around the path that circled the studios.

Even in daylight, there was something spectral and unworldly about the boat studio, so far removed from its natural element. Its weathered hull rested on a wooden cradle, and it was sheltered from the elements by a plexiglass canopy. Maybe the fact that it had sunk and had been raised from a watery grave accounted for its ghostly aura. While certainly picturesque, it was not popular with visiting artists because the narrow hull made for cramped working quarters. But Erika loved the way it allowed her to work at her computer and reach for her research files on the shelves behind her without moving from her chair. Laura looked for any sign of John Smith lurking among the pine trees, but she couldn't spot him. That didn't mean he wasn't there, of course. The way John Smith had zeroed in on Erika was as disturbing as his unpredictable behaviour. There didn't seem to be anything sexual about it, at least not in the usual sense.

The Evamy Studio made extensive use of glass and Laura could see Richard Madrin sitting at his desk deep in thought. Like the boat studio, it was designated for writers, but it was much more spacious, a feature

Richard appreciated since it gave him room to pace back and forth as he plotted the scenes of his novel. As Laura walked past, he got up from his desk, walked over to the window and gave her a friendly wave. Laura smiled, waved back, and continued on.

It was dynamite. Pure dynamite! Dare she use it? Without it her project would be little more than a scholarly treatise, unknown outside academic circles. If it got published at all. With it the book could be a publishing sensation. It might even make the *New York Times* bestseller list. Erika pinched herself. Get real, she thought. But a shiver, whether of fear or excitement she couldn't tell, ran through her as she bent over the computer printouts spread out on her desk. She was sure she was right. But what if she was wrong?

She took off her glasses, rubbed her eyes, and got up from the chair. She would draft the section to see what it looked like. To see whether it would turn out to be as sensational as she thought. Writing a draft didn't mean she was committed to using it, but she wouldn't do it today. She'd let it simmer in her subconscious while she worked on another, completely innocuous chapter. She paused for a moment, knowing that the bit about the subconscious was just an excuse to postpone putting the actual words down on paper. Erika wondered why she was so reluctant to start. It was because the whole thing was so unbelievably incredible. Incredible but true, she added to herself.

Equally incredible was the way in which her excitement over her discovery and the fact that her book was nearing completion had distanced her from Geoff. Until she had come to this remote and magical place, she never would have believed that she could think of

Geoff Hamilton without breaking up inside. After three years of an on-again, off-again relationship, he had decided to remain in his loveless marriage with two teenage children. A few days ago, he had called from New York saying he realized that he had made a mistake and wanting to come to Banff. She had astonished herself by telling him that she didn't want to see him. Not until her stay at the Centre was over, at least. That shocked him, as she knew it would. She had been so devastated when he told her he was ending the affair that now he couldn't seem to accept the possibility that she might not want him back.

The sudden ringing of the phone startled Laura so much that she almost dropped her brush. As it was, a broad smear of yellow was added to her already splattered bib apron. Every studio was equipped with a phone, but it was for emergency use only. In all the time Laura had spent at the colony, her studio phone had never rung. Her thoughts flew to her parents, cruising somewhere in the Caribbean on board their ketch, *Star Chaser*. She took a deep breath and reached for the phone. It was Kevin Lavoie, apologizing profusely for the disturbance, saying that Corporal Lindstrom would like to see her. Laura hesitated, then told him to send the policewoman to her studio. Laura rarely invited visitors to her studio, but when she did make an exception it invariably resulted in a pleasant surprise. Only the week before she had agreed to let Carl Eckart pay her a call.

She had agreed to the visit because the gruff Eckart was a musician, a professor of musicology in the music department and a composer of sorts. Musicians seemed to have special insights into her paintings. At the time of his visit Laura was playing a CD of some far-out jazz to energize her as she painted. Two days later he had presented her with a tape of the same music he had reproduced on his synthesizer. He had carried all the notes away from her studio in his head.

"Fascinating," murmured the policewoman, several minutes later as she gazed around the high-ceilinged studio with its north-facing skylight. "I've never been in an artist's studio before." Her eyes travelled along the paintings propped up against the walls. "I know I'm not qualified to give an opinion, but I like them. Especially that one." She pointed to a large painting of a room with a piano and a balcony overlooking a turquoise sea. "It looks so serene and peaceful."

"You have a good eye." Laura waved her to a chair and looked at her enquiringly.

"I'm here to enlist your help, Ms. Janeway."

"It's Laura."

"Great. I'm Karen."

Corporal Karen Lindstrom. How perfectly it suited her.

"I'm an artist," Laura said, "not a detective."

"That's precisely why I would like to have your help. All the players are artists and I'm not confident that I know what makes them tick. Especially after meeting Mr. Switzer."

Laura smiled. "I see what you mean. What did Jeremy have to say for himself?"

"He passes off the lawsuit as a nuisance, but he's bluffing. He couldn't stop tugging at his beard. The man's worried sick."

Laura nodded. "What did he say about last night?"

"He claims he has an alibi for the time of Montrose's death, but he won't tell me what it is. Doesn't want to ruin his lover's reputation, he says."

"Can he get away with that?"

"For the moment, yes. But, if the autopsy turns up anything suspicious, I'll come down hard on Mr. Switzer."

"It sounds as if you're not satisfied Alan's death was an accident?"

"No, I'm not. Partly because you're not. The autopsy could clear things up, one way or the other, but if we find that we have to carry on with the investigation, I would really appreciate your help. You could be my guide to the colony. What you told me about Switzer proved to be very helpful. While it was a frustrating interview, I felt I was able to meet him on his own terms."

Laura frowned. "I don't care much for the idea of spying on my friends."

"I'm not asking you to spy on anyone. It's more a matter of helping me understand the way these people think." Karen got up from her chair, walked over to the door, and then turned back with a smile. "Well, I suppose it *is* a bit more than that. According to Kevin Lavoie you have terrific powers of observation and that could be a tremendous help if this turns out to be a homicide. The public may not be aware of it, but the police do use gifted amateurs to help them solve cases where the circumstances are, shall we say, out of the ordinary. It doesn't just happen in crime stories. It happens in real life, too."

"I suppose we could give it a try and see how it works out," Laura agreed slowly. "But if I begin to feel compromised, I'll have to back off." She paused, then added, "Haven't you forgotten something? I could be a suspect myself. After all, I was the one who found the body."

"I haven't forgotten," Karen said as she closed the studio door behind her.

A little taken aback by the policewoman's parting remark, Laura glanced at her wristwatch, remembering that she was supposed to join Erika for a cup of tea. They alternated between their studios every Friday afternoon. Locking her studio door behind her, she walked down the path and knocked lightly on the boat studio's door and pushed it open. Erika was seated in front of her computer, deep in thought. Hesitating just inside the door, Laura said, "I don't want to interrupt if you're in the middle of something."

Erika hastily assured her that she had reached a good place to take a break. "I feel like I'm on a bit of a roll. Everything seems to be coming together just the way I want it."

"It's a natural high," agreed Laura as Erika began to make the tea. "I get the same feeling when I finally see how I'm going to approach a painting."

The two friends sat together on the narrow couch and companionably sipped herb tea. They were both in their mid-thirties, but there the similarity ended. Erika was small and quick, with short-cropped dark hair framing sharp, piquant features, while her brown-haired companion was built on a larger, more Junoesque scale. Erika's clear blue eyes sparkled with a bright, inquisitive sharpness, while Laura's brown ones glowed with sympathetic understanding.

The subject of Montrose was raised and quickly dropped as there wasn't much that could be said about it, and the conversation moved on to more congenial subjects. The easy flow of their talk was suddenly interrupted by a barrage of flashes outside the studio. Laura jumped to her feet and peered out one of the portholes. Unlike conventional portholes, these were large and square— more like windows. The colony was strictly off-limits to the public, but the polite "Please do not trespass" signs failed to inhibit some of the more thoughtless sightseers. Laura swore under her breath as she saw a tour group gesticulating and aiming cameras at the curious sight of an old fishing boat plunked down in a forest hundreds of miles from the nearest ocean.

"It makes me furious," she muttered. "It's one thing if somebody doesn't know any better, but that's a guided tour and they know damn well they shouldn't be here. I'm going to see them off." She brushed past Erika and went out on deck to politely inform the guide he had no business being there.

Laura's impulsive action didn't surprise Erika who was familiar with her friend's protective attitude toward the colony. Laura had been coming to the Leighton Artist Colony for years. Her art had benefited greatly from her frequent stays in the creative atmosphere and she was fiercely resentful of anything that threatened to undermine its unique character. She had also become a sort of den mother to her fellow colonists, showing them how the colony worked and emphasizing that its sole purpose was to encourage their creative talents. Her helpful hints had eased Erika's entry into the colony and enabled her to settle down to work much more quickly than otherwise might have been the case. In the intervening five weeks, the two women had become fast friends.

"I suppose I shouldn't let myself get carried away like that." Laura looked a little sheepish as she stepped back into the cabin. "But this place is important to me."

"You did the right thing," Erika assured her as they rinsed the cups and put them away. She glanced at her watch. "If we're going to be on time for dinner, we better go."

It was another of the survival tricks she had learned from Laura — be at the Banquet Hall when it opened at five-thirty while the food was still hot, and hadn't been ruined by sitting too long on a steam table.

As they scrunched along the path, Laura inhaled the thin, clean air that tasted cool somewhere deep in her lungs. Pointing at a clump of trees, she asked, "Do you see the deer?" Now that she knew where to look, Erika spotted the motionless grey shapes, which blended perfectly with the grey bark of the tree trunks. She had long since become accustomed to Laura's astonishing powers of observation; she was constantly pointing out things that had escaped everyone else's notice. She had once told Erika that it was because she was a visual artist, adding that visual artists are trained to see the normal, so that anything that fell outside the norm immediately attracted their attention. Unbidden, the thought of how much Geoff would enjoy going on nature walks with the observant Laura flickered through Erika's mind before she hastily banished it.

As usual, they would both return to work in their studios immediately after dinner.

Refreshed and relaxed after a late night swim and a session in the whirlpool that eased the strain of painting for hours with a tiny brush, Laura walked across the darkened parking lot and through the third floor side entrance of Lloyd Hall. The crime tape had been taken down from the stairwell, but she decided to use the elevator anyway.

She had just hung up her jacket when there was a knock on her door. "Who is it?" she called out.

"Marek Dabrowski. I know it's late, but could I talk to you for a few minutes?"

As expected, Dabrowski was distraught over the visit of Isabelle's husband. "He arrives in the morning. What should I do? I can't bear to see them together."

"Go away for the weekend. Rent a car and drive up to Jasper, or take a real break and drive out to Vancouver," she said, adding, "You should see some of the west while you're here anyway."

The composer shook his head. "I can't drive," he said in his accented English that added the final touch to his continental good looks.

"Then work. Lock yourself in your studio, take your meals there and sleep there. Create a masterpiece out of your emotion. I've found work to be the best panacea for a broken heart."

Marek looked at her with sudden interest. "You? What does the unattainable Ms. Janeway know of a broken heart? I have always thought of you as the one who breaks hearts. Ah, I remember now. Someone said you had once been married."

"It wasn't him." Laura waved a dismissive hand. "Have you and Isabelle given any thought to making your relationship permanent?"

"We've talked about it. But it won't work. It's her daughter. Isabelle is determined that Jessica will not be the victim of a broken home. Isabelle grew up in a loving home and she wants the same for her daughter. I try to tell her that children are tougher than she thinks, but she remains ...," Marek took a moment, as he sometimes did, to search for the precisely correct English word, then said with a faint air of triumph, "adamant."

He turned to go. "I will take your advice and remain in my studio, working on my concerto."

chapter three

A message flashed on the computer screen when the cashier took Richard Madrin's Centre Pass and punched in some numbers. The cashier, the chatty one with an earring and taped glasses, told him there was a package for him in the mailroom.

"It's probably my manuscript," Richard said. The drama student who worked part-time as a cashier was gratifyingly impressed. "I'll pick it up after lunch."

Kevin Lavoie with a potential donor to the artist colony in tow had joined some of the colonists for lunch. With a rueful shake of his head, he began to recount one of John Smith's recent exploits. The performance artist had dressed himself up as a magician and stationed himself in the foyer of the Eric Harvie Theatre to greet the guests arriving for the play. Pretending he was going to do a trick, he persuaded a number of them to hand over their credit cards.

"Then," continued Lavoie, "before anyone could stop him, he whipped out a pair of scissors and cut them in half. Two of his victims are big supporters of the Centre and they were not amused."

"That would only make it all the better as far as he's concerned," murmured Laura. "The victim's reaction is part of a performance artist's art."

"Just what is a performance artist?" asked Lavoie's guest. "I've heard the term, but I've never known just what it is they do."

The others looked to Laura to provide the answer. She thought for a moment before saying, "Performance art is hard to define and often harder to take should you be an unwilling participant. Performance artists do not create objects like a painting or a piece of sculpture. They act out a scene or a fantasy and often document it, they call it a 'happening', with a video camera. It's the only art form where the art is created before an audience rather than being presented as a finished product. The performances are frequently violent and dangerous, both to the artist and anyone in the vicinity. You may remember reading about the man in Paris who videotaped himself slicing off pieces of his penis with a razor?"

"Good Lord, yes."

"That was performance art."

"That's odd," interjected Richard, completely deadpan. "I always figured that was a do-it-yourself sex change operation."

Lavoie's guest laughed heartily. Meeting Richard was obviously the highlight of his visit to the Centre. Sensing this, Richard did his bit for the cause, discussing the characters in some of his novels and talking about the challenges and rewards of writing. It was the kind of talk he had given to countless book clubs and it was highly entertaining. He capped it by saying that the edited opening manuscript chapters of his new book had just arrived from his New York publisher and was waiting for him in the mailroom. Lavoie and Laura exchanged knowing smiles as he left. The donor would be putty in Lavoie's hands after that performance.

"Another bestseller, Mr. Madrin?" The mail clerk smiled as she handed over the parcel. *Original manuscript* had been typed on the customs form.

"I hope so," replied Richard as he tucked the package under his arm. "I still have a long way to go, though. This is just the edited version of the first five chapters."

Inside his studio, Richard sat down in front of his word processor, but didn't switch it on. Instead he carefully arranged a writing pad, erasers, pencils, scissors, and a roll of scotch tape on the long counter, like a surgeon preparing to operate. Only then did he unwrap the parcel. There was no title page, but that didn't worry him. The title would fall out of the book as the story unfolded. As usual, there was a lengthy letter from Thea Solberg explaining some of the changes she had pencilled in on the draft. She seemed genuinely excited by what he had written so far. Not only did it have the famous "Madrin action," she wrote, but this time he had succeeded in creating a truly sympathetic protagonist. The fictional James Hunt made mistakes, and had his share of human frailties, including a tendency to fall into jealous sulks. But he soldiered gamely on, and the reader knew he would prevail in the end.

After reading the part about the main character, Richard jumped up from his chair and walked over to the window. The Evamy Studio, named after the late Calgary architect who had designed it, boasted the most spectacular view in the colony — a tall, floor-to-ceiling window looking out on a cathedral aisle of pines framing the jagged peak of Mount Rundle, soaring above the tree line. But today Richard was oblivious to its grandeur; the editor's reaction to his new hero exactly mirrored his own thoughts. Maybe James Hunt deserved his own series; thrillers set in exotic parts of the globe featuring the likeable James Hunt with his baggage of human foibles and strengths. Richard's pulse quickened as he realized that the new book might lead to a television series. Having his stories and characters come to life on the screen had always been one of his greatest ambitions, but it had eluded him up to now. It meant that the hero could not get entangled in any long-term romantic attachments. But that was no problem. The female lead could always be killed off at the end of the book. Or, better yet, she could turn out to be the villain.

Exhilarated by the prospect of achieving the breakthrough he had always sought, Richard returned to his desk. As he expected, Thea's editorial changes were a lot less drastic than she seemed to think. From the tone of her letter one would think she was taking enormous liberties with his precious prose, whereas in reality her notations were little more than copy editing; substituting a word here, eliminating one there. But she liked James Hunt! That was the important part. Richard's contented smile deepened as he read.

Erika's stomach rumbled noisily, reminding her that, almost unheard of for her, she had forgotten to eat her lunch. She switched off the computer and shrugged into her jacket. She would eat out on the deck.

Winter was beginning to relax its grip on the mountains. The light morning snowfall had stopped and the sun had come out, melting the snow into little puddles on the path. Unzipping her jacket, Erika spread out the abundant lunch the kitchen staff, knowing her remarkable appetite, had packed. It was the shadow that made her look up. John Smith's bare feet made no sound as he mounted the solid plank steps, and Erika suddenly found herself staring directly at his genitalia. He stepped back several paces and said, "Hello, Erika," his voice echoing hollowly inside the donkey mask, which was all he was wearing. John Smith's sexuality might be problematical, but physically, he was undeniably a man, as his present costume, or lack of it, made abundantly clear.

"Hello yourself, John Smith," she replied coolly. "Aren't you rushing the season a bit?"

He shrugged to indicate her question didn't deserve a reply, then brought his right hand out from behind his back. "Look what I found in the woods. Do you know what it is?"

Erika stared at the dead bird with distaste. "As it happens, I do," she replied. Geoff was an avid birder and his interest had awakened her own. One of her first purchases in Banff had been a copy of *Birds of the Canadian Rockies.* "It's a nutcracker. Clark's nutcracker to be precise."

"That's right," John Smith's muffled voice sounded somewhat disappointed. "Do you know what a nutcracker does?" As he spoke he grabbed his scrotum with his free hand and began to squeeze. Horrified, Erika saw the tendons on the back of his hand standing out as he increased the pressure. She turned away and stared calmly into the distance.

His fingers relaxed their pressure and he stood there, still holding the carcass of the handsome grey and black bird in his hand.

"Finished?" she asked coolly. She heard the hiss of his indrawn breath as he stomped off.

"Oh, no!" Erika groaned aloud as she saw Isabelle leading her family down the path. Isabelle was giving them a tour of the colony and they were on a collision course with the naked John Smith who was in a sulk and liable to do anything. It would have been funny except for the little girl. But the child's presence must have inhibited even John Smith, for he turned aside and melted into the woods. Isabelle's husband, his hand covering his daughter's eyes, turned and stared disbelievingly after the apparition. He still looked shaken as they accepted Erika's invitation and joined her on the deck.

"I guess one has to be prepared for anything around an art colony," he said with a game smile as Isabelle introduced him. His name was Dennis, and the dark-haired little beauty was Jessica. The child's eyes were wide with unasked questions as she smiled shyly at Erika.

"John Smith is a little extreme, even for an art colony," Erika said. "I think he's put years on poor Kevin's life. Kevin Lavoie is the colony coordinator," she explained to Dennis.

"I've met him," he murmured noncommittally. And probably got a pretty cool reception, thought Erika. Kevin did not approve of visitors. He thought they were disruptive of colony life.

Saying, "We mustn't keep you from your writing," Isabelle stood up to leave the moment Erika finished her dessert, a generous slice of apple pie and a chunk of cheddar cheese.

Dennis blinked, then scrambled hastily to his feet. "I must say you're a remarkably dedicated bunch around here. I can scarcely persuade Isabelle to have dinner in town tonight with me and Jessica."

"I already explained it to you, Dennis," she said, the strain in Isabelle's voice was evident, and Erika's heart went out to her. "I'm way behind my schedule. I've still got two Schubert sonatas to add to my repertoire before I leave here. And I have a recording session in Chicago the third week of May."

"Our time here is a rare and wonderful chance for us to concentrate on our work free of distractions from the outside world," Erika said, unsure this was the most tactful way of putting it. But perhaps it would help the doctor understand why the family reunion was not turning out to be the joyous event he undoubtedly had anticipated.

Richard's euphoria over his editor's comments served him well that night. Henry Norrington was holding court in the lounge of the Sally Borden Building to an audience consisting of several of his graduate students and a few members of the colony. They were grouped around two tables that had been pulled together in the far end of the lounge. The celebrated writer-cum-lecturer, fuelled with a couple of after-dinner cognacs, was in fine acerbic form as he held forth on the subject of modern fiction.

"Sounds like you're practicing for our television show," laughed Richard when Norrington came to the end of a lengthy and perceptive discourse on the unlikely, but intriguing, parallels between the Argentinean novelist Manuel Garcia, and the American Roger Newbury.

Norrington's large nose swung majestically in Richard's direction. "I'm scarcely in need of practice for that," he sniffed.

It was only two days before the television "debate" between Norrington and Richard Madrin was scheduled to air. It was a much-anticipated event and one of the main topics of conversation in the colony. An Edmonton station, supported by public funds and with a mandate to spread culture throughout the province, frequently invited various luminaries who visited the Banff Centre to appear on its programs. The presence of both Henry Norrington and Richard Madrin on the campus at the same time was a natural. Norrington, as well as being the author of several widely acclaimed books on philosophy, was also a noted critic and a frequent, and much sought after, guest on television talk shows. Getting the famous guru as a visiting lecturer had been a real coup for the Centre. As part of the inducement for him to come, he had been assigned a studio in the colony — the award winning chapel-like studio designed by Calgary architect Fred Valentine, with its sloping roof and glassed-in porch. The consensus in the colony was that Norrington, with his sarcastic wit and biting contempt for the kind of books Richard wrote, would make mincemeat out of the thriller writer. But Laura wasn't so sure. Besides the kind of good looks that the camera would love, Richard had an easy-going self-confidence that might serve to blunt Norrington's barbs.

Now Norrington was telling Richard, in tones of one conferring a signal honour, that he was going to use one of Richard's books in his creative writing class.

"Oh?" Surprised and pleased, Richard asked, "Which one?"

Norrington shrugged. "It doesn't matter. I only managed to get halfway through one of them before giving up. But that told me all I needed to know. Any one of your books will serve as a perfect example of what and how not to write."

Norrington's mocking jest brought a sycophantic titter from one of the students, but the rest of his listeners sat in stony silence.

"Richard's books are enjoyed by a great many people," Laura said breaking the embarrassed silence.

"I appreciate your coming to my defence, Laura, but it's quite all right." Richard glanced at Norrington with a look that was almost amused. "Henry's just jealous that my books sell so much better than his."

This sally brought a gasp of outrage from Norrington, but a spluttered "Nonsense!" was the only reply he could muster.

This was the stuff of legend and Norrington's students were eating it up. But the undercurrent of animosity between the two men made Laura uncomfortable. She finished her glass of wine and got to her feet. Smothering a yawn, Richard said he would walk back to the residence with her. Outside the building, he paused to gaze almost reverently up at the night sky, the moon riding high among the stars. The air was so crisp and clear that the distant stars seemed almost to crackle. The eerie, high-pitched howl of a coyote floated down from somewhere higher up Tunnel Mountain.

"I love that sound," Richard murmured. "It's so wild and free."

"It sends chills up and down my spine, too," Laura agreed. "But it also reminds me of the time I put a coyote in a painting. Like everybody else I painted it sitting on its haunches and baying at the moon. A couple of months after the painting had been sold, I received a stern letter from a field naturalist saying that when coyotes howled they stood with all four feet planted on the ground."

"Did you reply?"

"Oh, yes. I wrote him a polite note thanking him for the information, but telling him that in my paintings, coyotes were free to do whatever they liked." She touched his arm. "Let's walk down the path. This night is too beautiful to waste!"

Moments later as they rounded a turn in the path they saw Veronica Phillips standing in front of Marek Dabrowski's studio.

"Oh, no," Laura exclaimed softly.

Veronica was listening so intently to the sounds filtering through the studio walls that she started visibly as the two approached. She held a finger to her lips until the music rose to a thundering crescendo then suddenly faltered to a halt. She turned to them with shining eyes. "It's going to be wonderful! He's writing it in C-major. It's the first time he's written a concerto in that key."

Marek began to pick out notes again and as Laura squeezed Richard's arm and turned to walk away, her eyes caught something glinting in the moonlight on the ground just off the path. When she narrowed her eyes to focus on it, she could make out that it was a microphone, partially hidden behind a fallen branch. Somebody was taping Marek as he worked on his concerto.

She glanced at Richard. His attention was riveted on her and he hadn't spotted the microphone. "You are very beautiful in the moonlight," he said softly.

"Thank you." She slipped her hand in his as they continued up the path. They walked in companionable silence to Lloyd Hall in the silver moonlight. The quizzical look was back in his eyes as they said good night at her door.

What should she do about the microphone? That question kept Laura awake and staring at the ceiling until she finally decided that in all good conscience she must tell Marek about it first thing in the morning. With that decision made, she fell into a restless sleep.

The microphone was still in place. After a quick glance around to make sure there was no one else in sight, Laura stepped off the path and tramped through the underbrush until she was standing over it. A thin black cord led her through the trees and down into the little ravine. The reel of the tape machine, hidden under a canopy of pine boughs, was revolving at a very slow rate. It contained enough tape to record for hours on end, and it would be an easy matter to change tapes without being seen since the ravine provided cover on all sides.

There was no sound coming from Marek's studio, but the outside light was still burning. Somewhat apprehensive of what her reception might be, Laura knocked on the door. She didn't know how she expected the composer to look after his self-imposed exile in his studio, but she certainly didn't expect the clear-eyed, freshly shaven Marek who opened the door. The only sign of fatigue were the dark smudges under his eyes.

"I hate disturbing you like this Marek, but there's something you should know about."

"Is it about Isabelle?" he demanded.

"No. It has nothing to do with her. Come with me and I'll show you."

"You are sure this has nothing to do with Isabelle?" Marek persisted as he followed her along the path.

"See for yourself," Laura said as she led him down the little ravine.

Marek stared down at the tape machine with its slowly revolving reel. "It's from the music department," he muttered. "Nobody else has a machine like that."

"But who would do something like this?"

"I think I can guess, but we'll know for sure soon enough. The tape is almost finished. Whoever it is will have to come back to change reels." Marek ran his fingers through his dark tousled hair. "The *andante* will be on there. That's what I was working on until just before dawn."

"But whoever it is couldn't use your music. Everybody would know."

"Change a note here and a few bars there. Better still, arrange it for violin rather than piano. The important thing is to have the structure to hang the notes on, and the tape would give you that." Marek was growing visibly angry at the thought of someone appropriating his music in this stealthy and underhanded manner.

The tape was almost down to the spindle. Even though it was broad daylight, Laura shivered. From somewhere down the ravine came the crack of a broken branch, followed by a muffled curse in German.

"It is just as I thought," whispered Marek. "Carl Eckart—a disappointed and bitter man whose music has been ignored by the world. My concerto would have been his masterpiece."

"What are you going to do?" Laura whispered as Eckart's thickset figure came into view through the trees.

"Protect my music," replied Marek. Telling her to stay hidden behind a tree, he moved off.

As she stood there, screened by the branches of a pine, Laura was immediately surrounded by a cloud of confiding chickadees looking for a handout. They had long ago learned that people in the colony could often be counted on for a treat of sunflower seeds or nuts.

Eckart was squatting over the machine, a reel of tape in either hand when Marek came silently up behind him. Both spools fell to the ground when Marek murmured, "I am flattered, Professor, but is what you are doing quite ethical?"

Eckart froze, too stunned to move. Then without lifting his eyes or turning around, he asked in a cracking voice what Marek intended to do about it.

"You are despicable. Beneath contempt. I should report you to the chair of your department."

Still on his knees, Eckart scrunched around until he was facing Marek. Hands clasped together as if in prayer, he implored Marek not to report him, saying that it would mean instant dismissal and he had no other means of support.

"Get on your feet," said Marek with distaste. "I *should* report you but I will not do so until I have thought about it. You will collect your equipment and bring it to my studio. Then you will bring me all the tapes. All of them, do you understand?" Eckart nodded, and Marek continued, "We will play them together to verify that I have them all."

From behind the cover of the pine tree, Laura watched Eckart gather up his equipment. She held her breath as he walked within a few feet of her, winding the microphone wire in neat coils. He was cursing in German to himself, and there was a look of despair on his broad, fleshy face. But there was something else there as well. Fury. The blind, unreasoning fury of one who believes he has been cheated by life.

chapter four

The malodorous flounder, sightless eyes staring heavenwards, lay on the doorstep of the boat studio like some unholy offering. Erika stared down at the unappetizing object with repugnance and something close to fear. It was the same fish that John Smith had been wearing around his neck at breakfast. Its smell had driven the others away and left him sitting alone at a table. He was so outrageously bizarre, it was scary, and to make it worse, he had obviously singled her out as his prime target. Holding her breath, Erika stepped over the fish and entered her studio. She was in a quandary. The performance artist was probably hiding among the trees, watching to see what she would do. If he saw her throwing it away, God only knew how he would react. Finally, she wrapped the fish in several layers of paper towelling and put it in the refrigerator.

Unsettled by the bizarre attentions of John Smith, Erika sat in front of the blank computer screen. She was definitely not in the right frame of mind to start writing up her astonishing discovery. Instead, she would recheck her research one more time. Booting her computer, she began to call up the document files and soon became totally engrossed in checking and cross-referencing the data.

She was so wrapped up in her work that at first she didn't hear the knocking on the door. She looked at her watch; lunch was at least an hour away. She was tempted not to answer the summons, but the knocking persisted. Sighing, she switched the computer off.

John Smith had decked himself out in a baggy clown costume, white with black and red diamond patches. His makeup was lugubrious, patterned after the heartbroken Pagliacci. Erika tried to block the doorway, but he pushed her aside none too gently and strode to the middle of the small room, his eyes searching every corner of the studio. Then he sighed, walked over to the fridge and opened it. Real tears coursed down his painted cheeks as he unwrapped his odoriferous offering. Placing it reverently on the counter, he whipped out a revolver, held it against his head, and pulled the trigger. It clicked harmlessly, but not before Erika screamed. John Smith looked at the revolver as if disappointed, then thumbed another chamber into position and once more raised the gun to his head. Erika tried to grab it from him, but he held her off easily with his left hand. It was as if her arm was caught in a steel vice. She kicked him on the shins and yelled at him to stop as he kept rotating the chambers and pulling the trigger. When the sixth and final chamber clicked into place, he smiled, held the revolver a few inches from his head and, looking straight into Erika's horrified gaze, pulled the trigger. A small white flag with BANG printed across it in red crayon popped out of the barrel.

"That's not funny." Erika collapsed into a chair, fighting to get her breathing under control. She frowned at the clown, who seemed ready to take a bow, and said, "I know these stunts," deliberately choosing a word that would insult him, "are your form of art. And I know they're important to you. But they can be very frightening to other people. And dangerous. What if I had a heart condition? I could have died."

From the way his eyes lit up, it was obvious that John Smith thought that would have been the icing on the cake. Something that would have made his performance truly memorable. Performance artists were a breed apart, totally egocentric and interested in other people only as potential props for their happenings, or as an audience. Erika knew that pleading with him to leave her alone would just make him concentrate on her all the more. Taking a deep breath, she rose out of the chair and said, as off-handedly as she could manage, "All right, John Smith, I've got work to do. Please take your toys and leave. Including the fish."

Offended, he drew himself up and headed for the door, leaving the dead flounder behind. He seemed to be favouring the leg she had kicked and that gave her a certain grim satisfaction. Swearing under her breath, Erika threw the fish out the door after him. To her surprise, the ichthyological missile found its target, hitting him between the shoulder blades. He stopped, made as if to turn around, then squared his shoulders, and kept on walking.

The dead flounder stared up at her reproachfully as she strode down the path. She was tempted to leave it lying there but realized its ripening aroma might attract bears. Controlling her temper, she returned to the studio for more paper towels. The kitchen staff would dispose of it in the garbage. The mention of John Smith's name would tell them all they needed to know.

It wasn't working. And Laura knew better than to try and force it. That would only lead to mistakes, and mistakes at this early stage could ruin a painting beyond repair. Later on, mistakes could be painted over, colour values could be adjusted. But in the early stages, when you were working out the basic composition of the painting and drawing it on the canvas, you had to be inspired. And this morning Laura was definitely not inspired. That degrading scene between Marek and the abject Eckart had eroded her creative energy. She sighed and put down the stick of charcoal.

Perhaps she'd browse through some art books in the library, an exercise that often helped put her back in the mood for painting. Cutting across the parking lot, en route to Lloyd Hall, she saw Richard, keys in hand, standing beside his rented Ford Taurus. His smile was understanding. "Can't paint? I can't write either. I'm going into town and drive around for a bit. Care to join me?"

Laura surprised herself by accepting. But she told Richard that she had a better idea than just driving aimlessly around. "Why don't we grab our swimsuits and go for a dip in the Upper Hot Springs?"

"Fabulous! I've been meaning to go there. Let's meet back here at the car in five minutes."

"This town has the damnedest street names," Richard remarked, as they drove downtown. He had just glanced up at a sign that read Wolf Street. "Then there's Caribou Street, Buffalo Street. It's like being in a zoo!"

"Don't forget Bear Street, Muskrat Street, Otter Street and various other members of the animal kingdom," smiled Laura. "There's even a Gopher Street. It's because Banff is in a national park. I think it's charming."

It was Sunday and Banff Avenue, the main street, was crowded with tourists hunting for souvenirs and bargains in the stores that lined both sides of the wide boulevard. Nestled in the beautiful valley of the Bow River, high up in the Canadian Rockies, the town of Banff has been a Mecca for tourists ever since the national park was created in 1883, after three labourers working on the construction of the Canadian Pacific Railway came across springs of sulphurous water seeping from the ground. Spring and fall were supposed to be the "shoulder" seasons, but the resort town had become so popular that in reality there were none. As March entered its third week, the snow was beginning to disappear around the town site, but the ski slopes in the higher elevations would remain open for another two months.

The light changed and Richard eased into the traffic. They followed a horse-drawn carriage filled with tourists along the congested street. The carriage turned off just before the bridge and Richard picked up speed. Following Laura's directions he turned left after crossing the bridge and then turned onto a winding road that climbed the pine-clad lower reaches of Sulphur Mountain.

A mile and a half up the road, a sign warned them to watch out for a flagman. The flagman turned out to be a flag woman with long blond hair underneath her red hardhat. She held up a stop sign as two giant earthmovers, travelling fast, bore down on the road.

"They're filling in an abandoned gravel pit," Laura explained as the first machine barrelled across the road in front of them. "They're going to build a shopping mall on it. A lot has changed since Banff became a town and got out from under the wing of Parks Canada."

The second earthmoving machine, belching smoke from its twin exhaust stacks, roared past them and the flagperson turned her sign from "Stop" to "Slow" waving them on.

"Those things always make me think of prehistoric monsters coming to life," said Laura as Richard accelerated up the hill.

"It's their sheer power that gets to me," Richard said. "They're like railway locomotives turned loose on the countryside."

As the roar of the gigantic machines faded in the distance, Laura leaned back against the headrest and said, "I always treasure the moment when you leave the town behind and there's just the mountains."

Richard pulled into the parking lot, shut off the ignition, and blinked in surprise as a deer stuck its head in through the Ford's open window.

"Meet the famous Upper Hot Springs tourist-friendly deer," said Laura as she climbed out of the car. "Every day, as soon as the pool opens, they gather in the parking lot to mooch food from the tourists. People aren't supposed to feed them, but of course they do."

The deer stood stock still as she petted it. Its coat was surprisingly coarse and bristly and felt something like a doormat. Seeing that no food was forthcoming, the deer nudged the rolled-up bathing suit Laura was carrying under her arm, then wandered off in search of easier pickings.

"It's much colder here." Richard tugged at the zipper of his jacket.

"It's because we're a lot higher up."

As they drew near the bathhouse the smell of sulphur permeated the air, leading Richard to mutter that he now understood how Sulphur Mountain got its name. A blackboard outside the entrance to the bath-house informed them that today's water temperature was 41° C or 106° F. After changing into their bathing suits, a short flight of steps protected by a glass wall led them from the changing rooms down to the pool.

Standing up to his neck in the water, his head enveloped in sulphurous steam, Richard felt the moisture on his hair begin to freeze. It crackled when he touched it, and he grinned and shook his head. "I've got to admit it's different. Bathing outdoors while the hair on your head freezes!"

Laura smiled. "It's even more wonderful during a snowstorm. I used to come up here a lot at night. You can look right down the valley and see the lights of Banff. It's magical."

There were other bathers in the pool, but the swirling clouds of steam made them virtually invisible. Now and then a breeze would gently blow the steam curtain aside and they could catch a glimpse of their fellow bathers, mostly members of a Japanese tour group, their faces wreathed in blissful smiles. They stayed in the hot pool for the recommended maximum of twenty minutes then climbed back up the stairs to the changing rooms. Laura told Richard she used the same time limit for the whirlpool at the Banff Centre.

"We definitely must do that again!" declared Richard as they drove back down Sulphur Mountain to Banff. They stopped for lunch and then Laura wanted to visit the bookstore on Banff Avenue. There was a book — a tome, really — on Matisse that she particularly wanted. It wasn't in the Centre's library, although in her opinion it should have been. She had a copy back in Denver, but it wasn't one of the books she had brought with her. Now she needed it. Oddly enough, it wasn't the paintings themselves but the written descriptions of the artist's approach to painting that never failed to inspire her. And inspiration was what she needed now.

Although famous for its selection of art books, The Banff Book & Art Den did not have the volume she wanted. However, to Richard's immense pleasure, it did have paperback copies of his two most recent thrillers in stock, as Laura already knew. Laura introduced the store manager to Richard. The visit of the well-known author caused a ripple of excitement. A clerk was dispatched up the circular staircase to fetch another clerk who was an ardent fan of Richard's books. A customer bought a copy of *The Blue Agenda* and asked Richard to autograph it for him. Several others, seeing that Richard was happy to oblige, followed suit. Before they left, he had signed all the remaining copies of his books and shaken hands with every member of the staff. The manager promised to move the autographed books to a prominent position just inside the entrance and invited him to drop in whenever he felt like it.

"You handled that beautifully," smiled Laura as they regained the street.

"I enjoy it. It doesn't happen often enough to become a nuisance and I like talking about my books. I can see how movie stars get to hate it, though. But book people are considerate; they don't try to tear the clothes off your back the way some movie fans do."

As he talked, Richard glanced down at the sidewalk. The breeze was sending a tiny glittery object scuttling along just in front of them. By some fluke of the wind, its pace was the same as theirs.

"It's a feather," Laura told him. "It looks like the breast feather of pigeon."

"It's almost as if we were taking our pet insect out for a walk," murmured Richard.

"What a wonderful image! And I love the idea of locomotives being turned loose on the countryside. You should put more little touches like that in your books."

They smiled at each other as a sudden gust of wind picked up the feather and sent it twirling above their heads.

"Are you prepared for the great debate?" she asked, wondering if she was doing the right thing by reminding him of it. Maybe that was why he had taken the day off — he could be too nervous and keyed-up to concentrate on writing.

But the TV show was obviously not preying on his mind, because he looked at her blankly for a moment before his expression cleared and he said, "Debate? Is that what they're calling it? They may be right at that. I expect old Henry will do his best to put me down. But I'm going to try and keep it on a higher plane. Take the high road as the politicians like to say—although they never do."

"When do you leave for Edmonton?"

"We'll drive down to Calgary first thing in the morning and catch a shuttle flight. We'll have to stay overnight in Edmonton as the program doesn't start until 10 p.m. and they're doing it live."

Although she was still upset by the flounder incident, Erika forced herself to go back to the studio right after lunch. As she walked along the path, she was so absorbed in thinking about her book that she didn't see the elk until she was almost upon it. Elk roamed freely in the colony woods, as they did throughout the Banff townsite: browsing on trees, helping themselves to whatever flowers and vegetables took their fancy, stopping traffic as they jaywalked across the downtown streets, and lazing about on front yards like giant lawn ornaments. Although their size was intimidating, Erika had accepted them as part of colony life. But now as a full-grown elk stepped out of the trees and advanced on her, tales of elk attacks came flooding back. After years of relatively peaceful cohabitation with their human neighbours, the elk had suddenly and inexplicably become aggressive. Some blamed it on the floods that had inundated their traditional calving grounds, others blamed it on the golf course that was constructed across their migration route, and still others thought it was the ever-increasing number of tourists that put pressure on the animals. Laura, who seemed to know about these things, said it was because of the fences that Parks Canada had built to keep them off the highway. According to her, the fences had the effect of funnelling the elk right into the Banff town site. Whatever the cause, the fact was that the number of attacks by elk was steadily mounting. *The Crag & Canyon*, Banff's local newspaper, carried stories of people having their noses broken and their legs slashed by the once peaceful animals. Since the colonists had to run the gauntlet of elk in order to get to their studios, these accounts were the subject of much mealtime conversation. On occasion, security personnel were called upon to escort the more timorous artists to and from their studios.

Now it very much looked as if Erika was about to become a statistic — the first elk victim in the colony. The cow elk — she assumed it was a cow because it had no antlers — was pawing the ground and pumping its head up and down in a way that said it meant business. Erika took a step back and looked over her shoulder, wondering if the elk would chase her if she ran back up the path. To her horror she saw that the rest of the herd had silently filed across the path behind her, completely blocking it. They stood there motionless, chocolate brown heads all pointing in her direction. Erika retreated a few more steps but the cow elk kept coming on. If only Geoff were here! With his understanding of animals he would know what to do. The elk made a curious whistling sound and lowered its head as if to charge. Petrified, Erika got ready to jump to one side.

And then suddenly, with a wild yell, John Smith was at her side. He was wearing his admiral's costume and he waved his three-cornered hat at the elk as he fearlessly walked toward the animal, yelling at the top of his voice. The elk stamped her forefeet at the apparition bearing down on her, then snorted, wheeled, and trotted back into the woods. With a sweeping bow, John Smith offered his arm. "Allow me to escort you to your studio, fair lady."

Erika took it gratefully. "Thank you, John Smith. You were very brave."

"Yes, I was, wasn't I?" Adjusting his hat so that it sat squarely on his head, he said, "It's too bad I wasn't properly attired for the occasion. My cowboy outfit would have been perfect. Or better still, I should have been dressed as a matador. That's what I was. A matador!"

Safely inside her studio, Erika wondered if she would be able to concentrate on her writing. The elk incident was a perfect excuse to put off once more dealing with the scandal. Did she have the right to invade people's lives and expose them like this, she asked herself for the hundredth time. She knew *that* was the real reason she kept postponing the moment when she would commit the story to paper. But the encounter with the elk had sent adrenaline coursing through her, giving her a sense of almost reckless well-being. Yes, she would write it, and now was the time to tackle it. She pressed the power switch on her computer.

After four hours of furious, non-stop writing, the first draft of the explosive chapter was almost finished. With it went all Erika's doubts about whether she should publish it. Seeing the words on paper made it seem more like an exciting game, complete with delightfully recherché clues. And it hung together beautifully. They would never dare sue her. Or would they? There were big reputations at stake here and they would undoubtedly deny her story outright. Then the pressure to put up or shut up might compel them to launch legal proceedings. Just like with Jeremy Switzer. But, unlike Jeremy's allegations, hers would stand up in court. Once the vital clues were pointed out, everything else fell into place. Erika banged the pages on the desk to straighten the edges and placed them in the manuscript box.

She glanced out one of the square portholes as she stood up. Night was fast overtaking the brief mountain twilight. It was the time of day, Geoff used to say, "when swallows turn into bats." Except that there were no swallows or bats in the Rocky Mountains in March. Her lips twisted in a bitter smile as she switched on the outside light. Once her stay in Banff was over, she would get on with her life.

Someone was sitting on the bottom step of her studio stairs. She almost groaned aloud when the figure sprang lithely to his feet and turned to face her. It was John Smith and he had changed out of his admiral's uniform into what she presumed to be his civilian clothes — black turtleneck sweater, black jacket and pants. His pale face gazed down at her as he fell into step beside her. Appalled, she heard him asking her to have dinner with him in town. Sure, it was only a dinner invitation, but the anxious look on his face told her it was much more than that. She had to put a stop to this before it got completely out of control.

Turning to face him, she said, "Look, John Smith, I am perfectly happy to be your friend, but I want you to understand that's all I can be. As everybody knows, I'm trying desperately hard to finish my book, and I don't have time for anything else." After a moment's hesitation, she added, "I'm involved with someone back in New York." It wasn't exactly a lie — she *was* still emotionally involved with Geoff.

John Smith, who had put his hand on her arm, snatched it back as if the contact burned him. "I should have known better," he snarled. "You bitches are all alike!"

Stunned by his outburst, Erika remained rooted to the path. After the "nut-cracking" scene, Laura had told her she should talk to Kevin Lavoie. She had put off doing it, but the time had come. Poor Kevin wouldn't appreciate being put in a position where he would have to deal with John Smith.

Erika was right about the colony coordinator's reaction. He shifted uncomfortably in his chair as she told him about her increasingly alarming encounters with the performance artist.

"You certainly are being harassed," he said when she had finished. The bureaucrat in him seemed to take comfort from that categorization of John Smith's actions. Harassment was an officially defined offence and could be dealt with on that basis.

Two hours later Kevin Lavoie reported back to Erika in her room. "Well, I've had my little talk with John Smith."

"And?"

"I don't think what I had to say made any impression on him whatsoever. He seems to have an ability not to hear what he doesn't want to hear."

"You don't suppose he's got one of those fixations you read about in the papers — you know, where a man gets the wild idea that a movie star is madly in love with him and writes her letters and follows her everywhere. Not even the threat of being sent to jail can convince him he's wrong about her secretly loving him."

"Something like that. It's as if he can't bring himself to admit that you really object to what he's doing."

"But he knows that I complained to you." Erika bit her lip. "That could have been a mistake. It might make him worse."

"I doubt it." Lavoie said reassuringly. "If he's convinced himself you really don't mind what he's doing, he'll have to ignore the fact that you spoke to me. I know it's annoying, but I don't think it's serious enough to worry about."

"It's more than annoying," Erika told him as he got up to leave. "It's goddamn dangerous."

Lavoie had decided there was no point in telling Erika that as John Smith exited his office he was muttering, "The little bitch! She's no better than the rest."

As he let himself out a side door of the residence, Lavoie saw an RCMP cruiser pulling away. Christ. Were the police still looking into Montrose's death? Drunks falling down stairwells and a weirdo harassing a female writer. What had he ever done to deserve a job like this — nurse-maiding a bunch of adult delinquents? So far, the media had treated Montrose's death as an accident. There had been no follow up to the initial story. But if it turned out not to be an accident ...! And if John Smith actually attacked Erika—which was how these things often turned out!

It didn't bear thinking about, and it couldn't be happening at a worse time. After a long courtship by Alec Fraser, the Centre's charismatic president, it looked as though the Chinook Foundation was finally ready to come through with a munificent donation. Alec was hoping for three million. The chairman of the Foundation was due to visit the Centre in a little more than a couple of weeks, and the provincial minister of culture was coming down from Edmonton at the same time. Everything would be in place for the big announcement. Somehow he would have to keep the lid on until then. The Chinook board of directors were notoriously conservative.

While Kevin was thinking these gloomy thoughts, Laura stepped back from a canvas and slipped out of her paint-smeared apron. Assailed with a mild case of guilt from taking the day off, she had gone to her studio directly after an early dinner. Instead of working on the painting she had begun to block out, she retouched a still life, deepening the green of the leaves to put them more in the background.

She wondered what the art world would make of her new works. Isaac, her excitable New York dealer, would have a bird when he saw the still lifes instead of the abstracts he was expecting. And the critics would probably say she should have stuck with the abstracts for which she was so well known. To hell with it. She needed a change of pace and the colony was the place for new beginnings. Laura checked her watch. There was plenty of time for a swim before the pool closed.

The pool, along with other athletic facilities, was in the Sally Borden Building — the Banff Centre, with its world-wide reputation and glamorous setting, attracts many benefactors and honours the most generous of them by naming buildings, theatres, and halls after them. Laura recognized the Tchaikovsky Second Piano Concerto thundering down from the speakers as she emerged from the locker room. That meant Michel was the lifeguard on duty — he had a passion for Tchaikovsky, particularly the three concertos, and liked to turn the volume up late at night when the pool was mostly deserted. Light from a late-rising moon streamed in through the glass roof.

Laura settled into the whirlpool with a grateful sigh, letting the powerful water jets work their wonders with her fatigued painting muscles. Then she dove, with a considerable splash, into the pool. At night she liked to swim on her back, looking up at her reflection in the sloping glass roof. By some trick of light, any part of a swimmer's skin that was not completely submerged, turned black. It was like swimming while wearing a black mask. The illusion never failed to delight her, and she was quite happy not knowing its cause.

Climbing out of the pool, she exchanged a few words with Michel, a graduate music student who was studying the violin, and continued on to the women's locker room to change. When she came out, Richard was standing at the counter getting a towel and locker key from the attendant. Impulsively, she went up to him, kissed him lightly on the lips, and whispered, "Thanks for today, and good luck tomorrow."

Startled, he reached for her. But he was too late. She slipped out of his grasp and ran laughing up the stairs.

chapter five

The TV lounge on the third floor of Lloyd Hall was rapidly filling up as colonists and art students streamed in just before ten o'clock on the following night. Marek Dabrowski was waiting for Laura and intercepted her as she was about to enter the TV room. Erika, who had ridden down in the elevator with her, said she would save Laura a seat. Instinctively, Laura looked around for Isabelle Ross but there was no sign of her. Her husband and daughter had left for home that morning, and, according to the grapevine, Dennis Ross had the look of a man in shock.

Drawing Laura to one side, Marek said, "Since you were the one who alerted me to what Eckart was up to, I think you should know what I have decided to do."

He paused as if expecting Laura to say something. When she didn't, he went on, "I called him down to my studio and told him that I had decided not to report him, much as he deserved it. I also told him that I would be monitoring everything he published and that if I heard so much as a single bar of my music in one of his compositions, I would ... blow the whistle." It was obvious from the careful way he pronounced it that Marek had learned the idiomatic phrase especially for the occasion.

"I think you made the right decision." Inwardly, Laura was relieved. If Marek had decided to report Eckart to the chair of the music department, she would inevitably have been drawn into the affair in the role of a corroborating witness. "I trust Carl was properly grateful?"

"Grateful? No, I wouldn't say he was grateful. At first, when he didn't know what I was going to do, he was humble, almost servile. When he knew he was off the ..."

"Hook," supplied Laura, and Marek went on, "Thank you. I always have trouble with your English idioms, much as I enjoy them." He paused and then said with a frown, "When Eckart realized I was not going to report him, he became his usual belligerent self again. It was as if the whole thing was somehow my fault."

"Hey, you two." Erika was waving at them from inside the television room. "The show's about to start."

The program opened with a close-up of the host, Kate Lewis — a good-looking woman in her late thirties, with straight dark hair framing a pale complexioned face and lively blue eyes. In some ways, she reminded Laura of Erika. She glanced sideways at Erika to see if she had caught the resemblance too, but her friend's face was expressionless as she watched the screen. Erika looked absolutely exhausted. She had told Laura that she had been writing in her studio since early that morning. To Laura's surprise, Erika had come equipped with a clipboard and ballpoint pen.

The talk show host began by introducing Norrington, describing him as a literary guru whose books of literary criticism and philosophy were required reading in every literature course in North America. The camera zoomed in for a close-up of Norrington's face, dominated by that large nose, which seemed to lead his head around. The rest of his face looked as if it had been assembled from disparate parts. His small mouth was pursed in a deprecating smile, but behind his thick glasses his eyes glinted with self-satisfaction.

The camera switched to Richard as Kate Lewis began to talk about his books. There was no hint of the reverential tone she had used to introduce Norrington as she described Richard as a writer of thrillers "that some reviewers have been known to call lurid." The introduction was insultingly offhand, but Richard appeared completely unruffled. His good-natured smile never wavered.

"Now, Dr. Norrington." Kate Lewis paused and looked archly at Norrington. "It is 'doctor', isn't it?"

Norrington smiled with false modesty. "I do have a doctorate in literature, and two universities have been gracious enough to confer honorary doctorates on me, so, yes, I think I can fairly be called doctor."

"I think so, too. Can you tell us something about the project you're currently working on?"

Again Norrington smiled, but this time the false modesty was replaced by condescension. "It's quite an ambitious undertaking. In fact, once it is completed, it will be my major opus. It has, I'm afraid, a rather formidable working title — *How The Post-Modern Novel Challenges The Boundaries Of Art.*"

"I'm impressed," smiled the TV host, leading him on. "What does it mean?"

Norrington launched into a lengthy discourse, replete with words like "self-reflexivity", "taxonomic categories", "genre distinctions", and similar jargon.

Erika was scribbling furiously, like a college student taking notes at a lecture. Once or twice she made a small sound as if agreeing with a point Norrington was making. The two of them were in the same field, so what Henry was saying was probably fascinating to her, thought Laura.

While Norrington droned on, the camera switched briefly to Richard. He appeared to be listening with keen interest. He was obviously following his game plan to stay on the "high road."

"I can understand why you have won so many awards for your scholarship," said Kate Lewis when Norrington finally wound down. Trying to inject some life into the program, she turned to Richard.

"I've heard people describe some of the sex scenes in your books as lurid."

Richard grinned. "Surely you don't expect me to let all the research I've done go to waste, do you?"

This brought a smile from the host and a hastily suppressed laugh from one of the camera operators on the floor.

Still smiling, Kate Lewis asked, "Have you won any awards for your books, Richard?"

Richard shook his head. "I don't write to win awards. The only award I'm interested in is that my books are read and enjoyed by a lot of people. Being on the bestseller list is good enough for me."

"Fair enough." The interviewer seemed to like that answer. "Do your books regularly make the bestseller list?"

"The last two have. In fact, *The Blue Agenda* got as high as fifth."

The camera followed him as he leaned forward, his handsome face animated. "My editor and I are really excited about the novel I'm working on now. I have the feeling it could be headed for a respectable run at the top of the list."

Norrington sniffed audibly, and Kate Lewis turned to him. "I gather you don't think too much of the thriller genre."

"Let's just say my sympathies are with the trees."

"Say, that's good!" Richard threw back his head and laughed. "I'll remember that one! But Henry is being too hard on the thriller genre. I think it's a versatile literary vehicle. You can explore almost any theme you want with it. For example, the book I am working on now is more psychological than anything else, and I like to think the main protagonist is a character with considerable depth."

"That's an intriguing thought. Let's explore it a little further." Richard's unaffected good humour was winning the host over and she knew it was having the same effect on the audience. The director of the show saw it too, and, to Norrington's obvious chagrin, the relaxed, likeable author received the lion's share of attention for the rest of the program.

When the credits rolled, saying that tonight's guests had been flown to Edmonton courtesy of Air Canada and would be staying at the MacDonald Hotel, there was general agreement in Lloyd Hall that Richard had clearly won the day.

"Henry's his own worst enemy," said Jeremy as he pressed the off button on the remote control. "He's so used to lecturing to a captive audience of students that he can't see how stiff and formal he comes across to the average viewer."

"I find that hard to believe," replied Laura musingly. "After all, he's not a stranger to television and should know what works and what doesn't. Maybe he just had an off night. I think Richard's casual attitude about things, including Henry's opinion, throws him off stride."

"Well, it's back to the studio for me," said Erika, as she stood up. Her air of fatigue seemed to have been replaced by one of excitement. There must have been something in Henry's monologue that I missed, thought Laura. Maybe to his peers old Henry was pretty hot stuff.

She looked at Erika with concern. "It's late. Why not get some rest? You've been going awfully hard."

"My book is almost finished and I can't stay away from it."

"That's wonderful," Laura congratulated her.

"I'll walk you there." John Smith swung a cloak around his narrow shoulders and fastened the clasp. "In case of an elk attack."

Tired and edgy, Erika snapped, "I'll take my chances with the elk, thank you." As soon as the hurtful words were out of her mouth, she wanted to call them back, but John Smith was no longer there.

Laura slept with the drapes pulled back so she could see the dark mass of Mount Rundle as she fell asleep. She could not remember if it was the faint orange glow or the need to go to the bathroom that woke her. But something did. Still half asleep, she turned her head on the pillow and watched as the ominous glow grew steadily brighter. Throwing aside the covers, she leapt out of bed and ran to the window. There was a fire in the colony! She tried to phone security but the line was busy. In the distance she heard the rising wail of the sirens as the fire engines raced through the sleeping town.

It must be one of the eight studios in the woods! Dear God, it might be hers! The flames lit her way as Laura, wearing a terrycloth robe over her pyjamas, rounded the first music hut and ran across the service road. With a whooshing roar, a towering pine exploded into flame. The path was filled with running figures shouting instructions to each other. Laura hurried across the footbridge and then stopped dead in her tracks. The boat studio was on fire. Except that it wasn't just a fire, it was a roaring, orange inferno that was literally vaporizing the dry, weathered hull. If Erika was trapped inside that holocaust she was beyond hope.

Laura scanned the gathering crowd for a glimpse of her friend. The flames leaping skyward lit the scene as if it were high noon. With growing desperation, she darted from person to person, searching each face. But none was the one she was looking for. A gasp went up as another tree burst into crackling flames like a giant firecracker. Erika must be sleeping in her room at Lloyd Hall. After all, it was two-thirty in the morning and she had been exhausted to begin with. Clinging to the thought, Laura headed back toward the residence, running against the tide of excited people, most of them with coats or jackets hastily thrown over nightclothes, streaming toward the fire. With a wailing crescendo of sirens and urgent blatting of horns, three fire trucks turned down the service road and ground to a halt. Firefighters, bulky in their yellow fire resistant gear, jumped down and ran toward the fire, unreeling hoses as they went.

Moments later, the police arrived, the lights of the cruiser flashing red and blue against the walls of the music huts. When Laura saw Corporal Lindstrom getting out of the passenger side, she changed direction and hurried over to the police officer. "Karen, that studio belongs to a friend of mine — Erika Dekter, you remember her, don't you?" The corporal nodded and Laura went on, "I can't find her anywhere. I'm going to her room to see if she's there."

"You do that," said the policewoman crisply. "And report back to me right away."

Frantically, Laura pounded on Erika's door. Rattling the doorknob, she yelled at Erika to wake up, but there was no answer. Maybe she had taken a sleeping pill and was dead to the world. Heart pounding against her ribs, Laura tore down the hall and ran back with a wooden chair, the one the janitor dozed on while he waited for his afternoon shift to end. She smashed it against the door until it finally broke apart in her hands. Dropping the remnants of the chair, she called out to Erika in a despairing voice. There was no answer. By now, she wasn't expecting one. Sleeping pills or not, no one could have slept through the unholy racket she had made.

The boat studio had burned to the ground and the firefighters had shifted their efforts to trying to save the rest of the colony. Streams of water arced skyward as they soaked the trees on the perimeter of the fire. Fortunately, there was no wind to send the flames leaping from treetop to treetop. Laura thought of her own studio and the months of work represented by the paintings in it. But that was swept aside by the unthinkable possibility that Erika had perished in the fire. Once again, Laura scanned the crowd of onlookers in the garish light of the flames, but this time with diminished hope. She saw Corporal Lindstrom panning the crowd with her video camera.

The Mountie wasn't the only one taping the fire; Laura saw John Smith at the edge of the crowd squinting through the viewfinder of his camera. He would probably use the footage in one of his performances. Or maybe the fire *was* his performance. The idea was not as preposterous as it first seemed.

Laura pushed her way through the crowd and tapped a Mountie on the arm. He turned around and she saw it was Constable Peplinski. He recognized her, and she told him she had to talk to the corporal. He waved Karen over, but she had already spotted Laura and was heading toward her.

"She's not in her room," Laura shouted frantically against the sound of burning trees, hissing and steaming as the streams of water hit them. The Mountie's lips twisted in a grimace and she motioned toward the fire chief who was standing nearby, glumly surveying the remains of the studio. It was reduced to nothing more than a pile of ash, blackened with the torrents of water that had been dumped on it. The boat's iron rudder still stood defiantly upright. It and the concrete piles on which the boat's cradle had rested were the only things left standing. The fire chief winced when the corporal told him that there might have been someone in the studio.

"It's completely saturated with water so it'll be cool enough for us to take a look," the chief said. "You going to join us, Karen?"

She nodded mutely, and he asked if she had ever seen the body of a fire victim. When she shook her head, he muttered something about there having to be a first time for everything in their line of work and, with the corporal following him, went off to detail two of his men to join in the search.

A few tendrils of smoke still rose from the charred branches and trunks of the burned trees, but the flames had been doused and sparks no longer flew. The other studios were safe. Laura registered that fact somewhere in the back of her mind, but all her attention was focused on the policewoman and the firefighters as they gingerly stepped onto the sodden rubble that had once been a studio. A murmur of excitement and apprehension rippled through the crowd as they realized the grisly purpose of the search.

Behind Laura, the colonists were clustered together at the barricade as if seeking comfort from each other. As usual, John Smith stood a little bit apart, his camera focused on the firefighters sifting through the rubble. Jeremy, wearing a fur coat over his pyjamas — trust Jeremy to have a fur coat — was pushing his way through the crowd towards Laura. "My God, do they think Erika's in there?"

His question put into words what they were all thinking. Taking a quick glance over her shoulder, she replied, "I don't know. But she's not in her room and I can't find her anywhere."

With Jeremy standing by her side, Laura turned her full attention back to the burned out studio. A firefighter was bending down to lift a charred timber that had once been a rib of the boat's hull. The fire chief was leaning toward Corporal Lindstrom, saying something in her ear.

"Smell that?" asked the chief.

Corporal Lindstrom sniffed and almost gagged. Mixed in with the acrid smell of smoke was another odour, so cloyingly sweet it stuck in the throat.

"She's in here somewhere," the chief grunted. He pointed to where the prow would have been. "That's where the couch was. See that piece of metal spring? If she fell asleep, this is where she'll be." He nodded to one of his men who carefully began to remove lumps of sodden ash with his gloved hands. It was awful, far worse than anything Karen could possibly have imagined. The object resembled nothing human. Rivulets of fat ran down the sides of the shrivelled torso, two pathetic stumps were all that remained of the legs, the head had shrunk to a third of its size and what had been a mouth now looked like the beak of a bird.

Karen gasped and turned aside, fighting back the nausea that rose in her throat. The fire chief looked away until she had regained her composure. "What a horrible way to die," she murmured, straightening her shoulders.

The fire chief nodded. "That's one of the worst I've seen, and I've seen more than my share." Motioning his men to cover what was left of Erika's body with a tarpaulin, the chief went on, "The fire must have been white hot to incinerate the body like that."

"Meaning it could have been set?" Karen's investigative instincts were now back in control.

"We won't know for sure until the arson squad checks it out, but everything points that way. The only times I've ever seen a body burned like that have been in fires that were deliberately set."

John Smith stepped up to the barricade and zoomed his camera in on Karen's face. "Erika's dead," he announced. "I can tell it from the look on that Mountie's face."

Laura felt her knees buckling and would have fallen if Jeremy hadn't grabbed her around the waist and held her up.

"Holy Jesus!" Jeremy muttered. All the hoses had been turned off and everything was still and eerily quiet.

John Smith shut off his camera and intoned sepulchrally, "She wouldn't let me protect her." It sounded as if he felt Erika deserved her fate.

"Are you all right?" Karen had come over and was looking anxiously at Laura.

"I'm okay now." Laura released her hold on Jeremy's arm. "Is it Erika?"

"We won't know for sure until we have the dental records checked. All we know at the moment is that there are human remains."

"How could it have happened?" whispered Laura as if asking herself.

"Did she smoke?" asked the fire chief. "That's how it usually happens. They fall asleep with a lighted cigarette and they're overcome with smoke before they wake up. At least that way they don't suffer," he added as if to comfort her.

"Erika didn't smoke."

Before the chief could reply he was called away by one of his men. "Can I speak to you alone, Corporal?" he asked when he returned.

"I'd like Ms. Janeway to hear what you have to say. She's been helping with my investigation of another unexplained death in the colony."

"I heard about that one. Guy fell down the stairs." The chief shook his head. "I've been telling Kevin Lavoie for years that damn railing was too low. Maybe now he'll listen." Shrugging massive shoulders, he said to Karen, "If you want the lady to listen in, that's okay with me. We're going to call in the arson squad from Calgary, but I don't need them to tell me the studio was torched. There are a couple of spots where you can see that the fire was especially hot. In fact, the heat was so intense that it actually burned the soil underneath. That's where the arsonist would have poured the gasoline or some other incendiary material, and lit it. Gives them away every time."

"One of those spots being underneath where we found the body?"

"Right. Whoever it was didn't want to take any chances."

"So it's murder," said the policewoman.

"The person who set the fire might not have known there was someone in the studio," Laura pointed out.

"It's still murder," replied Karen. "If someone is killed in the course of a criminal act, it's murder, regardless of intent."

chapter six

There was no sleep for anyone in the Centre that night, and the fire and the ensuing commotion brought many of the townspeople to the scene. At breakfast in the Banquet Hall, where there was an almost palpable silence instead of the usual hum of conversation, a hollow-eyed Laura watched Karen struggling to swallow a piece of toast, finally managing to wash it down with some milk. If what she had seen in the fire was enough to put a professional police officer off her food, it must have been truly awful. Laura pushed her bowl of granola to one side. The two women smiled wanly at each other.

Karen's cell phone rang. She listened to the brief message, said "10-4", and switched it off. "The Crime Scene Unit has dusted Erika's room, so we're free to check it out."

"Banff has a Crime Scene Unit?"

"It's just two regular officers who have been trained to do the work when necessary. As it is in this case."

Karen, energized by getting back into action, adjusted the angle of her cap and led the way out of the Banquet Hall.

"If your friend was murdered," Karen said, "the key might be something in this room. Let's check out things together. You could recognize the significance of something that I would overlook."

"Okay. Incidentally, your Crime Scene Unit will come up with my fingerprints. I've been in and out of this room practically every day."

"I know. We'll have to fingerprint everyone who had a legitimate reason to be in the room. For elimination purposes. I hope you don't mind?"

"Not in the slightest. So long as they're destroyed when the investigation is over."

"That's standard procedure. Let's get started."

Laura opened a bureau drawer and smiled sadly to herself as she gazed down at its contents. Like Erika herself, her things were exquisite. The bureau drawers were filled with neatly folded silk under-garments, and smartly-styled dresses and suits hung in the open closet.

"Everything is so neat and tidy, it's impossible to tell whether anyone has been here before us," Karen sighed as she unfolded a filmy garment and placed it to one side. "All they would have to do is put everything back the way it was. Well, let's try her desk."

"I can't understand why it's not here," Laura muttered after they had gone through the drawers of the built-in desk.

"What isn't here?"

"A copy of her manuscript. Or at least a computer disc." Laura went back over to the clothes closet and ran her hand along the top shelf. She stepped back and shook her head. "It's just not here. We've looked every place it could be. A manuscript isn't the easiest thing in the world to hide, either."

"Have you ever seen this manuscript?"

"Bits and pieces. She kept it in a locked drawer in her studio. She probably had some of it stored on discs, but they're not here either."

"Maybe her publisher will have a copy."

"She didn't have a publisher. She was writing the book on spec."

"You mean the book she was working on no longer exists?"

"It looks that way. God, how she would have hated that! To die without leaving something behind."

"Are we looking at a possible motive here?"

Laura shrugged. "She was writing a book of scholarly literary criticism. Not exactly the sort of thing one kills for."

"People can be mighty touchy about their reputations. Especially artistic types."

Thinking of the courtroom battles between Montrose and Jeremy, Laura had to agree. Hesitantly, Laura opened the card case they had found in the top drawer of Erika's desk. It contained her New York State driving licence, a couple of credit cards and, tucked inside the back flap, Geoff's business card. Until then, Laura had only known Geoff's first name, but here it was: Geoffrey Hamilton, partner in a law firm with a Wall Street address.

"Find something?" asked Karen.

Laura handed her the card. "That's the man Erika had a relationship with. But it's over. He broke it off not long before she came here."

"*He* broke it off?"

"Apparently he decided he couldn't leave his family. Erika was badly hurt, but I have the feeling she was beginning to get over it."

"If he's the one who did the breaking off, it doesn't give him much of a motive."

"Maybe I should call him at his office. He has a right to know about Erika. Do you have any objection?"

"I've been given an office in Donald Cameron Hall to work from. Let's make the call from there." Karen glanced at her watch. "They're probably out to lunch in New York, but it's worth a try. Here's a calling card number you can use."

Geoff Hamilton wasn't in his office, nor was he out to lunch. He was out of the country on business, his secretary said in imperious tones, but if Laura cared to leave her name and telephone number he would get the message when he called in and would be in touch with her. Karen frowned thoughtfully when Laura hung up. "Interesting that he's out of the country at the same time his ex-lover was killed. When he calls, Mr. Hamilton will have to verify his whereabouts for the last twenty-four hours."

As it turned out, there was no need to wait for his telephone call. Within minutes, the reception desk called through to say, in a hushed, conspiratorial voice, that there was a gentleman asking for Erika Dekter.

"What's his name?"

"Geoffrey Hamilton. He says he's a friend of Ms. Dekter."

Karen put her hand over the mouthpiece and looked up at Laura. "You won't believe this, but Geoffrey Hamilton is downstairs asking for Erika." Removing her hand, she told the receptionist to bring Hamilton directly to her office.

Geoffrey Hamilton was visibly shaken when he saw the uniformed policewoman behind the desk. Karen shook hands gravely and introduced herself and Laura. Laura could see why Erika had fallen for him. He was good looking, not exactly handsome but all the more attractive for that, and somewhere in his early forties. The most striking thing about him was the unmistakable air of intelligence that emanated from his keen, hazel eyes. In a way, he was not unlike Richard. Those hazel eyes were wary as he slowly lowered himself into a chair. "Is something wrong, Corporal?" The chevrons on her sleeve were not inverted as they would be in the States, but the rank was the same.

"Ms. Dekter's studio burned down last night."

"Dear God. She'll be dev—" He stopped and stared at the Mountie. "For God's sake, she wasn't in it, was she?"

"We're not sure yet. But you'll have to be prepared for that possibility. There were human remains and Ms. Dekter has disappeared, so there *is* cause for concern. We're checking the dental records and should have the answer shortly. We were able to get the name of her New York dentist from her mother, and he will fax her records to us." She paused, and then said, "I'm sorry to have to tell you all this, Mr. Hamilton."

He didn't seem to hear her. He slumped back in his chair and stared blankly at the wall behind her. Finally, Laura said softly, "Erika and I were good friends, Geoff. She told me about you."

"I came here to persuade her to marry me," he whispered.

The corporal cleared her throat and turned to a fresh page in her notebook. "Perhaps while you are here, I might have your statement. When did you arrive in Banff?"

"Just a few minutes ago. Wait a minute. Are you saying the fire wasn't an accident?"

"We have reason to believe arson was involved. If so, that makes it a homicide."

"You mean murder?" Hamilton was incredulous.

"It's murder in the first degree if the arsonist intended to kill someone. Otherwise it's murder in the second degree."

"Nobody had any reason to kill Erika." Geoff looked at Laura as if seeking her support. "Erika was an academic. She did some teaching at a small junior college in New York. She also freelanced as a book reviewer and that part of her career was really beginning to take off."

"Maybe someone whose book she savaged held a grudge," said Laura, dismissing the idea as soon as she said it.

"People don't commit murder over book reviews," Hamilton said, waving the suggestion aside. "Besides Erika ...," he hesitated over the tense, "... is basically a kind person. Her reviews are perceptive and quite often humorous, but she was never deliberately cruel or condescending. She had a reputation for being honest and fair."

"So you can't think of any motive?" asked Karen writing in her notebook.

"None whatsoever. The whole thing is crazy!"

"We're looking into it," the Mountie said. "Meanwhile, could I have a brief statement of your movements for the record?"

Geoff had flown to Calgary via Toronto, arriving at five o'clock yesterday afternoon. He had picked up a rental car at the airport and checked into the Westin Hotel where he stayed overnight. He had driven up to Banff that morning, leaving Calgary at nine and arriving at the Centre around ten-thirty. "When did the fire start?" he asked as he finished his recital.

"Around two o'clock this morning."

When his expression didn't change, Corporal Lindstrom said, "It doesn't seem to surprise you that she was in the studio at that hour."

"She often pulls 'all-nighters'. It's a hangover from her college days." He turned to Laura. "I'd like to talk to you when you have a moment. About Erika."

"Of course. Why don't you wait downstairs in the reception area, and I'll see you in a few minutes or so."

"He has no alibi," remarked Karen when she and Laura were alone.

"Technically, no. But there's no way he could have arranged that fire after arriving in Calgary at five yesterday afternoon. For one thing, he'd have no idea of the layout of the colony."

"That's true, but it's not impossible. He could have made an earlier trip up here and made all the necessary arrangements." Frowning, the Mountie leaned back in her chair, and said, "I'm not saying he did it, Laura. I'm just saying he could have."

"Are you sure you want to do this?" Laura peered dubiously into Geoff's drawn face.

"I'm sure," he muttered, and they continued along the path toward the colony. Overhead a helicopter dragon-flied in low sweeping circles over the burnt-out area. "That's the police," Laura told him. "Corporal Lindstrom said they had hired a helicopter to take aerial photos of the fire."

"I just can't get my mind around the fact that it was arson. There's absolutely no reason why anyone would want to kill Erika."

Privately Laura thought how presumptuous and foolish it was for someone to think they knew all there was to know about another person. But all she said was, "There seems to be no doubt that the fire was deliberately set, but whoever did it may not have known someone was inside."

Geoff's only comment was a skeptically raised eyebrow.

As they went past the large music hut, Laura glanced in through the open window. Isabelle was seated at the concert grand playing what sounded like a requiem. Her back was to them but the long dark hair cascading down her back was unmistakable. The image was so striking that Laura knew some day she would try to capture it on canvas.

The scene of the fire was still sealed off, but the Mountie on duty, after a quick, verifying glance at a photo the Centre had provided the police with, told Laura she and her guest could proceed to her studio. However, they would have to take the long way round by the road. This suited Laura perfectly because it would keep Geoff from getting too close a look at the place where Erika had died. As it was, all they could see were skeletal black tree trunks. The acrid smell of smoke and wet ash still hung heavily in the air. She let herself and Geoff in through the side door of her studio, the door that had been made extra high to allow large canvases to be moved in and out.

Geoff stood and stared in silence at the paintings, lingering longest on the large still life. "You are very, very good," he said finally with the air of one who knows. "Just as some musicians have perfect pitch, you have a perfect eye for colour."

Laura was impressed. Ever since her earliest days at art school she had been recognized as a superb colourist.

Still gazing at the paintings, Geoff murmured, "Thank you for letting me see that there may still be some worthwhile things in life."

"Erika meant a great deal to you." Without ever saying so, they had abandoned all pretense that Erika might still be alive.

"It took a separation to do it, but I came to realize that I couldn't live without her." He paused, then said, "But that's what I will have to learn how to do now, isn't it?"

"I take it Erika didn't know you were coming?"

"No. I wanted to surprise her. God help me."

You were taking a chance there, my friend, thought Laura. You could easily have found her involved in a new affair. Sometimes the mountains did that to people, especially those on the rebound.

"I really do want to see her studio," persisted Geoff.

"There's not much to see. Let me check it out with Corporal Lindstrom." Laura picked up the emergency phone. Today everything was an emergency. "Geoff Hamilton is here with me in my studio. He wants to have a look at Erika's studio and I thought I would ask if that would be all right with you," said Laura, emphasizing the "all right."

"The body's been removed, if that's what you mean. The dental records have arrived from New York and they're checking them now."

"That's fine then." Laura replaced the receiver with a sigh of relief. "We'll walk as far as we can down the path," she told Geoff. "We should be able to see it from there."

A huge black bird, at least three times the size of the average crow, plopped heavily down from a tree and swaggered along the trail in front of them, its tail insolently swinging from side to side. Geoff looked at it with something close to dread, as though it were an omen.

"Erika said you were quite a bird watcher," Laura found herself saying.

"I am. And that's the first northern raven I've seen. I hope to God I never see another one. I'll always associate it with what happened here."

"You're out of luck there, I'm afraid," said Laura matter-of-factly. "Banff is overrun with them."

Geoff took one appalled look at the site of the fire and quickly turned away. "Let's get out of here!" he said in a strangled voice.

Back inside Laura's studio, he took several deep breaths as he fought to regain his composure. "I wasn't ready for that." Moving agitatedly around the studio, he said, "I can't believe that I've lost her. Not now. Not when the way was finally clear for us to spend our lives together." He stopped his restless pacing to look at Laura. "I've asked my wife for a divorce."

"Are you going back to her?"

"No. That part of my life is over. It's been over for a long while. I just didn't face up to it in time."

Corporal Lindstrom was standing beside a cruiser in the parking lot, talking to the uniformed driver. She waved Laura and Geoff over as they rounded the music hut.

"The medical examiner has confirmed that the body is Erika's. I'm very sorry, Mr. Hamilton."

Laura heard Geoff's sharp intake of breath, then he said, "I guess we all knew that's how it would turn out. Still ..." Blinking rapidly, he fished in his pocket for a Kleenex and blew his nose.

The Mountie said, "May I ask what your plans are, Mr. Hamilton?"

Geoff looked a little taken aback by the question, but answered civilly enough. "I really haven't given it any thought. Maybe I'll stay around here for a few days and take Erika's body back to New York with me."

"I'm afraid it may be several weeks before her body is released. The medical examiner will want to have a number of tests done and ..." She let her voice trail off, but both her listeners silently finished the thought for her. There wasn't much left for the medical experts to work with. "It would be very helpful if you would remain in the area for a day or so. To give us some background on the victim," she added smoothly when the Wall Street lawyer shot her a sharp look.

"I'll be happy to help your investigation in any way I can," he said formally. Then he shook his head in disbelief. "I'm still having a hard time accepting that this might be a deliberate murder. As Laura says, whoever torched the place may not have known she was inside."

"I guess I was just trying to make myself feel better," Laura said and shook her head. "But I don't really believe it. If that had been the case, Erika would have been able to escape through one of the port holes."

"Are you suggesting she was tied up?" asked Geoff in a shocked whisper.

"Possibly. But it's more likely she was drugged. We'll know for sure when the tests are finished," the corporal said.

"That way she wouldn't know what was happening," Laura said in what she hoped was a comforting tone.

"I guess so." He didn't look very comforted. "I was thinking I might check out of the Westin and get a hotel room here in Banff."

"That makes sense," approved the corporal as Geoff unlocked his rental car, a black Chevrolet Caprice. "Let me know where you'll be staying."

"I talked with the Westin," she continued as she and Laura watched Geoff drive off. "He charged the parking fee to his room—which means he got a pass that allows him to drive in and out as he pleases."

"Oh? Did you check with the parking attendants to see if they saw him leave?"

"Apparently there was a big do at the hotel last night — the premier's dinner with more than 800 guests. You can imagine the parade of cars streaming in and out of the parkade. Nobody remembers seeing Geoff leave, but that doesn't mean a thing."

"But what about coming back? There can't have been many cars driving into the parkade at four o'clock in the morning."

"I thought of that. And he wouldn't have to, if he's the murderer. At that hour he could have left the car parked on one of the streets near the hotel."

"You've given this a lot of thought, haven't you?"

The policewoman shrugged. "I'm not saying he did it. It's just that I haven't been able to eliminate him." She made a few notes in her notebook, then said, "Speaking of possible suspects, have you come across that performance artist in your travels?"

"John Smith? No. Has he gone missing?"

"I wouldn't say that. It's just that I haven't been able to locate him. I'm sure he'll turn up in his own good time. But if you do see him, let me know right away."

chapter seven

Richard Madrin had returned from his TV stint in Edmonton in time for lunch, joining some of the colonists at their table in the dining room. He had heard about the fire on a couple of newscasts. Coupled with Montrose's death, which seemed less of an accident now, the fatal fire and the presence of the arson squad had ignited the interest of the press. So far, the identity of the victim had not been made public, but he knew it was the boat studio that had burned and he nodded quiet acceptance when Laura told him the dental records confirmed that it was Erika.

"What did she do? Fall asleep? She looked completely wiped the past few days."

"The police think she might have been drugged."

"You mean as in murder?"

"There seems to be no doubt that the fire was deliberately set, so it kind of follows, doesn't it?"

"I hear you spent the morning with her ex-boyfriend?" Jeremy Switzer's eyes were bright with curiosity as he leaned across the lunch table.

"Yes," replied Laura. "He's a Wall Street lawyer. He was going to ask her to marry him."

"His timing wasn't so hot, was it?" said Jeremy, then clapped his hand over his mouth as if realizing that his impulsive remark was too crass even for him.

Laura gave him a scathing look, then turned back to Richard. "I don't see Henry. Did he come back with you? Incidentally, I thought you were great."

"Henry decided to spend the day in Edmonton. He said there were some bookstores he wanted to visit."

"You sure showed him up," grinned Jeremy. "That's why he didn't want to travel back with you."

"If anything, Henry showed himself up," rejoined Laura.

Richard was looking at Jeremy, but it was clear he meant to address the table as a whole. "I can assure you I had no intention of showing Henry up. I just answered the questions that were put to me."

Jeremy shrugged and changed the subject. "Speaking of missing persons, has anyone seen our illustrious performance artist? The Mounties ..." Jeremy lingered on the word as if savouring its romantic flavour, "have been looking for him everywhere. Disappearing like that can raise some nasty suspicions."

"There he is now," remarked Richard casually.

John Smith stood at the top of the stairs, looking like something the grave had given up with considerable misgivings. He was wearing a black armband and his face was daubed with streaks of white and black makeup that made it look as if it were covered with ash. Oblivious of his fellow artists, he went to an empty table where he immediately proceeded to gulp down three large glasses of orange juice.

Murmuring something about going to the washroom, Laura slipped away and hurried up the stairs to Corporal Lindstrom's office where she found the policewoman at her desk munching on a toasted ham and cheese sandwich. Hastily swallowing the last bite, she sent a constable down to the dining room to collect the performance artist. "But wait until he's finished his lunch," she added.

To the extent that a face daubed with macabre makeup could be said to be expressionless, John Smith's was. He showed neither resentment nor interest, but simply stared with flat, dead eyes at the corporal through round-rimmed glasses.

"Mr. Smith ... ," the corporal began.

"John Smith," he interrupted. "Plain John Smith."

"Very well, John Smith. I will need to have an account of your movements last night."

"I didn't go to the bathroom once," he replied.

"That's not what I meant and you know it," Lindstrom snapped. "This is a serious business, John Smith. We know you were at the scene of the fire. It seems you are a video enthusiast."

"Just like you." The eyes behind the granny glasses suddenly gleamed with excitement. "I got some great footage. I'm going to use it in my project."

"What project is that?"

"The performance I'm working on. It's almost finished. It'll be the highlight of the year around here. I'll see that you get an invitation."

"That's very kind of you." The Mountie cleared her throat as if to get the interview back on track. "Now, if I could have an account of your ... of where you were last night? I noticed you were fully dressed at the fire."

"That's because I hadn't been to bed. John Smith does not sleep a third of his life away as other men do."

"Where were you when the fire broke out?"

"In my room. Meditating on the project. Alone," he added before she could ask the question.

"How did you feel about Ms. Dekter? Did you like her?"

"Yeah, I liked her. A lot. She didn't look down on my art the way most of the other characters around here do."

"The word is that she was becoming annoyed with the way you were following her around."

John Smith scowled, then quickly reverted to his usual deadpan expression. Holding out his hands, he asked in tones of mock terror, "Are you going to arrest me, officer? Put me in manacles? Shouldn't you read me my rights?"

"I'm not reading you your rights because I'm not going to arrest you, John Smith. Not now, anyway. But I do want you to make out a statement and sign it. Could you let me have it sometime this afternoon?"

John Smith paused at the door to look back at her. "I really did like Erika, you know. You'll realize how much when you see my performance."

"A dreadful business," said Alec Fraser. He and Kevin Lavoie were having a council-of-war over a sandwich lunch in the president's corner office with windows facing the Sundance Range. "And to have it happen now, of all times!"

"Have you talked to Harvey Benson?"

"At length. And I've also been on the phone with the minister. Not to mention the press. We're going to have to work up a press release."

"Did you get any feel of how Benson is reacting? He's the one who really controls the Chinook Foundation."

"Let me put it this way. If we were just starting to woo them, the events of the past few days would blow us out of the water. But we've been negotiating with the Foundation for months now, and they've made certain commitments. Not official or papered, unfortunately, but the understanding is there. On both sides. So Benson is still on board. But he made it clear that he's very concerned about the Centre's reputation with all this going on. If, God forbid, anything more happens, I expect he'll jump ship."

"Then April second is still on?"

"Yes." Fraser brightened. "Maybe this mess will have been cleared up by then, and we can put it behind us. Do you know if the police are making any progress?"

"It's early days yet. Two detectives from Calgary arrived this morning and are questioning people, including me. Anyway, I'll have a chat with Corporal Lindstrom."

"Do that."

Fraser's secretary came in to clear away the plates and cutlery as Kevin left. Alec Fraser walked down the hall to the washroom. Bending over the sink to wash his hands, he looked at himself in the mirror. You're nothing but a glorified fundraiser, he told himself. You're not running this great institution; your job is to suck up to donors and politicians, some of whom you can barely stand. That self-righteous prig, Harvey Benson, for instance.

Drying his hands on a paper towel, Fraser resolved to nail down the Chinook grant and then take some time to decide if his case of burnout was terminal.

When Karen asked for an appointment to talk about Montrose's death, she had made it very clear that she would like to meet in the studio so she could see the paintings again.

"I envy you, Laura," she said, gazing at the paintings that were taking up more and more space in Laura's studio. "You're creating something that will live on after you. In a way, you will be immortal. On the other hand, all I do is sift through the debris of other people's lives."

"What you do is every bit as important," Laura replied, although in her heart she knew it wasn't true. Even in her darkest moments when inspiration failed her, seemingly never to return, she never doubted the importance of making art. "Society couldn't function without the police," she went on as she poured the tea. *That* was true.

"I know police work is important and mostly I like what I do. But," Karen gazed around the bright, airy studio, and eerily echoed Laura's thoughts, "I also know it doesn't begin to compare in importance with this." Taking a sip of camomile tea, she said, "Speaking of police work, it looks as though you might be right about there being two murders in the colony."

"What have you found out?"

"Well, for one thing, Montrose's blood-alcohol reading was 0.11. If he had been behind the wheel of a car, he would have been charged with impaired driving."

"No surprises there."

"I'll get to that in a moment. According to the autopsy, his liver was slightly enlarged and he was forty pounds overweight, but there was no life threatening condition. But with all that extra weight, he would have no chance of surviving a fall like that. Not that anyone would, when you think about it. He suffered a head injury that ultimately would have proved fatal, but what killed him was a broken neck. It was what they call a 'hangman's fracture'. It snapped the same four vertebras that a considerate hangman will try to break with his rope. That way, death is mercifully quick."

"How interesting," murmured Laura, not knowing how else to react to this gruesome bit of trivia.

"A broken neck is consistent with a fatal fall," the Mountie continued. "If we only had the autopsy results to work with, I think we'd put it down as an accidental death. But before doing the autopsy the medical examiner sent Montrose's body to Edmonton for a laser scan and that came up with something interesting."

"Which you are about to tell me."

The policewoman smiled. "I guess I have been stringing out the suspense. The laser revealed signs of slight subcutaneous bruising just above both of Montrose's ankles."

"Are you saying someone reached down, grabbed his legs and flipped him over the railing?" Laura paused, then added thoughtfully, "That would account for the way he landed. Head first, I mean."

"We could use you on the Force," murmured Karen. "Of course, there could be other explanations as to how he got those bruises, but it's enough to keep the file open. Especially since there's no doubt about Erika's death being a homicide. By the way, I expect the detectives from the Calgary detachment will want another statement from you about how you found Montrose's body."

"No problem. Now that we're talking about two murders, I've been trying to think of some connection between Erika and Montrose. All I can think of is that they are both academics and writers who happened to be in the colony at the same time. So far as I know the only person here at the colony who had any previous connection with Montrose was Jeremy Switzer."

"I will be talking to Mr. Switzer. For him, push has come to shove."

"About his alibi?"

"Yes. If he's got one, now is the time to prove it."

"It's possible that Montrose's death may have nothing to do with the colony," Laura mused. "The outside doors of Lloyd Hall are never locked so anyone in the whole wide world is free to wander in. A man like Alan Montrose was almost bound to have picked up some enemies in the course of his life. He liked to lord it over people when he had the upper hand. Like the way he was taunting Jeremy that night over the libel action."

"We'll look into Montrose's background, of course. Starting with the university where he taught." Unexpectedly, Corporal Lindstrom smiled. "If the university I attended is any example, we'll uncover any number of possible motives — jealousy, professional rivalry, disgruntled students, you name it."

"Roy Hansen," Laura said suddenly and when Karen looked at her blankly, she explained. "Your mentioning disgruntled students made me think of him. He's the one who put Jeremy up to writing that article about Montrose having plagiarized his play. Now he's being sued by Montrose, along with Jeremy. He can't have been too kindly disposed toward his former professor."

Karen wrote his name in her notebook. "Now that we know the professor was murdered, we'll see if we can get a line on Mr. Hansen." Closing the notebook, she gazed once more around the studio. "You can say what you like, but I'd rather be painting."

The day was spring-like, a promise of what was to come. Laura paused for a moment outside her studio to breathe the air that soughed gently through the pines. A raven flew low overhead, rowing through the air with powerful strokes. Its wings made a whirring sound as if its feathers were made of metal. As her eye followed its flight, Laura saw that the men from the arson squad were still sifting through the remains of the boat studio, collecting samples, scooping up trowels of ash into plastic bags, and carefully labelling each bag. The area was still sealed off, so she took the service road, holding her nose against the blue miasma of diesel fumes as she hurried past idling tractors in the maintenance yard. More than once she had complained to Kevin about the tractors' engines being left running so close to the colony, but he had said he had no jurisdiction over the engineering department and there was nothing he could do.

"That smashing looking corporal was around again this afternoon asking questions about Montrose," said Richard. He and Laura had been for a swim and now were sitting in the lounge, sharing a bottle of wine with Henry Norrington. While Norrington might be contemptuous of Richard's books, he was, Laura noticed, always happy to accept the drinks that Richard bought. Predictably, Richard didn't seem to care one way or the other.

Laura could have told them what the laser scan had turned up, but she had decided not to reveal any information she picked up through working with Karen without the police officer's permission. It was the safest way to avoid saying something that might jeopardize the investigation. "I don't think the police are entirely satisfied with the circumstances of Alan's death," she said noncommittally.

"It was an accident," Norrington pronounced in a voice that brooked no argument. "Alan simply had too much to drink and fell over that criminally low railing."

Not wanting to pursue the subject, Laura looked away. Over in a far corner, Isabelle Ross and Marek Dabrowski were sitting by themselves.

"It looks as though the affair is on again," Richard remarked, following her glance.

Laura nodded. "She's taken her rings off again."

The bottle of wine was finished. Norrington, who had consumed most of it, excused himself.

"You're amazingly patient with Henry," Laura said as they watched Norrington's troll-like figure heading for the door. His malformed hips made him walk with a slightly rolling gait. "Some of the things he says about your writing are completely outrageous."

Richard shrugged. "It's just one man's opinion. Actually, I like the old guy. And in many ways I admire him. Fate, in the form of genetics, played a cruel trick by inflicting that ungainly body on him. But he does what he can to overcome the handicap with his daily swimming regimen. And he's used his brilliant mind to turn himself into a celebrity."

"You're very understanding," murmured Laura, surprised and pleased with Richard's reply. His usual manner was casual, almost flippant, but there were times when he displayed an acute perceptivity about people. "I will admit, however," he was saying with a laugh, "that there are times when the way he dumps on my books does get under my skin."

"That reminds me. With everything that's been happening, I keep forgetting to tell you I finished *The Blue Agenda*. I enjoyed it. It's a real page turner."

"That's what I like to hear," Richard said, and then sat back in his chair with a bemused smile. "I didn't know you were reading it."

"I've read all your books except *Mission to Mykonos*. I just received a second-hand copy of it and I'll read it as well."

"I'm flattered. And a little surprised. In the first place, I don't know how you managed to get copies of the earlier ones. They've been out of print for several years."

"I have my sources," Laura said, hoping to sound mysterious. "I'm quite good at research, you know." She leaned forward slightly. "When all this is behind us, I could discuss them with you, if you like."

"They're just entertainment," he said with a slight shrug. "I don't expect them to be taken seriously."

"I realize that. But there are times when they seem ready to break through to another level." Laura paused as she saw he was frowning. "You needn't worry that I'm out to change your style, or anything like that. I just thought it might be useful to have some input from an interested third party. But if you don't want to ..."

Richard looked uncomfortable. "I'm not sure how I feel about that, to be honest with you. You're a genuine artist with your own aesthetic. I'm not sure I could ever write at the level you would expect. Or that I would want to, if it comes to that." He looked at her. "I'm sorry, Laura. It's not that I don't appreciate your offer. I do. But ..."

Laura leaned forward and took his hand in hers. "There's no need to explain, or apologize. I understand. Consider the subject dropped."

chapter eight

The front-end loader, its scoop filled with sodden ash and charred bits of wood, snorted its way along the path, heading for a waiting dump truck. They were cleaning up the debris that had once been Erika's studio. Laura knew there would be no painting for her today. She turned her back on the noisy machines with their stinking diesel fumes and retreated back up the path. She still could salvage something from the day that stretched before her by doing what she had intended last Sunday, when she and Richard ended up going to the Hot Springs — look at some art books in the library.

The Centre's library had an impressive collection of art books. Laura roamed among the shelves, not looking for anything in particular, waiting for inspiration to strike. She paused as her eye fell on a familiar title, *Art and The Law* by Milstein. There was a copy of the legal text in her Denver studio; she had purchased it after a New York art dealer had sent her a twenty-page contract, heavily weighted in his favour. The final document that they signed was three pages long and heavily weighted in *her* favour. As she stared at the textbook, something that had been niggling at the back of her mind suddenly clicked into place. She remembered it because at the time she read it, it had seemed totally wrong. Picking up the text, she seated herself at a table and turned to the chapter on libel.

There it was. In black and white. The paragraph was short and to the point. "A libel action is extinguished with the death of the plaintiff." The statement was backed up by a number of judicial decisions, one of which was *Drake v. The Sacramento Times*, which meant that the legal principle applied in California where Montrose had brought his suit against Jeremy. The paragraph went on to say that a libel action was so personal in nature that the courts had held it should not survive the death of the defamed plaintiff. As it had when she first read it, it struck Laura as not being right somehow. It seemed unfair that a family couldn't defend a departed member's honour and reputation. But there it was.

What an incredible piece of luck for Jeremy! His fortune and self-indulgent lifestyle were safe. *If* it was luck. This was definitely something that Corporal Lindstrom should know about. She found Karen in her temporary office. She was on the phone, but she waved Laura in through the open doorway.

"That was Mr. Hamilton letting me know he has checked in to the Banff Springs Hotel," Karen said as she replaced the receiver.

"Look at this." Laura placed the legal text, open at the passage on libel, on the desk in front of Karen.

"It's a textbook motive, if you'll forgive the pun," Karen said with a low whistle after reading the paragraph.

"That book is kinda old. We should make sure it's still the law," Laura said. "I know. Let's give Geoff a call. He's a hot shot Wall Street lawyer and he should know the answer."

It turned out Geoff didn't know the answer. He specialized in securities and SEC work. But he would call one of his partners who did a lot of libel litigation and get right back to them. He did so within five minutes. The passage in the text was a correct statement of the law. He went on to say, maybe to excuse his own lack of knowledge, that it was such an obscure and little known rule that only a specialist in the law of libel would be expected to know about it.

"Jeremy would have consulted libel lawyers as a result of Montrose's lawsuit," Laura pointed out after Karen had hung up.

"That's true. But that point might not have come up—Montrose being alive at the time. But if Switzer *did* know about it beforehand, it gives him a picture perfect motive."

"Why don't you check it out with Jeremy's lawyer?"

"Won't do any good," replied the corporal with the air of one who has been there. "He'll just give me a runaround about solicitor-client privilege. Except I guess in the States it would be attorney-client privilege." Closing the textbook, she said, "I haven't managed to have my talk with Mr. Switzer since we found out about the bruises on Montrose's ankles. He's gone downtown shopping, according to Dr. Norrington who had breakfast with him. You know," she went on thoughtfully after a slight pause, "I think I'll have him picked up for questioning. That should attract his attention. If he's got an alibi, as he claims he has, now's the time for him to trot it out."

Leaving Karen to corral Jeremy, Laura pressed the elevator button in the hall outside the Mountie's office.

The door slid open and she gasped and took an involuntary step back. The cloaked figure inside the elevator wore a black eye-mask and broad brimmed black hat. It took her a moment to realize it was only John Smith in his Lone Ranger costume. He was taping a notice on the elevator's rear wall. She knew it would be pointless to tell him he shouldn't be going around scaring people like that. To him, it was all part of the ongoing performance that was his life. She entered the elevator and rode down to the ground floor of the Donald Cameron Hall with him. The crudely printed notice announced that John Smith would be giving a performance in the Walter Phillips Gallery at 8 p.m. on Tuesday, April first.

"Nice touch that, don't you think?" said John Smith as they got off. "Having it on April Fool's day, I mean." He had a thick sheaf of notices along with a roll of tape and a box of thumbtacks. It was clear that he intended to spread word of his show far and wide.

"Having the police around asking stupid questions is going to detract from my happening," he grumbled as he tacked a notice to a bulletin board inside the main entrance. "People won't be able to concentrate on it."

"Maybe everything will be cleared up by then. Let's see. Today is Thursday, the twentieth. That gives you what? Twelve days. A lot can happen in twelve days."

"The way they're stumbling around, hell will freeze over before they solve it. You'll be there, of course?"

"At your performance? I wouldn't miss it!"

"There's one." Laura pointed to a sheet of cardboard tacked on a telephone pole. She and Richard were on their way back to their respective studios after having lunched together in the dining room. He hadn't mentioned the good luck kiss Laura had given him the night before he went to Edmonton, but it was obvious his interest was aroused. Now he stopped and read the notice announcing John Smith's performance. His studio was directly across from the Thom studio that had been assigned to the performance artist, so he couldn't help but see the comings and goings.

"That promises to be quite a performance," he muttered. "He's enlisted some of the housekeeping staff to help him act out whatever it is he's got in mind."

Laura nodded. It was quite common for young actors, musicians, and artists whose grants had run out, or whose courses were completed, but who wanted to remain at the Centre, to take jobs with the housekeeping department. It was a pool of talent that was often tapped for bit parts in plays, extras in operas, and to augment visiting orchestras.

"It'll be interesting to see what he comes up with," murmured Laura.

"Not to mention bizarre. His assistants look pretty strange when they come out of that studio."

"That's all we need!" the Centre's president groaned as he looked up from the poster on his desk.

"I talked to John Smith and tried to get him to postpone his performance," said Kevin Lavoie, "but he refused. Said that doing it on April Fool's is an important part of the performance. I suppose we could always force ... ." He stopped when he saw Fraser shaking his head.

"We can't do that," said the president. "That would go against everything the Centre stands for. Our role is to foster and encourage art in all its many forms. We're not censors. I would like to steer Benson and the minister well clear of it, but I'm sure that won't be possible. Did I tell you that Harvey is going to bring his wife?"

"No, you haven't told me. Have you met her?"

"No." Fraser's smile was ironic. "I hear she's devoted to good works and is a pillar of her church."

"Beautiful! With police all over the place and John Smith doing his thing!"

As the dinner hour approached, Karen waited for Laura on the footbridge. "But I didn't want to interrupt your painting," she said as they fell in step together, "but I wanted to tell you about my little chat with Mr. Switzer. I think he rather enjoyed being picked up by the police on Banff Avenue. He said it saved him the taxi fare."

"Sounds like Jeremy. What did he have to say for himself?"

"He admits knowing that the death of the plaintiff puts an end to a libel action. He claims that he only learned of it after he talked to his attorneys and told them about Montrose."

"Do you believe him?"

"I'm still trying to make up my mind about that. He's so offhand about things that he's very hard to read. But it may not matter. He seems to have an unshakable alibi for the night Montrose was killed."

"Which you're not going to tell me about."

The policewoman shot the artist a sideways look. "There are times when you are positively uncanny. You're right, I'm not going to tell you what his alibi is. Not now, anyway. But it's fully corroborated."

"Which means he was with someone whose word you are prepared to accept."

The policewoman laughed. "Next you'll be telling me the name of the person."

"Not yet. But maybe it'll come to me." They stopped outside the side entrance of Lloyd Hall.

"What does this do to your theory about Montrose's death?"

"If it weren't for those subcutaneous bruises, I'd be inclined to put it down as an accident. The trouble is that the bruises could have been caused in any number of ways. He could have backed into something, for example."

"Knowing Alan, he could have bruised himself banging his heels against the footrest of a bar stool down at the Rose & Thorn."

"That's what I mean. They're just not conclusive, one way or the other." She paused, then added quietly, "But the evidence is pretty conclusive that your friend Erika Dekter *was* murdered. The results of the preliminary autopsy are in and it appears she must have been dead before the fire. They were able to determine that she hadn't breathed in any smoke."

Laura was silent for a moment, then said, "From the rumours I've heard about the condition of her body, I'm surprised they could tell."

"The pathologists have their little ways. If you want the gory details, there was no trace of soot in her trachea, and no carbon monoxide in her blood."

"Is this to be public knowledge?"

"No. I want to keep the murderer in the dark as much as possible."

Jeremy was in high spirits that night at dinner. Now that he knew the police were aware that the libel action against him had collapsed, he openly crowed over what he chose to regard as a great legal victory. As a final turn of the screw, he had instructed his attorneys to try to recover the costs of the action from Montrose's estate. They had advised him that successful litigants weren't entitled to recover costs under California law, but he had told them to go ahead anyway. Laura got the impression that if they didn't succeed, they would wait a long time for their account to be paid. Jeremy was a rascal, but a rather engaging one. In a way, it was sort of reassuring that there were people who could trip blithely through life the way he did.

chapter nine

The morning was so clear and fresh that Laura impulsively turned to Richard standing next to her outside Lloyd Hall. "You seemed to enjoy the Upper Hot Springs. Would you like to see something even more exotic?"

"If it means spending time with you, I'd be happy to watch paint dry. Let's go!"

"This place is out of control," said Laura as they crept along a congested Banff Avenue. "It's high time for them to put a lid on any more commercial construction. There are people who come here and never get beyond this street."

Richard smiled. "You expect a lot from your fellow humans."

"Too much, I guess." Laura relaxed and leaned back in her seat.

A line up of cars at a stoplight brought them to a halt in the middle of the stone bridge spanning the Bow

River. "I've got a bit of Banff trivia for you," Laura said as they waited for the light to change.

"What's that?"

"How the Bow River got its name. A bush called wolf willow grows along its banks. Because of its resiliency, the Indians used it to make their bows."

"Interesting. I might be able to use that sometime. Where are we headed, by the way?" he asked as they drove off the bridge and turned right.

"To the Cave & Basin. It's the lower of Banff's two hot springs."

"We didn't bring our bathing suits."

"The pool is closed for the winter. It's only the Upper Hot Springs that stays open all year round. I promised you something exotic and that's what we're here to see."

He parked in front of a low building made of dark Rundle stone, and she led him past an empty, deserted outdoor pool and down a long winding flight of wooden stairs. They hung onto the brightly collared ropes strung along the top of the railing as they picked their way down the steps, slippery with melting ice. There was a smell of sulphur in the air, and educational signs informed them that the run-off from the hot springs created a bizarre world where tropical fish thrived year round, and migratory birds happily wintered on the ice-free mud flats.

A boardwalk led out onto the marsh. Telling Richard to walk as quietly as he could, Laura pointed down to the tiny fish darting about in the open water.

"This is incredible!" he exclaimed, bending over for a closer look.

"There's a jewel fish." Laura pointed to a small cichlid hiding in the weeds. "And there's a black molly. There's another molly that's gone back to being silver, the way it is in nature."

"Aren't those aquarium fish?"

"Yes. Some amateur fish fanciers dumped them in the waterway back in the '60s to see what would happen. They've been breeding like crazy ever since. The park people were worried that they would wipe out a little native fish called the Banff long-nosed dace that lives here. This is the only place in the world where it's found." Laura pointed to several small streamlined shapes with deeply forked tails. "But they seem to be holding their own."

The boardwalk on which they were standing led out to a bird blind. As they walked along it, a robin flew up almost from beneath their feet, a killdeer winged low over the mud flats and several ducks upended their rumps and dove for food in the shallow pond.

Richard shook his head in wonder. "You know what this place and the Upper Hot Springs remind me of? Conan Doyle's *Lost World*. Tropical fish and robins in the winter, and swimming outside while your hair freezes!"

He walked back along the boardwalk to gaze down at the fish. "You seem pretty knowledgeable about these tropical fish. I wouldn't know one from another."

"I have a thirty gallon tank in my studio in Denver."

"Who looks after it when you're away?"

"My studio assistant," Laura smiled fondly. "The mortality rate in some species of tropical fish is notoriously high. Yet, whenever I return from a trip, no matter how extended, and look in the tank, I find the population is the same as when I left. We don't talk about it, but I'm pretty sure Diane goes to a pet store and buys fish to replace any that might have gone to the great aquarium in the sky. Like Picasso and his birds."

Richard was intrigued. "What about Picasso and his birds?"

"He absolutely doted on the birds he kept in an aviary. In order to spare him pain, his wife secretly replaced any that died. She thought she had succeeded in fooling him until one day she overheard him saying to a guest, 'My birds are immortal, you know'."

"What a charming story! I love it!" Richard took a long final look at the subtropical landscape and said, "I must come back here with a camera. It's a perfect setting for a story."

In the capricious way of mountain weather, a light flurry of snow had begun to fall by the time they reached Richard's car. He held the door open for her and as she turned to thank him, kissed her lightly on the lips. Neither spoke as they slowly drew apart.

They lunched at the Banff Springs Hotel, a massive pile of Rundle stone built to resemble a Scottish laird's castle. Laura swallowed a bite of her caesar salad, touched her lips with a paper napkin, and looked around the cavernous dining room. "I half-expected to run into Geoff Hamilton," she said. "He's staying here."

"Erika's ex-boyfriend? I haven't met him yet."

"He's nice. I like him."

"Quite a coincidence, his arriving on the scene right after she was killed. It must have been a hell of a shock for him."

"Traumatic."

"Is he a suspect?"

"No more than anyone else. The police seem to be flying blind. So far, at least."

"You and the dashing corporal seem very buddy-buddy."

"She's using me as a guide to the colony and its artistic ways. I agreed to help her, but sometimes I wonder if I'm betraying my friends. That bothers me. What do you think?"

"I think you should keep on helping her. Whoever set fire to Erika's studio, whether it's someone from the colony or not, can scarcely be considered a friend."

"That's pretty much how she put it. That makes me feel better. Thanks."

At the end of the meal Laura motioned for the check. It pleased her that Richard didn't protest, thanking her matter-of-factly instead. "We'll have our coffee on top of Sulphur Mountain," she said as they got up from the table.

As they passed through the lobby, Laura spotted Geoff Hamilton at the cashier's desk. A kilted bellboy stood a few paces away with his suitcase.

Laura intercepted Geoff as he finished checking out, picked up the briefcase at his feet, and turned to go. He had the drawn look of someone who has spent a sleepless night, but his eyes lit up when he saw Laura. She introduced the two men and they shook hands.

"Leaving so soon?" Laura asked.

"Afraid so. The office called. The SEC has launched an enquiry into the stock trading of one of my biggest clients and he's panicking. I've got to go back and hold his hand."

Seeing the question in Laura's eyes, he told her that he had checked with Corporal Lindstrom and she had no objection to his leaving. "She knows where to reach me," he added.

They followed the bellboy out through the revolving door of the main entrance. The sky had cleared again and they hastily put on their sunglasses.

"I was going to write and thank you for being so helpful and understanding," Geoff said to Laura.

"But now I can thank you personally. Which I do, most sincerely."

"If I helped at all, I'm very glad."

"You're right. He does seem like a nice guy," Richard said as he and Laura walked across the courtyard to the parkade to collect his car.

"I've heard of the Sulphur Mountain gondola lift, and I take it that's where we're going?" Richard asked as he steered carefully around a life-size statute of Cornelius Van Horne, one of the founders of the Canadian Pacific Railway, placed rather awkwardly in the middle of the courtyard.

"Right. It's next door to the Upper Hot Springs where we went last Sunday."

"God. Was that only last Sunday? So much has happened since then that it seems much longer."

"And Erika was still alive."

On the way up the twisting mountain road they were stopped by the same blond flagwoman. She seemed to recognize Richard and favoured him with a shy smile.

"She likes you," Laura murmured.

"Can I hope that you're jealous?"

"I'm not the type."

"No. You wouldn't be." Richard slipped the Taurus into gear as a huge earthmover thundered across the road, and the flagwoman waved them on. He gave her a wave and a friendly smile as they passed.

"They drive those behemoths at quite a clip, don't they?" Laura said, looking back to watch the giant machine banging and crashing its way across a field that looked as if a major tank battle had been fought on it.

"That's how they make money."

The gondola ride was swift and smooth. A sign inside the car said the summit was at an elevation of 7,500 feet and that the ride took eight minutes.

"I can never ride in one of these things without thinking of Alistair MacLean's *Where Eagles Dare,*" said Richard, watching the mountain dropping away beneath them.

"I've never read the book, but I watched the film on video," Laura said. "That scene where they were fighting on top of the gondola is unforgettable. Your books have a lot of the same kind of action."

"You couldn't have said anything that would have pleased me more." The door slid open and Richard followed her out onto the platform.

"This is a great way to get yourself oriented." Laura held on to the railing of the observation deck and pointed down to where the valley was spread out below them. "There's the Banff Springs Hotel where we had lunch and those dark brown buildings across from it on Tunnel Mountain are the Banff Centre." She frowned. "They called it that because they were going to drill a tunnel through it for the railroad, but they never did. I like the Indian name much better."

"Which is?"

"Sleeping Buffalo Mountain. That's exactly what it looks like from certain angles. Especially from the golf course. They should change it back."

"I agree." Richard smiled. "You know something? I've found the setting for my next novel." Richard breathed deeply and fell silent as he drank in the panoramic view.

From behind her sunglasses, Laura studied him as he gazed intently into the distance. He was, she decided, devastatingly good looking. The nice thing about it was that he never seemed to be aware of it. He took it for granted, like a lot of other things in his charmed life. He also was wonderful company. Secure in the knowledge that she could have just about any man she wanted, and completely dedicated to her art, Laura was ultra-cautious about taking on any romantic entanglements. When she was in high school her mother had said to her, "Let the boys practice on the other girls," and that advice still lingered. Still, there was no denying that pleasant buzz of excitement that being with him seemed to bring. He turned suddenly and caught her looking at him. He didn't say anything, but both of them knew something was happening.

"Have you seen enough?" Laura broke the silence. When he nodded, she said, "Then let's get that coffee."

"Rumour has it," Richard placed his cup back in the saucer with exaggerated care, "that there's a boyfriend in Denver."

"I planted that rumour myself," Laura told him after a lengthy pause. "A preventive measure on my part."

"Clever. But now you've blown your cover."

"So I have." She took off her glasses and looked directly at him. "But I'm not ready for anything just yet. I'm thinking about a painting that's so challenging it almost scares me. It will require every bit of energy I have."

"And when it's finished?"

"It will be worth the wait." Laura looked at her watch. "Let's go back. All of a sudden I have an urge to paint."

Karen was surrounded by reporters in the parking lot outside Lloyd Hall. One of them recognized Richard and called out, "Hey, Mr. Madrin, are you going to use this in a book?"

Richard shook his head. "Not me. I write thrillers, not murder mysteries."

chapter ten

Returning to her studio after an early dinner, Laura decided to do something fast and energetic. Something she could finish quickly. She had brought a number of small canvases, already stretched and gessoed, with her from Denver. She would use one of them to paint a colourful abstract that was already taking shape in her mind.

Freed from the constraints of the still life, Laura laid on the paint with quick, sure strokes. Exhilarated by the way the painting was taking shape, she worked on into the night. The blob of pink paint landed with a soft splat precisely where she wanted it, but she could feel the energy draining out of her. She had better stop before she made a mistake that would ruin the painting. She stepped back from the canvas and looked at her watch. Ten o'clock. Time for a restorative visit to the whirlpool.

Richard and Jeremy were already in the whirlpool when she arrived. As she joined them, Richard's thigh brushed lightly against her as he moved sideways along the bench to let a jet massage his lower back.

Laura pulled the straps of her bathing suit down over her shoulders and lowered herself onto the bottom bench so the jets could reach her shoulder muscles. When it reached the point that the hot water became enervating rather than relaxing, she stood up and announced that she was going for a swim.

"It's time for me to get in some laps, too." Richard climbed out after her.

From the whirlpool, Jeremy gazed at Laura's shapely back as she stood by the edge of the pool. She was what he really wanted, but he knew it would never happen.

Richard, who was a strong swimmer, ploughed up and down the Olympic size pool with a smooth, powerful crawl. Laura had never really mastered the crawl, so she did a few laps with her serviceable side stroke, then rolled over on her back to look up at herself reflected in the glass roof, delighted as always to see the black mask.

"People can be funny, can't they, Richard?" Laura mused as they rode up in the elevator. "I feel so badly about Erika, and miss her terribly, yet I'm happy because a painting is working for me."

"I understand that," Richard said as they got off at the sixth floor. "Art has a life of its own, altogether separate from the workaday world. I hope that's not the only reason you're happy," he added teasingly.

Laura made a face at him and stopped at his door, which was next to the elevator. "Good night, Richard," she said, turning up her face for a kiss.

He kissed her, then took her arm.

"I'll walk you down the hall." Her room was at the far end of the corridor, next to the stairwell. Richard went past her door and looked into the stairwell. "They still haven't done anything about that low railing. You'd think they'd at least put up a warning sign."

"They won't do anything until all this is history." Laura fished in her bag for her room key.

Laura let out a small sigh of exasperation when the cashier pointed to the message on the computer screen. Corporal Lindstrom wanted to see her as soon as she finished breakfast. Laura was beginning to entertain second thoughts about having agreed so readily to assist the police. She depended on her sojourns in the colony to get a great deal of work done. She was already beginning to feel the pressure of the September show she had committed to do for Isaac's Gallery.

At home in Denver there were so many demands on her time that her productivity suffered. Her friends thought that as a single, unattached female she had all the time in the world to paint. They could never comprehend how much of her time and energy had to be devoted to purely clerical and administrative tasks. While having a part-time studio assistant helped to some extent, Laura was the one who had to make arrangements for paintings to be shipped, to deal with galleries and art consultants, to arrange for shows of her work, to send out invoices, and pay the bills as they came in. Until this time, her stays in the colony had been gloriously free of such non-creative demands and interruptions. But now the outside world was intruding with a vengeance.

Remembering Erika and the horrible way she had died, Laura scolded herself for being selfish and self-centred. But, damn it, her art *was* important. She still felt a lingering resentment as she climbed the stairs to the floor where Karen had her office.

Karen looked rested and fit, which did nothing to improve Laura's mood. But her welcoming smile soon faded and her expression darkened as she said, "I just can't seem to get anywhere with this case."

"It's early days yet," Laura remarked.

"I know. But it's the first few hours that are important. That's your best chance of getting a break in the investigation."

When Laura made no reply, Karen began to flip through the pages of her notebook as if hoping to find an answer there. "I'm told Erika Dekter was very tense in the days prior to her death?"

Laura nodded. "She was tense, but it was a creative tension. She was very excited about the way her book was going."

"Geoff Hamilton is the only one we know who had a close connection with Erika Dekter." Karen was watching Laura's face, trying to read her reaction.

"He wanted to marry her."

"So he says. Would she have married him?"

"No, I don't think so," Laura surprised herself by saying. "I have the feeling that in the time she spent up here, she was beginning to distance herself from their relationship. To become whole again, if you like."

"He wouldn't have liked that. Especially after the way he burned his bridges with his wife and family. He's moved into a hotel in midtown Manhattan, by the way. The Algonquin. You don't suppose," Karen went on thoughtfully, "he could have called her from New York, perhaps proposed to her and been turned down. That could account for the stress she was under."

"I really think you're wrong about her being under stress. It's more a matter of her being totally wrapped up in her writing. And how can you get around the logistics? How could Geoff have done all that needed to be done in the available time?"

"Difficult, but not impossible. There's such a thing as preparing the ground beforehand. I've asked the Calgary detachment to go back to the Westin hotel and poke around some more. Check his outgoing calls. Something might turn up."

"Speaking of outgoing calls," Laura said thoughtfully, "there's a way you could put your theory about Geoff calling from New York to the test."

"I'm listening."

"Erika didn't want a phone in her room. That means that any calls for her would have to go through the central switchboard. You could talk to the operators and see if they remember any calls coming in for her."

Karen closed her notebook with a snap and got to her feet. "I'm on my way." Opening the door for Laura, she added, "That's why you're so valuable. You know how this place works."

Galvanized by the need to make up for lost time, Laura put aside the nearly finished small abstract and attacked the largest blank canvas. An image had been festering in her subconscious since the night Erika died, and it was time to get it out of her system. With vigorous, confident strokes of charcoal she began to sketch in the outline of a male ballet dancer, wearing a mask, and dancing with Death as his partner. By early afternoon she had reached the stage where she could start to work with paint. She put on a CD that mixed bird songs with background music, humming contentedly to herself as she mixed colours in the empty yoghurt containers she favoured for the purpose. Five hours later, she knew that the painting would be powerful and also that it would demand a great deal of creative energy. Things that had been pent up inside her were now exploding on the canvas. Her stomach rumbled quietly, reminding her that she had worked through the lunch hour. It was also getting dark as the sun began its descent behind Sulphur Mountain, blocking the setting sun and shortening the hours of daylight at the Centre. She shivered and, after carefully cleaning her brushes, locked the studio door behind her and started down the path.

Richard, accompanied by a young woman laden with a camera, tape recorder, and notebook, was standing on the path in front of the blackened patch where the boat studio had once stood. Was he giving an interview to the press about Erika's murder? That would be too much! He waved at Laura, and he and his companion walked up to join her at the junction of the circular path. The young woman was a reporter all right, but she wasn't there to do a story on the murder. Richard explained, with that air of ingenuous enthusiasm that Laura found so appealing, that *The Crag & Canyon* was going to do a profile on him and his writing. His attitude was a refreshing change from the jaded, why-do-I-have-to-put-up-with-all-this approach affected by some other writers Laura knew. He openly revelled in the attention his books brought him, and it was nice to see.

The distant skirl of bagpipes made the three of them stare at each other and then look up the path. John Smith, with a plaid blanket wrapped around his waist as a makeshift kilt, and a ghetto blaster slung over his shoulder, was marching his motley crew down the path. As he came up to Laura and her companions he switched off the music and shouted, "Parade Halt!" Laura recognized three of his four assistants. The most striking was a long-limbed black woman whose name was Desiré. She was from Martinique and was studying modern dance. The other woman had taken a printmaking course and now worked in housekeeping. She had close-cropped blond hair and was known to be a lesbian. What was her name? Charlene. That was it. The young man, with the dark, slicked-back hair, glasses held together with tape, and a gold earring in his left ear, was a cashier in the Banquet Hall. His name was Justin; Laura couldn't recall his last name, if she had ever known it. He had an amusing line of patter and aspired to be an actor. Laura didn't know the other man, but was pretty sure that he too was studying drama.

When John Smith learned that the woman with Richard was a reporter, he immediately handed her a notice of his upcoming recital and pressed her to attend. "You're free to take as many pictures as you like," he assured her. "Remember it's the Walter Phillips Gallery on April Fool's day." Then he switched on his tape machine and his little band marched off to the strains of "Scotland the Brave."

Staring after them, Richard muttered, "If there isn't a medical term for that guy's behaviour, there should be."

The reporter gave an appreciative chuckle as she folded the notice and placed it in her notebook. "I just might take him up on his invitation. It sounds as if there could be a story in it."

"I can almost guarantee that," Richard grinned. He turned to Laura. "That Phillips guy must be a pretty generous donor to have a gallery named after him."

The reporter made a small choking sound and Laura quickly interjected, "Walter Phillips was a famous Alberta artist. He made wonderful woodcuts. But there's no reason for you to know that."

"I confess that I'm not very well informed on the

local art scene. But," he smiled cheerfully at Laura, "you've got to admit I'm doing my best to catch up!"

They walked the reporter to her car and, as she drove away, Richard turned to Laura. "Your painting went well. I can tell from the look in your eyes."

Laura nodded happily, and put her arms around him as they kissed. Hand in hand, they walked into Lloyd Hall.

"Listen to this one!" Jeremy exclaimed gleefully. One of his plays had been produced in New York and a friend had sent him the reviews. Jeremy had attended the opening night, but had left for Banff long before the reviews appeared. It was remarkable that the play was reviewed at all. The fact that they were so scathing is what probably led to their finally being printed. Laughing uproariously, he was regaling his fellow artists with them.

"'Never was the famous advice *Run, don't walk to the nearest exit* more fitting than in the case of Jeremy Switzer's self-indulgent excuse for a play, *The Function of Ten*.

"And how about this one? 'Stay home and do yourself a favour.'"

Carefully folding the press clippings, Jeremy picked up his friend's letter and read from it. "I ran into Anita Goldstone, your wealthy socialite friend from East Hampton during the intermission. She was absolutely livid and was shouting 'someone will pay for this' as she swept out the door."

Hooting with laughter, Jeremy spluttered gleefully, "The best part is that *she's* the one who will pay. She financed the whole production!"

Even Henry Norrington was amused; his heavy

shoulders shook with laughter as he asked, "I take it this production is off-off-Broadway?"

"Not only is it off-off-Broadway. My friends had to travel to the wilds of Queens to see it."

Shaking his head, Richard said, "I don't know how you can be so casual about those reviews. I admire your attitude, but ..." He shrugged and let his voice trail off.

Jeremy laughed. "I've got some real zingers from my previous plays in a scrap book. If I get enough of them, I'll publish them in a collection."

"I've never met a writer quite like Jeremy," mused Richard as he and Laura left the Sally Borden Building. Mount Rundle's sharp peak was biting a wedge out of the full moon. "He doesn't seem to care what people think of his plays."

"And what about you?" Laura turned to face him. "I recall reading some reviews of your books that weren't exactly flattering. But it doesn't seem to bother you."

"Maybe not outwardly. Besides, I don't think it's quite the same. In my case, the unfavourable reviews are really directed at the thriller genre, not at me specifically. Book review editors delight in giving the kind of books I write to academics who can be counted on to trash them. That I have learned to accept and live with. But I couldn't stand the personal humiliation and ridicule that Jeremy seems to revel in."

"I don't think his plays are all that important to Jeremy. I have this theory that they're just an excuse to allow him to live the kind of life he wants to live."

"That explains a lot about his attitude. Anyway, the book I'm working on now will knock their socks off."

On the steps of Lloyd Hall he took her by the arms

and turned her to face him. "As I have said before, and will again, you are very beautiful in the moonlight," he whispered and kissed her gently.

When they broke apart, she took a step back. "Remember what I said about the painting. I started it today and, as I expected, it's going to take every ounce of energy I can muster."

Brushing his lips against her forehead, Richard murmured, "I will wait. How long?"

"Depends. Maybe only a couple of days, if I can maintain the pace."

chapter eleven

"What are you staring at?" demanded Laura.

"It's Corporal Lindstrom. She's in civilian clothes." Richard was giving a rapid-fire commentary like an on-the-scene reporter at a news event. "She's wearing a skirt, would you believe? Her legs are gorgeous, by the way. I was wondering about that." With his instinctive courtesy, Richard stood up as Karen, carrying a tray with nothing on it but a cup of coffee, approached their table and asked if she could join them.

"It's my day off," she announced somewhat defensively as she sat down. "I'm not going to take the whole day off," she added as if this would be unpardonable. "But I'm entitled to spend a few hours at least with my daughter."

Richard looked around as if expecting the daughter to suddenly materialize before them, while Laura realized with a mild sense of shock that it had never occurred to her to wonder about Karen's home life. Somehow one didn't associate public functionaries like the police and firefighters with such ordinary impediments as spouses, children, and all the domestic concerns that go with them. Karen stirred her coffee as if unsure of what to say next. Richard, sensing that it was Laura she wanted to talk to, piled his dishes on the tray and excused himself.

"I talked to the telephone operators as you suggested," Karen said.

"And?"

"In all the time she was here, Erika received only one phone call. It was a man. The operator remembers that he had a sexy voice."

"That could be Geoff."

"It was. I called him in New York. He admitted making the call."

"Did he tell you what it was about?"

"He wasn't all that forthcoming. He said they talked about her book and their possible future together. He said it was after that phone call that he decided to come here."

"Sounds pretty close to what we talked about. She could have turned him down."

"True." Karen didn't seem to want to pursue the matter any further. It was obvious she had something else on her mind.

Changing the subject, Laura said, "I didn't know you had a daughter."

The policewoman seemed uncharacteristically unsure of herself. She took a deep breath before saying, "She's the reason I'm here. Knowing how busy you are, and how precious your time is, I would never ask this favour on behalf of anyone else. I've told Ingrid, that's my daughter's name, all about you and she is dying to meet you. She's only seven but she's taking art lessons at school and they tell me she has real talent. From the drawings that she brings home, I think so too. I know she loves it. She's never met an honest-to-God artist and talking to you would be a real inspiration. So I was wondering if you could possibly take the time to come to my apartment and have lunch with us. I know it's an imposition, but ...."

This was precisely the sort of intrusion that Laura resented. But she had become fond of Karen and, as a professional artist, she had some obligation to encourage a gifted child. Besides if she painted as vigorously as she planned to this morning, she would probably be powered-out by noon anyway. "I have a better idea," she said. "Why don't you bring the lunch, and you and Ingrid meet me at my studio around noon? That way she can see the paintings and also get an idea of what an artist's studio looks like."

"That's more than I dared hope for. Are you sure you don't mind?"

"If I minded, I wouldn't do it." Laura smiled, then went on, "I'm a little surprised you haven't mentioned your daughter before. Especially since she's interested in art."

"I've wanted to. But police personnel try to keep work and family life as separate as possible. I'm sure you can understand why. But I like to think you and I have become pretty good friends. Maybe this being my day off had something to do with it as well. Makes me feel more like a civilian, I guess."

"I understand." Laura gave a tentative cough before going on. "Please excuse my curiosity, but I've always thought how perfectly your name suited you. It's so classically Nordic. But now I guess Lindstrom may not have been your maiden name? I know it's none of my business ..."

"You're right about Lindstrom not being my maiden name. But it was something equally Nordic. It was Finnsdtter, no less. Pure Icelandic. My ancestors came over from Iceland and settled in Gimli, Manitoba, way back in 1875." She paused for a moment, and then added, "While we're on the subject of me and since you'll be meeting Ingrid, you should know that her father is dead."

"I'm so sorry. How long ago did he die?"

"Two years next month. Larry was a policeman, too. He was a member of Calgary's Tac-Team and he was killed in the line of duty. He and his partner went into the basement suite of a house where a suspected killer was living. The neighbours told the Tac-Team that there were two young children sleeping in the basement. The police wanted to get them out before they stormed the house so the killer couldn't use them as hostages."

"What an incredibly daring thing to do."

"They almost made it. But the three-year old boy Larry was to bring out woke up and started to yell before Larry could put his hand over his mouth. The killer ran to the top of the stairs and shot him just as he reached the window. Larry was wearing a flak jacket, but the guy was a handgun expert and shot him at the base of the skull where he had no protection. But he managed to push the kid out the window to his partner before he went down."

Laura reached out and squeezed Karen's hand. There was nothing to say.

"I sometimes used to wonder if the reason I'm so enthused about Ingrid's artistic bent is that it means she won't become a cop. It does run in families, you know. Larry's father was one." It was as if Karen was thinking aloud. "But then I realized it wasn't that at all. If Ingrid really does have a talent, then I want her to have the opportunity to take it as far as she can."

"I'm looking forward to meeting her," Laura said with a smile. "Why don't you have her bring along some of her drawings?"

Ingrid was a paler version of her mother. Tall for her age, she had Karen's wide shoulders and narrow hips. Her flaxen hair was parted in the middle and braided in a long ponytail. Her pale blue eyes seemed to have no depth, until she smiled. Then they came alive with a cool, composed intelligence. She was, thought Laura as she welcomed the child, the obverse side of the mirror to little Jessica, Isabelle's dark-eyed daughter.

Ingrid, holding a leather portfolio in front of her, stood silently in the middle of the floor, raptly gazing at the paintings that were stacked and hung everywhere. Laura had turned the big painting she was working on face to the wall. It was becoming steadily more macabre as it progressed and it would be deeply disturbing to a sensitive child. Ingrid breathed deeply, inhaling the mixture of paint and cleaner as if to draw the essence of the studio inside herself.

"I've never seen anything like these before," she murmured finally. "I don't know what to say."

"Don't say anything," replied Laura. "Just look. We'll talk later."

Without taking her eyes off the paintings, Ingrid placed her portfolio beside some art books lying open on the coffee table and walked over for a closer look at the individual pieces.

"The colours! Everything is so full of colour!" she exclaimed after working her way along the south wall.

Laura raised an impressed eyebrow at Karen and said, "Colour is colour, but colour value is something else. Let me show you something." She led Ingrid over to where a still life stood on an easel. Pointing to the petals of a rose, she said, "For instance, this yellow is too bright. It stands out more than it should. Can you see that?"

Cocking her head to one side, Ingrid nodded agreement.

Picking up a brush, Laura lightly daubed the offending flower with orange paint. It was as if the rose had taken a step backward into the painting. "I haven't changed the colour," Laura explained. "It's still yellow. I've just changed its value. Colour values range from black at the bottom with a zero, to white with a value of ten."

Guiding Ingrid over to another painting, Laura said, "Let me show you something else about colour. What do you see?"

"Red. Red everywhere. The table, the walls, the carpet. Except for the flowers. They're white. And some blue accents."

"Do you see anything else?"

Puzzled, the young girl peered closer. "There's a black line that tells you where the table stops and the wall begins."

"Perfect! That shows you how even a little touch of colour can create depth. You have an eye, Ingrid."

Ears straining to hear every word, Karen laid out the salad, sandwiches, and fruit she had brought. Before they sat down, she glanced meaningfully at Ingrid's portfolio. "Maybe you should show Ms. Janeway your drawings now, dear." Laura smiled to herself. Scratch a policewoman and you find a doting mother.

Smiling encouragingly at Ingrid, Laura braced herself. Ingrid had a good eye, but so did lots of people.

That's what made collectors. The question was, did she have the talent? Unaware that she had been holding her breath, Laura let out an audible sigh when the drawings began to appear. It was all right. The child could draw. In fact, she could do more than draw. The first drawings were faithful renderings of the object — a box, a sunflower, a bowl of oranges — but in the more recent ones, Ingrid had begun to simplify, to suggest rather than to meticulously record.

"You're a colourist, Ingrid," Laura said at last.

Karen stared blankly at the drawings. They were all done in thick pencil strokes or charcoal. There wasn't a hint of colour anywhere. Ingrid looked expectantly at Laura who said, "The great master colourist, Matisse, once wrote, 'A colourist makes his presence known even in a simple charcoal drawing.' I see a colourist in these drawings."

With Ingrid's talent so happily authenticated, the lunch turned into a celebratory feast. Karen had brought a bottle of wine, but since she was going to assign herself back on duty that afternoon, declined to have any herself. Laura put the unopened bottle away for future use, and made iced tea. As they munched and talked, Ingrid's eyes returned again and again to the paintings.

"You know, Ms. Janeway," she said with a mischievous smile, "if Mrs. Green, our art teacher, were to mark your paintings, I don't think you'd pass."

"Because of perspective you mean?"

Ingrid nodded, and Laura laughed. "Perspective is something you learn and then use or not use as you see fit."

"I've wondered about that," admitted Karen. "In some of the paintings, it looks as if the dishes will slide off the table. But the colour is so wonderful you forget about it."

"That's just what you're supposed to do. Perspective is just a matter of making distant objects look smaller, but in these paintings I give equal value to all the objects. The viewer's imagination can provide the perspective."

Laura crossed over to where some books were stacked on a shelf. She took down one titled *Art of The Twentieth Century* and knelt beside Ingrid's chair. "This is for you. All the great artists are in there. It tells you something about their lives and shows you what their paintings look like."

Eyes shining, Ingrid held the book as if it were the key to the future. Impulsively, she flung her arms around Laura and kissed her on the cheek.

While they were engrossed in the book, Ingrid turning the pages with little exclamations of delight, a scratching sound made her look up and glance toward the balcony.

"That's my pet squirrel," said Laura. "A substitute for my dog while I'm here. Would you like to feed him?"

Ingrid nodded eagerly and Laura handed her a biscuit and opened the sliding glass door onto the balcony. She closed it behind Ingrid to keep the squirrel from coming into the studio.

"Knowing you as I think I do," said Karen, as she began to gather up the plastic bags in which she had brought the food, "you would never have been so encouraging towards Ingrid unless you genuinely felt she has talent. Am I right?"

"In my view, she has the capability to become a visual artist. How that talent develops remains to be seen, of course."

"That's what I wanted to ask you about. What should I be doing to help her?"

"For the moment, very little. She should continue with her art lessons, of course. At this stage Mrs. Green can't do her any harm. You might suggest to Mrs. Green that she tape a charcoal to the end of a three-foot stick and have her students draw with that. That will teach them to draw freely and not worry about tiny little strokes of the pencil. However, Ingrid will soon outgrow Mrs. Green. Then we'll have to find her a teacher who can take her to the next plateau. As long as you're stationed in Banff, that won't be a problem; there are some outstanding instructors right here in the Centre. If you like, I'll make some enquiries."

"That would be wonderful. I should be here for another couple of years at least. Of course, you never know. I could be posted to Moose Jaw or Tuktoyaktuk tomorrow." It was obvious that Karen was worried about how the demands of her own career might clash with what was best for her daughter.

"You should be able to work around that. What they can do today with computers and correspondence courses is incredible," Laura assured her. Laura could still feel the spot on her cheek where Ingrid had kissed her. She was aware that her own biological clock was fast winding down and that if she were ever going to have a child it would have to be soon. As she always did when this mood struck her, she looked around at her paintings. *They* were her children.

"With Larry gone, Ingrid and I are completely on our own." Karen's thoughts were still on her daughter's future. "If anything happened to me, I don't know what would become of her."

Laura realized it would be useless to say that nothing could happen to her. They both knew better.

"When you're out on patrol and spot some guy driving a stolen vehicle and pull him over late at night, you haven't a clue what you're going to be faced with when you walk up to that car. You could be met with a blast from a sawed-off shotgun, or cut in two with an automatic rifle. It's crazy out there."

That kind of thinking could affect a person's ability to respond in an emergency. As if reading Laura's mind, Karen sat up straighter and said, "We're trained to block everything out except how we're going to handle the situation without people getting hurt. After Larry was killed, they made me take a refresher course. It works."

The balcony door slid open and Ingrid came back into the studio. She slid the latch home before turning to look at her mother. She seemed composed, but her pale cheeks were slightly flushed.

"There's a strange man out there, Mummy. A clown."

"Did he say anything to you?"

"No. He was juggling some balls in the air. I came right in."

"You did the right thing, dear." Her mother gave her a hug.

Laura stormed out the front door, intending to tell John Smith where to get off, but as she expected, there was no sign of him. She would get to him later.

"The squirrel ate all the biscuit," Ingrid volunteered, as if to ease the situation.

Laura smiled at her. "He loves biscuits. They're better for him than nuts."

After the remains of the lunch had been packed in Karen's cooler, Laura announced she was "painted out" and would leave with them. Locking the studio behind her, she joined them as they went up the path. "Oh, oh," she muttered when they rounded a bend and came in sight of the parking lot. John Smith, clad in a rather sinister-looking clown outfit — rakish black fedora, black jacket and pants, his face made up with white greasepaint and green eye shadow — was being interviewed by a television reporter and cameraman. The media coverage which had reached a fever pitch in the days immediately following Erika's death had dwindled down to the occasional follow-up item. It would flare up again if there were any more sensational developments, such as another death, or an arrest. Lavoie had pleaded with the colonists not to talk to the media, but that of course wouldn't deter John Smith.

John Smith's painted lips broadened in a smile as Laura and her two companions hurried past. Karen frowned when she heard the reporter ask about the possibility of there being a serial killer on the campus. A rumour like that would bring reporters swarming like a plague of locusts. She quickened her pace so that they were practically running by the time they reached her minivan. She barely allowed Ingrid time to say goodbye before hustling her into the passenger seat and closing the door. Leaning against it, she said to Laura, "I hate him knowing I have a daughter."

"I don't think I'd worry too much about that," Laura tried to reassure her. "John Smith likes to touch the world, but he doesn't like to be touched back."

"I just don't like him knowing about Ingrid. It makes me feel kind of vulnerable somehow."

Laura almost came out with the quote from Francis Bacon—"He that hath wife and children hath given hostages to fortune"—but checked herself in time. The word "hostages" was bound to have painful associations for Karen. Still, if you brought the cynical old essayist into this century by making him gender neutral, he was expressing precisely the same thought as Karen had when she talked about being vulnerable. Everything that happens has happened before and someone had a word for it.

Ingrid blew Laura a kiss as the minivan drove away.

chapter twelve

It was finished! Laura's excitement mounted as she painted an ear hole on the evilly grinning skull. Stepping back from the canvas, she knew it was good. It was better than good. It was great. She had a feeling it was destined to be an icon. But not yet. She would keep it to herself for a while. It would not travel to New York with her show, although there probably was a market for it there. Later maybe. A sudden shiver ran through her body. She lifted the painting down from the easel and placed it face-first against the wall. With the eerily powerful painting hidden from view, the others in the studio seemed to come back to life. Laura looked at the still lifes and abstracts, vibrant with colour, and smiled. That's what she would paint for the remainder of her stay.

Picking up her flashlight, she switched off the studio lights and went outside into the darkness. She would celebrate with a glass of wine. It was more than a celebration; she needed the wine to calm herself down.

"It's finished," she whispered to Richard as he held a chair for her. He, Norrington, and Jeremy were sitting around a table, sharing a bottle of wine.

A delighted smile spread over his face. "When?" he asked.

"Maybe you could buy a girl dinner tomorrow night?"

"Done."

"What are you two whispering about?" asked Jeremy.

"I was just telling him I've finished a painting," Laura replied blandly.

Jeremy sniffed, but didn't probe further.

He knows there's something between me and Richard, thought Laura. But who cares? We're both adults.

The conversation, like every conversation in the Centre, returned to the subject of the unsolved deaths. "I'm beginning to wonder," intoned Norrington, "if we don't have a thrill killer in our midst. There seems to be a complete absence of motive in the killings. Except of course, for you and Montrose," he added with a sideways glance at Jeremy.

"The police are completely satisfied with my alibi."

"So it would seem. I wonder what it is?"

When Jeremy showed no sign of enlightening them, Laura said, "The police have ruled out a serial killer."

"I was speaking of a killer who kills for the thrill of it, not a serial killer. As if it were a game."

"If you're looking for a thrill killer," Jeremy said, "John Smith's your man. It could be one of his performances."

"Even he wouldn't go that far," protested Laura.

Jeremy shrugged. "The guy's a sociopath. That's all I know."

That seemed to bring the conversation about the deaths to a dead end. Norrington turned to Richard. "How is your new masterpiece progressing?"

"Very well, as a matter of fact. As I said on the television program," Norrington winced, but Richard didn't seem to notice as he went on, "I think my new hero has a number of layers ..."

"So does cardboard," Norrington interjected.

"I think he has the staying power to sustain a series."

"A *series*!" Norrington almost squeaked. "May the good Lord have mercy on us!"

Laura put down her empty glass, and stood up. "I'm off. It's been a long day."

"I'll go with you." Richard drank the last of his wine and put the empty glass down on the table. Seeing there was some wine left in the bottle Richard had paid for, Norrington and Jeremy elected to stay.

"I honestly don't know how you can stand it." Laura's face was flushed as she and Richard left the Sally Borden Building.

Richard laughed. "If you think that was bad, you should have heard him earlier. He announced to at least ten people that it would be a boon to the world of literature if my word processor were to self-destruct."

"What an appalling thing to say!"

"It was pretty extreme, I agree," Richard shook his head thoughtfully. "There are times when he sounds really bitter. Almost venomous. Tonight was one of them. I can't think why. Lord knows I've never done anything to him. Except buy him drinks. Anyway, it's his problem, not mine."

Laura slipped her arm through his. "You really don't care what Henry thinks, do you?" When Richard shook his head, she said, "Then I shouldn't let myself get so worked up."

"Except that it becomes you so." He held her close and kissed her. "Tomorrow night seems an awfully long time away."

"Twenty-four little hours, that's all."

Richard walked her to her door and kissed her goodnight. Before Laura fell asleep, she decided that first thing tomorrow she would check out one of Norrington's books from the library. She might come across some weaknesses and absurdities that Richard could use as ammunition to defend himself with. If Norrington wrote the way he talked, he would be highly susceptible to parody.

The librarian showed Laura where Norrington's books were shelved, and lifted a heavy tome down from the shelf. "This is probably the best one to start with."

Laura read the title aloud, "*Demystifying Deconstructionism* — not exactly escapist literature, is it?"

The librarian smiled. "It's easier to read than you might think. He's got quite a way with words. When you finish with that one, you can move on to *Decoding Paradise*," he said as she signed for the book. "It's pretty metaphysical, but it's worth the effort."

"While I'm here, I'd like to have another look at the tape of Chagall. Could I borrow it?"

"Sure, I'll get it for you." He went over to a rack of videotapes and brought one back to her. The library was in the basement of Lloyd Hall and had an extensive collection of audiovisual materials and equipment.

Laura switched on a VCR and began to watch the video. The tape was an interview with Marc Chagall shortly before his death and took place in his garden. So many of the great European painters took inspiration from their gardens, Laura thought. It undoubtedly had to do with colour.

The revered artist's lined face was luminous with pleasure as he talked about *Daphnis & Chloe*, his series of jewel-like lithographs. Laura was so absorbed in his comments it took her a moment to realize something liquid was dribbling down the screen. Ripping off her earphones, she jumped to her feet. Now she heard the soft splat as another drop landed on the TV set and began its downward journey. Slowly, almost reluctantly, her gaze travelled up to the ceiling. A dark crimson stain was spreading across its surface. Another drop fell, then another. A male dancer who had been watching a ballet video on the set next to hers, leapt to one side to get out of range. "Jesus Christ, is that *blood*?" It was as if he had been confronted with a cobra, its evil hood outspread.

"Come over here!" Laura called out to the librarian and the urgency in her voice brought him running from his office. The hushed quiet of the library gave way to an excited babble of voices as staff and visitors dropped whatever they were doing and gathered round the television set. Warning them not to do or touch anything, Laura used the librarian's telephone to call Corporal Lindstrom's extension. To her intense relief, the Mountie answered on the first ring.

"There's something weird going on down here at the library. Can you come over right away?"

"What's happening?"

"It looks like there's blood dripping down from the ceiling."

"I'm on my way."

"What's upstairs?" Corporal Lindstrom asked only a few brief moments later. She was gazing up at the dark stain, now considerably larger than when Laura had first seen it. Laura frowned, trying to recall the layout. A security guard, his walkie-talkie squawking excitedly, answered for her. "A small conference room. It isn't used very much."

"Do you have a key?" Karen asked. "Let's go then," she said when he patted the key ring on his belt. Telling the others to stay put, she turned to Laura. "I don't know what we're in for, but I'd like you to come along."

Laura gestured for her to lead the way and followed her and the guard out of the library and up the circular staircase. Standing to one side of the door, Karen reached out and tried the knob. The door was unlocked. Motioning the others to stand back, she pushed it all the way open. Holding her revolver in a two-handed grip, she sprang into the room. Sweeping the gun in a slow arc, she cautiously looked around. The walls were paneled and there were no closets or other places to hide. After checking behind the door, she waved at her two companions to join her.

"This looks like some of John Smith's work," Laura said as she gazed down at the floor.

"You're sure?" asked Karen.

"I can't think of anyone else who would pull a stunt like this."

"Jesus Christ!" the security guard said as they stared at the mess on the floor — a large pool of viscous red fluid, flecked with globules of white matter.

"Is that white stuff what I think it is?" asked Karen.

"It looks like semen to me," replied Laura, adding dryly, "That will be John Smith's personal contribution."

"Is it really blood?" The security guard looked as if he wanted to bolt out of the room. How people's attitude to the life-giving fluid had changed, Laura thought.

"It certainly looks and smells like blood all right. But I very much doubt it's human blood," replied

Laura. She pointed to the guard's walkie-talkie. "Shouldn't Mr. Lavoie know about this?"

The guard quickly pressed the switch and began to talk.

"Blood and semen," said Laura. "In this, the age of AIDS, the message is rather clear, don't you think?"

"And gross," muttered Karen.

When Lavoie joined them, they went back downstairs to the library. "What I can't understand," he said, staring up at the library ceiling as if wondering how much it would cost to repair the damage, "is how so much seeped through. That conference room has a hardwood floor."

"I imagine John Smith found a way to help that along." Laura said. "When that mess is cleaned up, I think you'll find a few tiny holes drilled in the floor. Having the blood drip through the ceiling would be part of the performance. And so would the reaction of those who saw it." As she spoke, Laura's gaze was roving around the library. "There it is," she said, pointing with her finger. "Over there on top of that bookcase. I knew it had to be here somewhere."

The video camera was wedged between some books so that it was completely hidden, except for the lens. Standing on a chair, Laura squinted into the eyepiece. "He's got a nice wide field of view. It takes in the entire area where people sit to watch the VCR screens. I'm not sure how I feel about appearing in one of John Smith's feature performances," she added as she stepped down.

With Corporal Lindstrom's permission, the librarian moved the television set and placed a pail under the spot where the blood was dripping down. The sweetish smell of blood — sheep's blood, as it later turned out to be — hung in the air. "What do you want to do about this?" the police officer asked Lavoie.

"Do?" He frowned at her in some puzzlement. "What do you mean 'do'?"

"I mean laying charges — destruction of public property, public nuisance. There are a number of criminal charges that could be made to fit."

Lavoie looked shocked. "This is Art! It's a creative act, not a crime." He turned to Laura. "Do you think this performance is finished?"

She spread her hands in a gesture that said how could anyone know when one of John Smith's performances was over.

"Well, I'm going to have it cleaned up anyway," Lavoie said, walking away. Laura watched him go with a thoughtful expression on her face.

Leaning back in a lounge chair with his feet propped up on a table in front of him, Richard grimaced with distaste as Laura recounted the episode of the blood and the semen.

It was mid-afternoon and the lounge was deserted, except for themselves and two men from the grounds staff playing pool. Like many men at the Centre, they wore their hair in ponytails. Their hair was thin and sparse, leading Richard to think, as he often did, that "squirrel tails" would be a more apt description. The clicking of the billiard balls was inordinately loud in the otherwise silent room, and Laura and Richard had retreated to the far end of the lounge to escape from it.

Suddenly Richard jumped to his feet. "What do you think you're doing?" he demanded, hastily pushing back his chair. But John Smith was too fast for him.

With a quick snip of his scissors, he deftly cut a lock of Laura's hair, popped it into a small plastic bag, and was gone, leaving Laura and Richard glaring speechlessly after him.

Laura fingered the spot where her hair had been cut. If she was vain about any part of her looks, it was her luxuriant, golden-brown hair. "He's got me on his video, and now he's got a lock of my hair. I once knew an artist who collected bits and pieces from people because he wanted to be a warlock. He thought he could gain power over people by doing that."

"I'll get it back." Richard started for the door through which John Smith had disappeared, but she grabbed his arm. "No, I don't want you to do anything. Not yet, anyway. Let's see what he's up to."

Outside the Sally Borden Building, they ran into an annoyed and puzzled Marek Dabrowski. "That John Smith," he said through clenched teeth. "I was sitting on my deck outside the studio going over some sheet music, when he suddenly appeared out of nowhere and grabbed a sheet from my hand. I was going to call security, but I found it shoved under my door a few minutes later."

"After he made a copy of it," Laura murmured.

Marek frowned. "What is going on here? First Eckart and now this. Why are they trying to steal my music?"

"What did he mean about Eckart stealing his music?" asked Richard after a fuming Marek strode off in the direction of Donald Cameron Hall.

"I don't think Marek intended to let that slip, but now that he has, here's what happened," Laura said, and told him about Eckart's attempt to tape Marek's concerto and how Marek had dealt with it.

"Marek would realize that if he made an issue of it, he would be diverted from his concerto," Richard said.

"You're right, of course. And I would have been dragged into it too."

Looking into her eyes, Richard said, "I hope all this excitement hasn't made you forget we're having dinner tonight?"

Laura smiled. "See you at seven."

"Is that you, Laura?" The chief of security came closer and peered at Laura as she stood beside the passenger door of the Ford Taurus, waiting for Richard to unlock it. Her hair was upswept and she was wearing an elegant off-the-shoulder black dress. "For a minute there, I thought it was a member of the Board of Governors."

Laura laughed. "Can't a poor working artist get dressed up once in a while?"

"You could wear a flour sack and still look like a Greek tycoon's wife," murmured Richard, holding the door open for her. He was rewarded with a devastating smile.

With so auspicious a start, it was not surprising that the dinner date was a great success. They dined at Le Beaujolais, the soft candlelight suffusing Laura's bare shoulders and lighting her brown eyes with a warm glow. With that disturbing and powerful painting behind her, her artistic conscience was at peace.

"The squirrels stole one of the paintings I'm working on," Laura said as Richard tested the wine and nodded approval."

"The squirrels stole your *painting*?" he asked incredulously.

"Not the painting," she laughed. "The props. When I went to my studio this afternoon I found that they had gotten in somehow and climbed up on the table and made off with the apple and pears I was painting. Don't ask me how they managed it, but an apple and two pears were out on the balcony with big bites out of them."

"Maybe you should paint them that way."

Laura cocked her head to one side. "Now that's an interesting thought."

As the evening progressed, Richard soon realized that this remarkable woman was the most delightful dinner companion he had ever known. She had a unique way of looking at things, a different and highly intelligent perspective, and an entertaining way of expressing her thoughts. Some of her throwaway lines were so apt Richard found himself committing them to memory for future use. When he mentioned the "virtual reality" group of artists at the Centre, she dismissed them by saying, "When all's said and done with that bunch, it's more said than done."

Once she paused and said, "I know what you're doing. Jeremy does that too, only he's completely open about it. He scribbles things I say down in a little notebook he carries with him."

"He should use more of your material. He'd get better reviews. If it bothers you, I promise never to use them."

"I don't mind. I seem to have an endless supply. You might give me a footnote, though." She smiled at him over her wine glass.

"You should be a writer. No, I'm serious, Laura. You really should try it. With the way you express yourself, you'd be a natural."

Laura shook her head. "You're a writer because you write. You put words down on paper. I don't. I may say some amusing things from time to time, but it's just dinner party wit that doesn't transpose to the printed page. I don't write. I paint."

Richard reached across the table and took her hand. "And you paint superbly."

They were quiet on the drive back to the Centre. Once he smiled and reached out his hand, and Laura pressed her lips against it.

"You can come in if you like," she said softly, handing Richard her room key.

"I like," he said, fumbling with the key. In his excitement it took him a couple of tries to get the door open.

She came willingly into his arms. There was no pulling back as she moulded her firm curves against him. He slowly unzipped the back of her dress, thrilling to the feel of her cool skin. The dress slipped around her waist. She wasn't wearing a bra.

Richard bent to kiss her breasts. She gave a low moan and reached for him. When this lady decided it was time to make love, she didn't hold back. Her passion matched his own as they breathlessly undressed each other.

"Let me look at you," He took a step back as they came out of a long, passionate embrace. "You're beautiful!" he breathed, awed by the naked splendour of her magnificent body.

"So are you." Deftly, she slipped a condom over his erection, then took him by the hand and led him over to the bed. She gasped with pleasure as he entered her. Despite her whispered pleas not to hurry, he was so excited by her beauty and unrestrained passion that he reached orgasm while she was still groaning with passion.

"Touch me!" she cried fiercely, and his caressing finger swiftly brought her to a back arching, soaring climax. "I come with instructions," she said with a demure smile when the spasms tapered off and she was still.

He laughed delightedly and said, "I've got a bottle of wine in my room. Why don't I slip across and get it?"

"Put some clothes on first."

When he returned, she had wrapped herself in a terry cloth robe and was standing on the balcony. "I love balconies," she said. "You can see things from them, but somehow you're protected from what's going on out there. That makes me a bit of a voyeur, I guess."

"You're not a voyeur, you're a painter."

They stood together sipping wine, before the chill of the night drove them back inside. Glass in hand, Richard walked over to inspect her bookshelves.

"I have to admit it gives me a bit of a thrill to see my books all together like that."

"You have every right to be proud. Those books are a major achievement."

"Despite what old Henry says?"

"He doesn't matter. What matters is that your books are a good read. All of them. You're probably right when you say he's jealous of your success."

Knowing that she would be bringing Richard back to her room, she had hidden Norrington's book out of sight. She had an idea that seeing it might bother him. It would be soon enough to talk about it after she had had a chance to read it.

Turning away from the bookcase, Richard untied the belt of her robe and she let it fall from her. When they had both climaxed in their different ways, she smiled up at him and playfully tweaked his nose. "Don't look so macho and worried. That's the way I like it. I told you I came with instructions. But my stomach muscles are going to be sore for a week. It's a good thing I don't paint with them."

She refused another glass of wine, saying she wanted to have a clear head. "Because tomorrow it's back to painting for me and writing for you."

Preparing to leave, Richard opened the door and took a cautious peek down the corridor. “The coast is clear.”

“Richard?” Laura called softly from her bed. “I like you,” she said when he turned around.

“And I like you,” he whispered, and closed the door quietly behind him.

chapter thirteen

"Our musicology professor, old Eckart, was going on about the influence of Handel's London oratorios on Haydn, yesterday afternoon," the music student was saying, "when John Smith walks into the lecture hall. He goes to the tape machine, turns it on, listens for a bit, then takes out a pair of scissors and cuts a piece of tape. Eckart looks like he's going to have a major heart attack. Then John Smith waves the tape in Eckart's face, and runs out of the room, holding it above his head like a pennant."

Seated across from each other at the breakfast table, Laura and Marek exchanged glances. So John Smith knew about Eckart's attempt to steal Marek's concerto. That didn't surprise Laura. The performance artist prowled around campus at all hours of the day and night, and could easily have come across Eckart's bulky tape machine during one of his forays in the woods. It would be completely in character for him to keep quiet about his discovery until he was ready to use it for his own purposes.

Laura got up to leave. Richard, grinning wickedly as he saw her wince, picked up his tray and followed her out. "John Smith steals a lock of my hair," Laura said as she and Richard left the Banquet Hall together. "That's about as personal as you can get. He steals a sheet of music from Marek and music is at the core of Marek's being. He walks into a lecture hall and makes off with a piece of tape from Carl Eckart."

"And we know what the tape represents to Eckart."

"Our performance artist is building up to something, Richard."

"That strikes me as a dangerous game for him to be playing. Dangerous for him."

"Which would make it all the better as far as he's concerned," replied Laura. "Danger has always been an element in his art."

"Are you sure you don't want me to go to his studio and retrieve the lock of your hair?"

Laura shook her head. "No. I'm not superstitious."

They walked companionably down the path towards the studios. "I'll see you at lunch," Laura said as they embraced at the point where the path to her studio branched off.

A harried Alec Fraser walked into Kevin Lavoie's office and slumped in a chair. "I just had a call from Harvey Benson," he said.

"Is the Chinook Foundation pulling out?" asked Kevin with bated breath.

Fraser shook his head. "It hasn't come to that. Not yet anyway. But he made it very clear that he and the Foundation's board of directors are very concerned about what's been going on around here. I can't say I blame them. Two violent deaths on the campus and a killer still at large."

"And with John Smith's performance still to come," said Kevin with a shudder. "Shouldn't we try to postpone their visit until after this mess is cleared up and John Smith's show is over?"

"I've thought of that and decided it's too risky. The sooner we can get the funding agreement signed and the public announcement made, the better. The more time they have, the more likely they are to back out." Fraser got to his feet. "We'll just have to tough it out. Somehow," he added with a heavy sigh.

"You've shown me some of the wonders of Banff. Now it's my turn," Richard said as he and Laura finished lunch. He seemed to be struggling to keep a straight face. "But first let me ask if you've been to the Walter Phillips gallery recently?"

"No, I've been meaning to, but there just hasn't been time."

"After my gaffe over its name, I figured I should at least check it out. Which I did this morning. There's a real treat in store for you. But they'll be taking it down to make way for John Smith's performance so we don't have much time."

"Then let's go now."

The gallery was deserted except for a student attendant, who didn't bother to look up from the book she was reading. Glancing around the gallery walls, huge with large, undistinguished paintings that all seemed to depict a nest of copulating snakes, Laura muttered, "This is pretty boring. Is this what you brought me to see?"

Grinning, Richard took her by the arm and marched her across the main gallery to the smaller one at the far end. Shapes, made of plaster and glaringly white under the bright lights, were grouped together on the floor.

"They look like so many toad stools and mushrooms," said Laura. "Do you know what they're supposed to be?"

"Did I not promise you a wonder?" Richard waved his arm expansively. "Welcome to the *Urinary Garden*!"

Laura glanced again at the installation, then went over to read the write-up stapled to the wall. "That's the best part," said Richard. "It's hilarious."

The write-up explained how the artist had been exploring aspects of sexuality by making works that referred to the female body — usually her own. The series, called the *Urinary Garden,* had been produced during the artist's two-week residence in the colony. The works were "biological images made from life" — plaster casts of female and male urinations in the snow.

"I remember hearing about an artist from Wales waiting for the right snow conditions," said Laura. "Now I guess we know why."

"Keep on reading, "Richard told her. "Look at all the grants she received for this project. The lady is a grant junkie."

"She certainly knows how to work the system," agreed Laura as she read the grateful acknowledgments of grants from the Canada Council, the Guggenheim, and two other foundations whose names she didn't recognize. Under the heading *Contributions*, the artist thanked all those who had contributed to the project. Laura recognized a couple of names: Charlene Adams, the lesbian printmaker, and, among the men, Jeremy Switzer. Trust Jeremy to get involved in something like this. He would load up with a couple of beers and laugh with delight as he peed into the pristine snow.

The attendant was still immersed in her book as they left. Richard, who was enjoying himself enormously, stopped at her desk to tell her how fortunate they were to have caught the exhibit before it was taken down.

"Oh, but it's been extended for another month," she said.

"That's odd. I thought it had to come down to make room for John Smith's performance."

"That's been moved. Haven't you heard? There's been so much interest in his recital that they've decided to transfer it to the Eric Harvie Theatre. Look at the poster by the main door as you leave."

They stopped to examine the poster, which was just inside the front door. A wide band of paper announcing the change in venue—"by popular demand"— had been pasted diagonally across the poster.

"What do you think of that?" John Smith suddenly appeared in the doorway. Uncharacteristically, he seemed almost excited.

"Congratulations," said Richard. "This should make you famous."

John Smith's thin lips tightened. "Fame means nothing to me."

"Come off it," Laura scoffed. "You're a performance artist and, by definition, performance artists need audiences. The bigger the better."

John Smith gave her a measured look, then drew himself up. "As usual, you are right. When John Smith creates Art, he wants the world to know about it," he chuckled as if suddenly struck by an amusing idea.

"I'd like to show you something," he said, falling into step beside them. "Why don't you both come to my studio?"

Richard cocked an inquiring eyebrow at Laura, and she nodded. Viewing John Smith's art usually meant being the victim of it. Nevertheless, she was curious to see what went on in his studio. He had the Ron Thom Studio, designed by the late Toronto architect, located directly across from Richard's studio and next to where the boat studio had once stood.

John Smith unlocked his studio door and waved them in with a low bow. Inside, five female mannequins, all of them naked to the waist, were the first things that caught the eye. They were grouped by themselves in a dark corner. Thinking there would be a video camera somewhere, Laura kept her face expressionless as she gave them a cursory look. One mannequin clutched the bars of a small cage, another was lashed to a cross, the third was tied to a chair, and the remaining two were shackled together.

But John Smith didn't seem interested in the mannequins. Maybe they were props from a past installation, or part of a project he had abandoned. He didn't so much as glance at them as he led his guests over to a paint-daubed bench beside an equally splattered sink — the Thom Studio was normally used by painters. He had assembled what looked like a junior crime lab on the bench. There was a small microscope, a magnifying glass, a fingerprint kit, a test tube rack, and various small jars and plastic bags. The display looked like the sort of thing that a pre-teen playing detective might have put together. Laura looked for her lock of hair among the objects littering the bench, but it didn't seem to be there. But there were plenty of other items with a human connection: a cigarette butt smeared with lipstick, a sheet of music — Marek's probably — the notorious slice of tape, a number of Polaroid prints, one of which, disturbingly, showed the interior of

Laura's studio. Richard swore under his breath and picked up a typed sheet of manuscript covered with penciled notations.

"This is mine. What are you doing with it?"

"I like to have little mementos of my friends," replied John Smith looking amused when Richard folded the page and put it in his pocket. Laura was sure he would have a copy somewhere. He made no attempt to explain what he was doing with the equipment and the bizarre collection of personal items. He seemed content to have them know they were there. As so often was the case with him, the symbolism seemed more important than the reality. While he hovered over the bench, Laura glanced around the cluttered studio, looking for the video camera. Intentionally or otherwise, John Smith had transformed the studio into a surrealistic happening. Masks and costumes were strewn about everywhere; some were hanging on the walls, others were lying on the floor and along the back of the sofa. A muffled whirring sound gave away the camera's location. It was hidden inside a grotesque mask that John Smith had once worn to a "Bad Dreams" party at the Centre. The mask had a gaping mouth that accommodated the camera's wide-angle lens. It was probably capable of filming almost everything that took place in the studio.

Laura decided to ignore it, and turned back to John Smith with a look that seemed to ask, "Is that all there is?" He smiled thinly, pulled a lever, and a figure, arms flapping wildly, sprang up from behind the sofa. Its blue mouth leering horribly, it swayed from side to side before finally coming to rest.

"This is quite a collection of toys you have here." Richard gave the dummy a push, making it sway on its springs again.

"It's better at night with the lights off," John Smith said, with a look of childish disappointment. "His face glows in the dark."

Laura, who was beginning to relax and enjoy herself, sat down on the sofa, ready for whatever other treats John Smith might have in store for them. A Bible lay open on the coffee table. Wondering whether it would explode in her face, she picked it up. It was opened at the Book of Revelation. Watching her, John Smith nodded approvingly. "That's what I'm going to call my performance. Revelation."

"Revelation about what? Or need I ask?"

"You'll find out at the proper time." John Smith tried to look omniscient, but only succeeded in looking smug.

"Is it all right if I move this?" Laura pointed to a gorilla mask glaring over her shoulder.

"If it bothers you, yes." John Smith seemed to feel he had scored a minor victory.

"It doesn't bother me. It's just in my way." Turning to pick up the mask, Laura saw a large paper dragon lying on the floor behind the sofa. It looked oddly pathetic, as if it were dying. Then Laura saw that what she at first had taken to be wounds were just the spaces where John Smith had yet to finish covering the bamboo frame with crepe paper. The dragon was red, or would be when it was finished. Looking more closely, Laura saw that it was designed to be worn as a costume. There was an opening in its belly where an actor, presumably John Smith, could put it on.

Revelation. Laura's parents had dutifully sent her to Sunday School until she convinced them that her time would be better spent painting. By then, however, she had been exposed to the apocalyptic visions in the Book of Revelation. It was a nightmarish watercolour she did of the fifth angel, his trumpet blaring while a blazing star fell from heaven, and fire and smoke rose from the bottomless pit that finally persuaded her parents to let her stay home.

"The great red dragon. Wasn't he ...?" Laura picked up the Bible, turned some pages and began to read aloud. " 'And another portent appeared in heaven; behold a great red dragon, with seven heads and seven diadems upon his heads. His tail swept down a third of the stars of heaven, and cast them to the earth.'" She closed the Bible and placed it back on the table. "Is the great red dragon going to be your messenger?"

"Very good, Laura. You're very quick. But you'll have to wait for the night of the performance."

But Laura wasn't listening. One of the mannequins had moved! The telltale movement was almost imperceptible, just a slight rise of a breast as she eased the pressure of the thongs that bound her to the cross. Laura was mildly surprised that she hadn't spotted her before, but John Smith had cleverly managed to divert their attention. Now that she knew what she was looking for, it was easy to detect the slight movement of the model's chest as she took a shallow breath. A quick glance at the other figures confirmed that they were "real" mannequins. Once again, John Smith had stood reality on its head.

"She must be terribly uncomfortable holding her breath like that," Laura remarked casually.

"She likes it," John Smith snapped. He looked thoroughly put out. Laura was puzzled as to what the "fake" mannequin was doing there. John Smith couldn't have known she and Richard would be coming back to the studio with him. Maybe it was a rehearsal, or more likely, John Smith had deliberately gone looking for some unsuspecting victims he could lure into the studio and startle out of their wits when the mannequin suddenly came to life. He must have been hugging himself with glee when she and Richard agreed to visit him.

"Are you all right?" Richard asked the woman with genuine concern. While this had all the earmarks of one of John Smith's performances, it was possible that she had been tied up against her will.

"I'm okay," she said, shrugging her shoulders.

"It's Charlene, isn't it?" Although her shorn blond hair was covered with a black wig, Laura recognized the printmaker who worked part-time in housekeeping. Laura had seen a revealing collection of Polaroid's in Charlene's studio in the art building. The walls were lined with pictures of Charlene and her girlfriends laughing, drinking wine, hugging and kissing one another.

"Yeah," she replied with another shrug. Suddenly the thongs fell away from her wrists, dropping to the floor with a soft thud. Rubbing her wrists, she stepped away from the cross and unhurriedly took her shirt down from a hook and slipped into it.

Richard signalled that it was time to leave. As they walked toward the door, John Smith placed his hand on Laura's arm. "You're very good, you know. Very observant. I like that. How would you like to assist me with my project?"

Remembering how the performance artist had fixated on Erika in the days before her death, Laura wondered if she was to become his next subject. She had no intention of letting that happen.

"I'm sure that would be very interesting," she said. "But I'm totally wrapped up in my own work at the moment. As a fellow artist, I know you will understand."

Put that way, John Smith had no choice but to accept her refusal. But there was something threatening in the scowl that darkened his face as Richard held the door open for her and followed her out.

"Listen," said Laura as she and Richard crossed the footbridge. "It's Schubert," she said as the gentle notes wafted through the air. "That must be Isabelle practicing the sonatas."

The window was partially open and a gentle breeze tugged at the lightly woven drapes, spreading them slightly apart. Isabelle was seated at the Baldwin, her back to them as her fingers moved over the keys. They lingered for a few moments while Laura fed the scene into her visual memory book. She would paint it, sooner than later.

"Are we going to see each other tonight?" Richard asked as they resumed their leisurely stroll.

"Not tonight. I've got some serious reading to do." Laura paused and laid a hand on Richard's arm. "I took one of Henry's books out of the library. I need a block of time to really delve into it."

Richard stared at her for a moment, then shrugged, and said, "Everyone to their own taste," as they walked on.

Propped up in bed, Laura opened *Demystifying Deconstructionism*. Its weight made her grateful that she had brought her portable reading stand from Denver with her. She had expected Henry's book to be heavy going, but soon found that it was highly readable. The sarcasm and condescension that marred his every day conversation were totally absent in his writing. It helped that she agreed with his central thesis — that deconstructionism was a self-destructing philosophy that failed to recognize that the whole could be more that the sum of its parts. Looking up from the page, Laura nodded to herself. Henry's book itself was an example of what he was saying. In addition to the words and the ideas, there was also his prose style, sure-footed and lucid. If, as the deconstructionists would have it, you took that away and broke the text down into the individual words, attaching equal weight to each one, the whole exercise would become meaningless. Unavoidably perhaps, Norrington occasionally lapsed into professional jargon, twice forcing Laura out of bed to consult her dictionary. But she always enjoyed learning new words, no matter how arcane.

"Right on," she found herself murmured as she read a paragraph that stoutly declared there was nothing wrong with fiction "constructing rather than reflecting realty."

Her eyes were beginning to burn. Marking her place with the flap of the dust jacket, she was surprised to see that she had read almost half the thick tome. Holding it with both hands, she placed in on the bookshelf next to the row of Richard's novels. There's plenty of room for both of you in the world of literature, she thought to herself. Richard knew that, but Norrington refused to accept it.

She turned out the light and stepped out onto the balcony. The dark mass of Mount Rundle was limned with moonlight. With a slight shudder Laura realized it was eerily like the way it had been lit by the fire that took Erika's life.

chapter fourteen

John Smith must have worked all night, thought Laura as she read one of his new posters on her way to breakfast. He would be determined to fill the theatre. Having it only half-full would be an intolerable blow to his pride. The poster confirmed the change of venue and promised startling revelations when John Smith, "who knows all, would reveal all." There was no mention of what the "all" might be, although, under the circumstances, there was a clear inference that it had something to do with the mysterious deaths on campus.

Those deaths continued to remain mysterious, Laura mused as she stood before the poster, lost in thought. With the subcutaneous bruising, Montrose's death might well have been murder although Jeremy, the only one known to have a motive, apparently had an unshakable alibi. Erika's death was almost certainly murder, but what was the motive? It was Geoff Hamilton who had made the one telephone call she received, and she might well have told him that they were through. Karen obviously thought of him as a possible suspect.

Laura snapped out of her reverie when Richard walked up to stand beside her. Scanning the poster, he muttered, "So we are going to have 'revelations' are we? And John Smith is going to reveal all."

"Knowing him," Laura said as they turned away and headed for the Banquet Hall, "it could simply mean that he will take off his clothes."

"How did you get along with Henry's book?"

"Amazingly well. I was thinking of it as kind of a 'duty' read. I see him every day and I thought I should know something about his work, but it was fascinating. He writes beautifully. He comes across completely differently than in person. Have you read any of his books?"

Richard blinked in surprise. "Good Lord, no."

Constable Peplinski brought a copy of the poster into Karen's office where she was working at her desk. She frowned as she read it and told the constable to find John Smith and bring him in for an interview.

This time there was no difficulty in locating the performance artist. Within minutes Peplinski was back. Closing the office door, he told Karen that John Smith was waiting in the hall. His eyes widened as he told her that he had found him in his studio painting an image of Satan on the body of a girl who was stark naked. So complete was the paint job that at first Peplinski had thought she was wearing a costume. "Her face was all made up with slanted eyebrows and her pubic hair had been shaved off," he told the bemused corporal. "To make it easier to paint her," he added helpfully. "He even introduced me," he said in a tone of wonder. "Her name is Charlene."

Karen gave a tight-lipped smile and asked him to show the performance artist in. She waited a few moments before acknowledging John Smith's presence. Glancing up from the poster spread out on her desk, she said, "I'll get right to the point. If you know anything about the murders, it's your duty to tell me."

"So it's 'murders' now, is it? You're finally admitting that old Montrose was murdered."

"I'm treating his death as murder, until proven otherwise. Exactly what is it you know about these deaths?"

"What makes you think I know anything about them?"

"You're telling the whole world that there's going to be a revelation, that you're going to reveal all."

"The poster doesn't even mention murder."

"It won't be long before everyone will think you intend to reveal the identity of the murderer or murderers. Are you saying that's not true?"

"I guess everyone will have to wait to find out."

Although she knew it wouldn't do any good, the policewoman tried to pressure John Smith into telling what he knew. Knowing that appeals to his duty as a law abiding citizen would only amuse him, she warned him that he had foolishly placed his life at risk and that the only way to protect himself was to tell the police what, if anything, he had found out.

"That makes it all the more interesting, don't you see?" John Smith seemed exasperated by her obtuseness.

"What I see is that this whole thing is one of your performances. Was setting fire to Erika's studio one of your performances, too?"

"I liked Erika. She was my friend."

"You told me that before. But I hear that she was frightened of you."

John Smith, white with fury, stood up. “May I go now?”

“Yes. But if it’s true that you really don’t know anything about the murders, I’d advise you to make that known as soon as possible.”

“But who would believe me?” John Smith asked as he quietly closed the door behind him.

Carrying the lunch the kitchen staff had packed for her, Laura was determined to remain in her studio all day, working on the structure of the first panel of a large triptych she was planning to paint. The problem was what object to put below the open window with a view of the mountains in the background. Seated at her desk, Laura penciled in several designs in her sketch-book. None of them worked.

Her subconscious must have continued to mull over the problem, because, as Laura ate her lunch, she suddenly knew it should be a wooden stool with a violin and bow lying across it. Hastily finishing her fruit salad, she began sketching in the outline with rapid, confident strokes of the charcoal pencil.

She drew the bow in several positions before deciding it worked best lying beside the violin. Late in the afternoon, she put down the charcoal. The colours she would decide on tomorrow. Colour was never a problem for her. It was the composition that had to be thought through, a process that could sometimes require her to spend hours studying a painting, lying on the floor or climbing a stepladder to look at it from all angles.

Exhilarated by the breakthrough she had made, Laura locked her studio and headed back to the residence. Looking to her left she saw Henry Norrington trudging with that rolling gait of his up the path from his studio, and decided to wait for him. The depth and clarity of his perceptions had both astonished and impressed her, and she wanted to tell him so. As an artist, she knew how rewarding it was when someone responded to one's work, and understood and appreciated what it was about. Norrington's ego was inflated enough already, but like all art, his work had a value and an existence of its own, entirely apart from himself as a person.

"I was reading one of your books last night, Henry," she said as he came up to her.

"Oh. Which one?"

"*Demystifying Deconstructionism*. It's fascinating."

"I'm glad you think so," said Norrington, visibly preening himself. "I, of course, wrote about deconstruction in writing, but much of what I said could also apply to painting. The proponents of that misguided doctrine would have it apply to all the arts."

"I agree with them on that, at least. There should be no boundaries in art."

"'In my Father's house are many mansions'," Henry quoted gravely. "And so it should be with art." He paused as if to allow time for the thought to sink in, then said, "Your own paintings, I am glad to say, are the very opposite of deconstructionist. If I read them correctly, they themselves are the object, and not some hidden, underlying agenda. Incidentally, they are, to my untutored eye, quite beautiful."

Laura smiled to herself as she thought of the recently completed Dance With Death. But that was an aberration, altogether apart from the mainstream of her art.

"Thank you. It pleases me to hear you say that. And you're not fooling me with that business about an 'untutored eye'." Laura smiled, at him, then went on thoughtfully, "I think that the creation of a beautiful image, is, as you say, what I am really out to achieve. In my recent paintings I'm trying to capture not so much the thing itself, but the *effect* of the thing on the viewer. Some of my fellow artists criticize what I'm doing, saying that my work is irrelevant and that I should be seeking to reveal the great unifying principles that underlie everything. Your comment that instead of unifying, the deconstructionists only succeed in putting everything asunder, was a revelation to me."

"Hmm. Yes." Norrington's glance fell on one of John Smith's ubiquitous posters tacked, against all the rules, to the side of a music hut. "I have become quite wearied of that word recently."

"I know what you mean. But his promise of a revelation seems to be working. I hear they expect to fill the theatre. Listen." Laura stopped abruptly at the edge of the service road. Music, glorious music, was pouring out of the large music hut across the way. Someone, it could only be Isabelle, was playing a piano with verve and great virtuosity.

"That has to be a concerto," she said as the music soared and thundered out through an open window. "And I bet I know whose it is. Let's see."

The curtain had been pulled aside and the window was wide open. It was as though the pianist wanted everyone to hear this magnificent music. Isabelle was seated at the Baldwin concert grand, her trained fingers flying over the keys. Marek, eyes half-closed in concentration stood beside the piano, his right hand conducting an imaginary orchestra.

Laura and Norrington lingered on the cinder path and let the music wash over them. Ordinarily, Laura would have felt uncomfortably like a voyeur, but not this time. The two lovers were so wrapped up in the music that it wouldn't have mattered to them if the whole world stood outside their window. Concertos are designed to showcase the soloist, and Marek had provided ample scope for his beloved to display her virtuosity. Isabelle had been right when she predicted it would quickly become part of the standard repertoire. Concert pianists would fall upon it with delight, recognizing it as a perfect vehicle to show off their talents. They would vie with one another as to who could decorate each phrase most elaborately.

The music thundered to a crescendo, then abruptly ceased. Norrington started to applaud, but Laura grabbed his hands and jerked her head to indicate they should move on. Intent on getting Norrington out of there before he did or said something that would break the spell, Laura failed to notice John Smith standing motionless in the trees at the far end of the hut.

But there was no overlooking Veronica Phillips. The beautiful young cellist, hidden from the music hut by a curve in the path, stood as if transfixed. Seeing the tears glistening in her eyes, Laura murmured a greeting and kept on walking. But Veronica put a hand out to detain her.

"Wasn't that beautiful, Laura? I'm so proud of him."

Veronica's attitude thrilled Laura. It was art at the highest level; an act of creation transcending personal considerations and being hailed as the masterpiece it was. She smiled at Veronica. "The world of music is a much richer place today. I feel privileged just to be here."

"I'll wait for you in the parking lot," Norrington said gruffly, seeing that Veronica wanted to talk to Laura.

"Is it finished?" asked Laura. "I don't know enough about music to know."

"Not quite. There are some missing passages in the *andante,* and he still has some of the third movement to write. But he has plenty of time to finish it before he leaves." Veronica's lip quivered at the thought of Marek leaving and she dabbed at her eyes with a Kleenex. "When it's finished I'm going to ask him to transcribe it for the cello."

"That would be nice," Laura murmured diplomatically, knowing it would be the last thing Marek would want. The piano concerto was his song of love to Isabelle and he wouldn't want to dilute it in any way.

"That's what's so wonderful about this place," said Laura as she joined Norrington in the parking lot. "There's always something to inspire you."

"That was truly inspiring," he agreed. "An epiphany, if you like."

"Well, my dear," he said with a courtly little bow as they rode the elevator to the sixth floor. "I greatly enjoyed our little talk. Perhaps we could continue it after dinner. I suppose Richard will tag along with you, but I doubt that a discussion of deconstructionism will be of much interest to him."

"You shouldn't underestimate Richard," she chided Norrington. "He's a very intelligent man. And I like his books. I've got them right beside yours on my bookshelf. I was thinking last night that there was plenty of room in the literary firmament for both of you."

"Humph," sniffed Henry, opening the door of his room. "If that's so, his would be a mighty dim star."

"I thought you told me Charlene was a lesbian." Richard nudged Laura as they walked into the lounge and pointed to Jeremy and Charlene chattering animatedly at a table overlooking the pool.

"She is. And Jeremy is bisexual. Maybe she is too. Anyway, gay people are often the best of friends with the opposite sex." As if to confirm what Laura was saying, Charlene threw her head back and shook with helpless laughter.

"Maybe he's telling her about the reviews of his play," grinned Richard. "Whatever it is, she's eating it up."

But there's somebody who isn't, thought Laura. Kevin Lavoie was standing just inside the entrance, a strange, almost bewildered, look on his face. Laura waved at him, but he didn't seem to see her. He turned on his heel and left.

"Your usual, Dr. Norrington?" The barman asked as the trio passed by on their way to a table.

Norrington nodded, and Richard said, "And we'll have a bottle of Chambertin."

"Have you seen this?" Laura held up a copy of the Centre's newsletter as Richard pulled out a chair for her. When both Richard and Norrington shook their heads, she showed them an item headed "Colony Resident Accepts University Post."

"Dr. Marek Dabrowski," it read, "has accepted an appointment to the prestigious Indiana School of Music. He will take up the appointment in September. Dr. Dabrowski, a resident artist in the colony since January 15, said in an interview that he will have a light teaching load and will be able to devote most of his time to composing. While at the colony, Dr. Dabrowski finished writing a sonata in C-minor and is currently at work on a concerto for piano and orchestra."

"That is, indeed a very prestigious appointment," murmured an impressed Norrington. "It will do much to further his career. Not," he added, "that he is not already well established and highly regarded in the world of music."

"That could give Marek and Isabelle the perfect opportunity to begin a new life together," said Richard.

"Marek is going to dedicate his concerto to her," Laura told them. "It will be called the 'Isabelle Concerto' and she will give its premiere performance. According to her, every orchestra in the world will want to make it part of their repertoire."

The drinks arrived and Norrington, in a tone of voice that brooked no denial, changed the subject to the philosophy of deconstructionism.

"Many deconstructionists believe that depicting something monstrous and deformed by itself amounts to a philosophy," he intoned.

"That explains some paintings I've seen," murmured Richard.

"Just so," agreed Henry, taking an appreciative sniff of his brandy. "They purport to believe that rational discourse, such as we are enjoying tonight," he added benignly, serene in the knowledge that virtually all of the rational discourse would be his own, "obscures the real meaning of life." He shook his massive head at such heresy. "Instead of rational discourse, they treat words as 'constructs' that must be decoded in order to discover their true meaning. I admit there is the occasional instance when this seems to work. Take 'menopause', for example. It doesn't require all that much imagination to interpret that as the time when a woman may 'pause' in her relations with 'men'. It's not hard to see why the philosophy of deconstruction is so popular with feminists. In fact, they have virtually taken it over."

"That sounds like an exception that doesn't prove the rule," Richard interjected.

"An apt way of putting it." Norrington raised his brandy snifter as if to salute the felicity of the phrase.

"But if you carried this idea, or philosophy or whatever it is, to its logical end, wouldn't it lead to the deconstruction of deconstructionism itself?" asked Laura.

'Precisely," Henry beamed at her. "I addressed that very point in an article I wrote called *The Paradox of Deconstruction*. It did not endear me to the deconstructionists," he added with a complacent smile. "Incidentally, that article is the last thing I wrote or intend to write about deconstructionism. I have turned to larger, grander themes."

"As in *How The Post Modern Novel Challenges The Boundaries of Art*," murmured Laura. "A subject like that should give you all the scope you could possibly want."

"And I am taking full advantage of it. That is the opus I want to be remembered for. As I am sure I will be."

"Still, it was your early work on deconstruction that originally got you tenure at the university, wasn't it?" asked Richard.

"And I am duly grateful. But deconstructionism is only an insignificant blip in the literary panorama I am dealing with now."

"I'm here to paint, and you're here to write," Laura reminded Richard when he made as if to follow her into her room. She let him hold her close for a moment, then gently pushed him away.

"I never realized before that making love and making art were mutually exclusive activities," he grinned. "In fact, I had the impression it was just the opposite."

"Maybe for some people. But with me it's a matter of energy. I need to conserve it in order to paint at the level I want to achieve. That doesn't mean I don't like you, though," she added in a subdued voice.

"I know." He kissed her lightly on the lips. "You go to bed and conserve energy and I'll see you in the morning."

Laura, stimulated by Norrington's ideas and also, she admitted to herself, by the brief physical contact with Richard, knew she wouldn't be able to fall asleep right away. She smiled to herself as she looked at the collection of Richard's titles on the shelf. Taking *The Blue Agenda* down, she opened it at random. Although she had read it before, she was soon caught up in the action, the pages seeming to turn of their own volition. From time to time she paused, silently mouthing the words as if to capture the rhythm of the passage.

A sudden yawn made her glance at the clock radio on her bedside table. Nearly one o'clock. This was no way to store up energy for painting. Worse, when she did slip between the cool sheets, her mind refused to switch off. Words and phrases kept tumbling about in her head.

chapter fifteen

The next morning Norrington intercepted Laura on her way to her studio and insisted that she join him in his studio for a cup of coffee.

"Wasn't that incredible yesterday? Hearing Isabelle playing Marek's new concerto?" asked Laura, taking a careful first sip of coffee. "Those two seemed made for each other. Musically and romantically."

The portly pundit folded his hands across his middle and smiled like a benevolent toad. "Dabrowski will drop the delectable Mrs. Ross as soon as his stay in the colony is over."

"You don't know what you're saying. They're madly in love."

"I know perfectly well what I'm saying. Don't forget I'm a veteran colonist. I've stayed in art colonies all over North American and Europe. So has Dabrowski. Our handsome composer has quite a track record. He invariably enlivens his stay with a passionate affair, complete with all the romantic trappings — vows of eternal love, jealousy, ardent looks, the whole gamut. Maybe it inspires him to compose. Maybe he just likes the drama of it all. I don't know. But I do know there is a consistent behaviour pattern. When he takes up his post at the Indiana School of Music, he will have an affair with some student. And then break her heart. And then another. And another. I know of one woman who committed suicide when he dropped her."

"That's appalling." Laura wanted to deny the shocking things Norrington had said but he spoke with an air of such calm conviction that she knew he was telling the truth. What should she do about Isabelle? Should she try to warn her? Try to prepare her in some fashion for the shock she was in for?

Norrington was speaking again, breaking into her thoughts. "It would not surprise me if we have another death in the colony."

"Why do you say that?"

"It would be designed purely to cause confusion. Maybe even to suggest there's a homicidal maniac at work. It would have to be completely motiveless, to divert attention from the real motive for killing the real victims. Like Jeremy's motive for wanting Montrose dead."

"The police haven't arrested Jeremy," Laura pointed out, without mentioning that Jeremy claimed to have an unbreakable alibi.

"Ah, but there's the motive. And I'm sure if the police dig deep enough into Erika's background they will find a motive for killing her. That's why I say the next murder will appear to be completely random. To throw the police off the track." Henry paused, "I see it being made to look like a suicide at first but with enough clues to show it was murder." He paused and gave her a quizzical look. "Why are you smiling at me like that. I didn't think what I said was particularly amusing."

"You know, Henry, you're a bit of a fraud," she chided him playfully. "An entertaining fraud, but a fraud nonetheless."

"What do you mean?" he demanded huffily.

"You make a big fuss about not reading Richard's books. How you only managed to get part way through one of them. You claim they're completely beneath you. And yet that scenario you've just described comes right out of *It Stalks By Night*. And it wasn't revealed until near the end."

Norrington shrugged. "There's nothing original about the idea of a red herring murder. It's been used countless times. In fact, because of its lack of originality, I'm not surprised that it found its way into one of Richard's books."

"If you say so, Henry." Laura rinsed her mug in the sink. "Thanks for the coffee." She refrained from thanking him for the troubling conversation.

Men! Seething with anger over Marek's self-centred duplicity, Laura closed her studio door with unnecessary force, vowing to never again let herself fall into the trap that was about to snap shut on Isabelle.

Her anger gradually subsided as she mixed paints and began to add colour to the design she had drawn on the canvas yesterday. The predominant colour was a soft shade of blue with the reddish brown of the violin providing the contrast. Satisfied with the morning's work, she decided to take the afternoon off to do some shopping in town.

It was a pleasant walk down the mountainside to town. Laura purchased some toiletries, another art book, and fresh flowers for her room, then treated herself to an ice cream cone. With time on her hands, she decided to drop in at the RCMP headquarters and see if Karen was on duty.

The RCMP office was on Lynx Street down by the railway tracks. The building itself was modern and commodious, but the reception area was the size of a jail cell, with walls lined with dark Rundle stone, giving it a forbidding, cave-like appearance. "All hope abandon ye who enter here," thought Laura with a shudder as she pressed a button on the counter.

The duty constable came out and told her that Corporal Lindstrom was in charge of an honour guard at the funeral of a park ranger who had been killed in a helicopter crash trying to pluck an injured climber off Mount Assiniboine. Laura nodded. Lindstrom had been on parade duty at the formal opening of a new wing to the Whyte Museum. "Just tell her that Laura Janeway came by to see her. It's not urgent."

The constable who obviously recognized her name, glanced at a wall clock and said, "She's due back in about fifteen minutes. Why don't you wait?"

Ten minutes later Karen came out to the reception area to greet Laura. She was resplendent in full dress uniform: wide-brimmed Stetson, scarlet tunic, britches, and brown riding boots complete with spurs.

"Excuse the Rose Marie get-up." She spoke lightly, but there was no mistaking her pride in the famous uniform. "I had to attend an opening."

"I know. I think it's very dashing."

Karen glanced back over her shoulder as she led the way to her office. "You probably don't know what I meant by the Rose Marie crack, do you?"

"I most certainly do. It's an old Hollywood chestnut starring Nelson Eddy and Jeanette MacDonald. It had some wonderful songs."

"It also made a generation of movie goers believe that Mounties spend their time riding black horses through the snow, wearing Stetsons and scarlet tunics, and singing their heads off."

Karen led Laura across the brightly lit interior to a small office and closed the door to shut out the squawking of radios and jangle of telephones. The walls were bare except for a framed certificate verifying that Constable Karen Lindstrom had been awarded the Distinguished Marksman Award. A row of books were lined up on top of a heating vent.

"I shouldn't be taking up your time," Laura said.

"Don't worry about that." Smiling, Karen waved Laura into a chair. "Would you like some tea?"

"Oh, no. I just dropped in to tell you my theory about Jeremy's alibi."

Karen looked amused. "Which is?"

"Kevin Lavoie. They spent the night together. Right?"

"I told you before that you should be on the force. How did you guess?"

"The look on Kevin's face when he saw Jeremy chatting up a girl from housekeeping. He looked absolutely betrayed. And that time he walked away from the mess John Smith made in the library. It was more of a flounce than a walk."

"I take it you knew Jeremy was gay?"

"He's bisexual, actually. It's like Jeremy to want to have the pleasures of both worlds. I didn't know about Kevin, though."

"I have an idea this is a fairly new development in his life," Karen mused. "It cost him quite an effort to admit that he was with Jeremy when Montrose was killed in the stairwell."

Her telephone rang and she picked it up. She listened, then said, "I'll come out." She told Laura she had to sign a report but it wouldn't take a minute. "Don't go away," she added, "I want to ask you something."

While she was gone, Laura glanced over the row of books. Most were police manuals, but there were two legal texts, one on court procedure and the other on the rules of evidence.

"I've been taking Lavoie's word at face value," Karen said as she came back, closing the door behind her. "You know him. What do you think?"

"I think that if Kevin said he was with Jeremy, then he was with Jeremy. Especially since it required him to admit he had a homosexual encounter."

"That's how I feel about it, too. Are you going to tell anyone about this discovery of yours, Laura?"

"No. Not so much for Jeremy's sake — he wouldn't care — but for Kevin's."

"This could be habit-forming." Richard stretched luxuriously.

"It does have its moments," Laura, lying naked beside him on the bed, conceded with a smile.

"I want it to have more than moments. A lot more." Richard turned his head to look at her. "I don't want this to end when we leave the colony. If it's all right with you I could spend time with you in Denver. Serious time. I'm completely portable. I can write wherever I happen to be, and all I need to carry on my business is a cell phone and fax machine. How about it?"

"We could try it," Laura said slowly.

"That's all I can ask for." Richard gave a deep sigh of relief that turned into a gasp as her cool lips began to travel down the length of his body.

chapter sixteen

On Sunday morning, John Smith stood on the proscenium stage of the Eric Harvie Theatre and gazed out at the amphitheatre of empty seats. On Tuesday night they would be filled with people curious to see what his "revelation" would bring. He was sure the Mounted policewoman would be there. The plainclothes detectives who had invaded the campus in the first few days after the fire, then disappeared from the scene, would almost certainly be present as well. His publicity campaign had really snowballed; the switchboard was jammed with inquires about the performance. People were even driving up from Calgary to see the show. He should have been selling tickets, but money wasn't important. What was important was that his recital, preserved on videotape, would become one of the icons of performance art. But there was still much to be done.

As if in answer to his unspoken thoughts, Charlene, a proud, possessive smile on her face, led

Jeremy out from the wings. "I told Jeremy about our being short-handed, and he volunteered to help. He really knows his way around a theatre."

John Smith, not altogether pleased with the fond looks his assistant was bestowing on the bearded playwright, stared at the unlikely twosome. "I thought you specialized in 'bridge and tunnel' theatres," he finally muttered.

"They're still theatres. With exactly the same equipment this one has. I've done everything from prop man to stagehand to director, but," Jeremy shrugged, "if you don't want my help, I've got other things to do."

John Smith was about to turn away in dismissal when the mutinous look on Charlene's face warned him that she might leave along with Jeremy. He couldn't afford to lose her. Not at this point. Besides, he really could use another pair of hands. Particularly experienced hands. "Okay," he conceded reluctantly, "I'll take you below and you can start working on some props."

On the way to the underground workshop, they passed Desiré limbering up at the barre. Even in baggy warm-up pants and thick leggings, the tall, black dancer was spectacular. "Desiré will be a star after Tuesday night," John Smith informed Jeremy in a voice loud enough for the dancer to hear. She smiled into the mirror behind the barre and gave him a thumbs up with her free hand. "Her costumes will blow the men right out of their seats," he went on as they waited for the elevator to take them down to the subterranean depths of the theatre. "And some of the women too," he added as the elevator door slid open.

The props in the workshop were unlike any Jeremy had ever seen. A giant red dragon leaned against a tall gilded altar. Next to it stood an altar of a very different kind — a wooden pole surmounted with a conical thatched roof. Doll heads, painted white, dangled from hooks, and bottles of rum and black candles were arranged on a breast-high circular shelf. Even to Jeremy's uninformed eye, it smacked of voodoo. Or at least John Smith's version of it. Doubtless, this was where Desiré would star. Jeremy felt a stirring in his crotch at the thought.

John Smith handed him a can of gold paint and told him to start putting a second coat on some wooden trumpets. "After you finish that," he said, "you can start on the swords. Silver for the blades and black for the handles." The performance artist went over to another workbench where he picked up a half-finished mask and began to work on it.

"You're a fast worker," allowed John Smith with grudging approval as Jeremy hung the last sword on a hook to dry. "Do you know how to use a power saw?"

"Show me a prop man who doesn't."

"Good. You can start cutting out spears. Here's the pattern. We need six of them."

"I hear John Smith's got you building props." The cashier with the earring and taped eyeglasses smiled at Jeremy as he punched numbers into the cash register. "That's great, man."

"It's great to be back in a theatre again. There's nothing else in the world to compare with it."

"That's where I'm going to spend my life." The cashier stuck out his hand. "Justin Sterling is my name. I'll see you over at the theatre later this afternoon."

"Now there's a name that will look great on a marquee," said Jeremy as they shook hands. And undoubtedly chosen for that very reason, he thought to himself.

"I've never seen props quite like that before," he went on. "Have you seen the script?"

The cashier stared at him. "Script? With a performance artist? It's all in John Smith's head, and he keeps changing it as he goes along."

The other cashier hissed, "Break it up, Justin. The customers are getting impatient."

Jeremy smiled apologetically at the line-up behind him and picked up his tray.

"Let's knock off for a beer. We deserve it." A fine dusting of sawdust flew up as Jeremy brushed the front of his sweater. They were in the workshop in the basement of the theatre building.

"Give me a moment to finish this skirt." Charlene rapidly stapled the two pieces of patterned paper together, and said, "Okay, let's go," as she set the finished skirt aside.

Jeremy had been surprised to find that most of the costumes were made of paper. Charlene had explained that they had neither the skills nor the money to use cloth. "Besides," she added, "John Smith likes the idea. He says the paper costumes will add to the ephemeral, impermanent nature of the performance. It's only meant to be given once, not like a regular play."

"Some of my plays have that ephemeral quality, too," grinned Jeremy as they walked along an underground passage leading to a door that opened beside the orchestra pit. He opened the door and they stepped out onto the main concourse in front of the ascending rows of seats. Above them on the stage John Smith and Desiré were working on a routine. Desiré, now wearing a black body stocking, bounded about the stage in soaring, graceful leaps. She carried a wooden spear, similar to the ones Jeremy had just finished making, and lunged at John Smith as she flew by in ever decreasing circles. John Smith, who appeared to be in some sort of a trance, stared unblinkingly out at the empty amphitheatre. If he was aware of Jeremy and Charlene gazing up at him, he gave no sign.

Charlene and Jeremy's eyes met as they turned away. "We both want her, don't we?" murmured Jeremy. "Maybe we can both have her."

"You mean together?" Charlene's voice was a choked whisper. The slapping, slithering sound of Desiré's slippers followed them as they walked up the aisle.

"You'd like that, wouldn't you?" asked Jeremy.

"I think so," she replied uncertainly. "Do you think you can make it happen?"

"It's worth a try." But Charlene didn't hear him. "Oh, my God," she muttered. She was staring across the foyer at a black and white poster pinned to the wall, "I forgot about Malvina's performance. It's on right now. She'll kill me if I don't show up. Literally. But there's still time."

"Where is it? I'll come with you."

"At the gallery. But I don't think it would be a good idea for us to go in together. You can come in a few minutes after me."

Intrigued, Jeremy followed Charlene as she hurried across the campus to the Walter Phillips Gallery. On the way, she told him that Malvina was a student in the art department and that the performance was her graduation project. "I used to see quite a lot of her and I don't want her to see us together." She motioned him to stand back as she opened the door to the gallery.

Grinning to himself, Jeremy counted slowly to sixty before following her in. A figure, looking like a cross between an astronaut and a deep-sea diver, hung suspended by steel cables from the ceiling of the hallway outside the main gallery . The cables were attached to a harness fitted under her crotch. Malvina, for a sign propped against a wall proclaimed that's who it was, was clad in shiny metallic-looking material. A heavy-featured, mournful face stared out from under a football helmet painted silver. The artist was an extremely large woman; Jeremy estimated her at six-foot-two and at least one hundred and eighty pounds. Thin wires ran over pulleys and down to a small booth, open on two sides.

The booth was empty and Charlene slipped inside and, after a quick glance at the brief instructions taped to a wall, reached for one of the levers. An electric motor whirred to life, the cable slipped down a notch and, with much clanking of metal, Malvina began to roll forward. Charlene shoved the lever forward and Malvina stopped with a sudden jerk, swinging on the wires like a giant pendulum. Charlene pulled another lever, and Malvina shot back up, helmeted head almost banging into the ceiling. A sideways movement of the lever and she began to rotate. There was a sudden shower of sparks and the electric motor short-circuited. Charlene, her face ashen, emerged from the booth and headed straight for the door, without looking back at her outsize friend dangling from her disabled contraption.

"It had to be me," Charlene wailed when Jeremy caught up to her. "I had to be the one at the controls when everything blew up."

"She can get down all right. All they have to go is lower the cables."

"I know. But that's not the point. She'll be furious. She's been working on that project for months."

"What was it all about, anyway? It looked like some weird form of torture."

"It is supposed to be an exploration of the body in relation to space. Malvina's big on exploring the body."

"She's got a lot to explore," interjected Jeremy.

Charlene ignored the quip. "She would deny that her project has anything to do with torture. But, of course, it does. Deliberately rendering yourself helpless, and providing the machinery for other people to jerk you around is sheer masochism."

She hesitated at the foot of the steps leading up to the Sally Borden Building. "Maybe we should forget that beer and go back to work. There's still an awful lot to do."

"I need that beer. My throat feels like sandpaper after inhaling all that sawdust."

"Okay. But just one."

"The motor giving up like that wouldn't bother your friend John Smith," Jeremy said as he plunked two draft beers down on the table. "He'd simply make it a part of his act."

"There's a world of difference between what you saw back there and John Smith. He's a master artist while Malvina is still an amateur trying to figure out which way she wants to go. John Smith is a perfectionist. If something goes wrong in one of his acts it's because it was meant to."

"Really? I've seen some stuff of his that looks pretty crude and handmade. That donkey head of his for one. And his elkmobile. That's just an elk hide draped over a bicycle with antlers tied to the handlebars."

"That's how those things are supposed to look. It's a form of abstraction. You'll see what I mean on Tuesday . He's going to push everything right to the edge."

"For example?"

"Are you pumping me, Jeremy?"

"Not at all. But when somebody makes a statement like you just did about John Smith going to the edge, they should be prepared to back it up with a for instance."

"You remind me of a lawyer I once knew."

"He was right."

"It wasn't a he."

"Sorry. I should have known better."

"I'll tell you this much. He's going to be playing with fire."

"Fire? With all those paper costumes." Jeremy's fingers combed his beard. "That's pretty close to the edge all right. Do the authorities know about this?"

"No. And they're not to know. I shouldn't have told you. Promise that you won't tell anyone."

"My lips are sealed."

"Justin will be standing in the wings with a fire extinguisher. When we get to the fire part."

"The skinny cashier? With the earring? Now that's what I call reassuring."

chapter seventeen

Laura held the elevator door open for Norrington. He was wearing a bathrobe over his swim trunks and was bound for his daily late afternoon session in the pool. He smiled his thanks and nodded distantly to Richard as he stepped in. The small, glassed-in elevator offered a scenic view of Bow Valley on the short ride to the ground floor of the Sally Borden Building. They parted company in the lobby, Norrington going down the stairs to the pool, while Laura and Richard went into the lounge.

"Oh, oh! The pool's closed. Henry won't like that," said Richard, looking down at the deep end of the pool where technicians were stringing up lights and loud speakers.

"That'll be for Joyce's show tonight. We promised to attend. Remember?"

"Thanks for reminding me. Hey, get a load of this."

Norrington, an impressive sight in fluorescent yellow trunks, shiny brown bathing cap, and dark goggles, strode purposefully along the edge of the pool, ignoring the frantic protests of the pool attendant who danced along in front of him. Arriving at the deep end, he dove in and began to swim with a powerful breaststroke. Nothing was allowed to interfere with his daily ritual of swimming fifty laps.

"If one of those lamps falls into the pool, he's toast," muttered Richard. But the supervisor was waving his arms at the crew, telling them to shut everything down. Henry swam serenely on.

"He doesn't look it, but Henry must be in pretty good shape," Laura said, watching him surge through the water with a bow wave that a tugboat might envy.

"As I've said before, I kind of admire the guy." Richard handed her a glass of wine. "He never lets anything stop him. Look at the way he handled that pool attendant. It was as if he wasn't there."

"It would kill him to admit it, but I think he admires you, too."

Richard stared at her. "Where have you been all this time? Haven't you heard him put me down every chance he gets?"

"I know. But, believe it or not, I think Henry is a secret fan of yours."

"You've got to be joking!"

Laura smiled. "I admit it's just a guess on my part. Yesterday morning, he described a scenario that was right out of *It Stalks By Night.*"

"Oh? What was that?"

"The third death that looked like suicide was really murder, and it was meant to be a red herring to distract attention from the killer's real motive."

"I don't think that means much. The idea of a red herring murder is pretty trite. In fact, I was a little embarrassed about using it."

"That's what Henry said as well. Still, it's kind of a neat idea, isn't it? Old Henry heaping scorn on your books in public, while secretly devouring them."

"Dream on," Richard laughed.

The academic year was coming to an end, and the bulletin boards were festooned with notices of recitals, lectures, readings, and performances. It was impossible to take them all in, not even those of particular interest. But Joyce Evans, a senior multimedia artist from England, had become friendly with most of the colonists during her stay. She had made a special point of personally inviting Laura and Richard to her presentation, and they had agreed to come. Using the pool as the venue was an unusual twist and Laura was looking forward to it.

At dinner that evening, Richard rounded up Jeremy Switzer and Norrington to accompany them, telling Henry with a laugh that after all the trouble he had caused in the pool that afternoon he owed it to Joyce to attend.

Henry drew himself up indignantly. "I caused no trouble. I merely exercised my rights."

"Good for you," said Richard. "But you realize you could have been electrocuted?"

It was obvious the idea had never occurred to Henry. "Nonsense!" he expostulated after giving Richard a startled look. "They wouldn't dare."

A goodly crowd had assembled in the lounge and along the shallow end of the pool by the time the little contingent from the colony arrived. When it was announced that "due to unforeseen circumstances' the show would be delayed a half-hour, some drifted away, intending to spend the half-hour taking in some other event.

"How does it feel to be an 'unforeseen circumstance', Henry?" asked Richard with a grin. Henry tried to remain deadpan, but he couldn't resist grinning back.

A rippling high-pitched wave of sound announced the start of the show. There was a moment of complete darkness, then spotlights bathed the swimmers in a rainbow of colours. There were seven of them, all women, lined up along the edge of the pool at the deep end. The lights shifted, changing colours as the performers dove cleanly into the pool one after another.

The atonal sound glissaded down the scale to be replaced with the melodic tinkling of bells. Applause broke out as the swimmers spread out to form a wheel. The wheel gathered speed, then broke apart to form another pattern. What followed was basically a sound and light show augmented by synchronized swimming and a kaleidoscope of images flashing on and off a giant screen suspended over the pool. It was pleasant, but unfulfilling. Laura felt that she should be grateful it carried no message, since virtually every performance at the Centre was heavy with social comment and symbolism. Nonetheless, she had expected more, and it was with a faint sense of disappointment that she joined in the polite applause that greeted the end of the show. Joyce Evans stood spotlighted on the diving board to take her bows. She was turning to leave when a voice came over the loudspeaker. "Ladies and gentlemen, for a *real* show, remember it's Tuesday night at the Eric Harvie Theatre when the great red dragon will speak." A computer picture of a dragon appeared briefly on both sides of the giant screen and then was gone.

"Talk about stealing the show!" said Richard as he paid for the drinks.

"John Smith shouldn't have done that," said Laura. "He knows better."

"Knowing better never stops our boy," replied Richard, leading the way to a table near the bar.

"Jeremy, you've been helping out at the theatre," said Laura. "Do you have any idea of what's going to happen?"

"Some. Enough to know that it will blow what took place here tonight right off the wall. But if you're asking me if I know what the big revelation is, the answer is no."

"I keep thinking that it will turn out to be another one of his stunts. He's quite capable of leading people on and then leaving them empty-handed."

"Anything's possible with that guy," Jeremy agreed.

"Dangerously possible," added Norrington.

Carl Eckart was walking over as if to join their little group, but turned away and went over to stand at the bar when he saw Marek approaching them.

"Did you see Joyce's show?" Laura asked Marek as he pulled up a chair and sat down. "I didn't see you in the audience.

"Alas, no." Marek spread his hands in a gesture of regret. "I would have liked to, but my concerto is at a very demanding stage. I am anxious to finish it so that Isabelle can have it before she leaves."

"A farewell present?" Norrington asked innocently.

"It is not meant as a gift. It is a tribute to her artistry," Marek replied smoothly, giving Norrington a tiny shake of his head as if to warn him off.

Norrington lifted the brandy glass to his nose for a long, luxurious sniff. "Ah, yes. Is it not wonderful that the art world is so full of beautiful and talented women?"

Marek pretended to be oblivious to Henry's innuendo. "Ah, yes," he replied with a soulful sigh, "we are truly blessed in that regard."

"There was Joan the violinist," Henry said in a reminiscent tone, ticking them off on his fingers, "Olga the pianist, Irene the composer, and of course we can't forget poor Evelyn who met with such an unfortunate fate."

"I must return to my work." Marek abruptly stood up and strode off after jerking a formal bow in Laura's direction.

"Not exactly subtle, my friend," murmured Richard. "That was a list of Marek's conquests, I assume?"

"A partial one."

"I wonder if the fair Isabelle knows about this?" As always, Jeremy was alert to the possibility of mischief.

"No. And you're not to tell her," said Laura.

"I have no intention of doing that," Jeremy replied with a show of indignation.

"So Marek has a past?" Richard mused as he and Laura rode up in the glass-sided elevator to the floor that connected with Lloyd Hall.

"A spectacular one according to Henry," Laura told him. "Henry unloaded all this on me yesterday. I wish he hadn't."

"You're not thinking of telling Isabelle, are you?"

"No. It wouldn't do any good. If Marek runs true to form, she's in for a heartbreak sooner or later. Warning her now would only speed up the process."

"I'm going to contact a real estate firm in Denver tomorrow and have them start looking for a condo I can rent. If that's all right with you? I promise not to take up too much of your time," Richard added hastily as he saw the look on Laura's face. "Okay?"

"On that condition, okay," Laura smiled.

They said goodnight at her door, both of them aware that their relationship had reached a new plateau.

Preparing for bed, Laura thought about this new development in her life. Having Richard as a more or less permanent part of it was exciting, but first there must be no secrets between them. She took *Mission to Mykonos* down from the shelf and leafed through it until she found the passage she wanted. She nodded to herself. It was as she remembered.

Snow had fallen during the night, blanketing the bare ground and making everything seem new and pristine. Laura had slept badly, but her spirits lifted as she walked through the glistening white landscape on her way to breakfast. Veronica Phillips, her cheeks flushed and looking almost unbearably beautiful, was on her way back from the Banquet Hall.

"Guess what?" she called out as she drew closer.

"Professor Dabrowski ... Marek ... wants me to apply to the Indiana School of Music. He's sure I'll be accepted."

"With Marek's backing I'd say you're a shoo-in," Laura said. "Congratulations!"

As an ecstatic Veronica turned and walked away, Laura thought to herself, that arrogant, scheming bastard!

Laura had finished her breakfast and was drinking herb tea. Her lips twisted in a grimace of distaste as she thought about Marek and how neatly he had arranged for his next romantic interlude. It was almost as if he stored women until he needed them, like some species of spider that wrapped their victims in a silken shroud and hung them up in the web until they were ready to be sucked dry. And she had been so sympathetic to Marek and his star-crossed love!

"If looks could kill, there'd be another death in the colony," Karen said as she slid into a seat opposite

Laura with a cup of coffee. As usual, the cashier had refused to let her pay for it. Free coffee was one of the universal perks of the police.

"Men can be absolute bastards at times, can't they?" mused Laura.

"Some men more than others," the policewoman agreed. "Is this something personal to you?"

Laura looked shocked. "Good God, no!"

"Does it have any bearing on the case?"

"I don't think so." Laura hesitated. "But you better know about it, so you can judge for yourself."

"What a sleaze bag!" Karen exclaimed when Laura finished her little tale of duplicity. "And he's such a handsome son of a bitch!"

Laura expected to hear the thundering notes of the concerto as she approached the hut on her way to her studio. Instead, she heard the furious voice of Isabelle Ross. "If you think I'm grateful to you for telling me this, Carl Eckart, you are very much mistaken!"

"I just thought you should know," replied the musicology professor as he emerged through the hut's open door in quick retreat. He stopped short when he saw Laura, then brushed past her without a word, his thick lips twisted in a triumphant smirk. He must have overheard Norrington taunting Marek in the crowded lounge last night. It would be his revenge for the humiliation of being caught trying to steal Marek's music.

Now that she had driven her tormentor off, the impact of what she had heard was hitting home to Isabelle. She was clinging to the doorjamb for support, her face drained of colour and numb with shock.

Laura hurried up the walk to her side. "Are you all right?"

Isabelle swallowed, and blinked her eyes as if trying to bring things back into focus. "I'll be okay in a minute." She took the Kleenex Laura handed her and wiped her eyes.

Laura put a protective arm around Isabelle's shoulders and led her over to a chair.

Isabelle gave Laura a grateful smile, but her eyes had the same hurt, bewildered look that Kevin Lavoie's had when he saw Jeremy chatting up Charlene. But there was something else there too. The lady was thinking. Her expression cleared as if she had reached a decision.

"Marek ..." A tremor crept back into her voice. "Marek says he will have a complete score by the end of next week and my agent has talked to the conductor and he's agreed to make it the centrepiece of my concert in Chicago."

Isabelle clearly intended to put aside her grief for her newly lost love for the sake of the concerto. Laura got to her feet. "Well, if you're sure you're all right, I'll let you get on with it."

Isabelle followed her to the door. "Nothing, nothing whatsoever must be allowed to interfere with the concerto," she muttered fiercely, as if to reinforce her determination.

"I know Marek feels the same way." Laura paused on the doorstep. "I'm sure both of you are headed for a great success with it."

Isabelle made as if to say something, then changed her mind. Closing the door behind Laura, she hurried across to the piano, flexing her long fingers in anticipation.

Although there was less than an inch of snow on the ground that would melt away before noon, the support staff had run a snow blower over the path. They try to take such good care of their artists, Laura thought. And yet here we are, dropping like flies. She shook her head at the irony of it.

chapter eighteen

Charlene parked the rented pickup truck outside a service entrance to the theatre building. Jeremy climbed out of the passenger side, his nose wrinkling at the smell of kerosene. Charlene lifted the canisters out of the back of the truck and placed them carefully on the ground. "You can help me carry them in, if you like."

Feeling like an accessory to a criminal act, Jeremy picked up two of the canisters and followed her into the theatre. "Your boyfriend sure likes playing with fire," he muttered.

"He's not my boyfriend, he's my mentor. And fire is his preferred method of expression."

"As in the boat studio?"

She turned around to stare at him. "You're not serious?"

"I guess not. But," he added as they continued on their way down the concrete corridor, "it's the only theory that makes any sense."

Charlene stopped at a door with a replica of a human hand nailed to it. The hand pointed to a sign that said *Prop Storage*. As Jeremy expected, the room was crowded with props from past performances that were still used to rehearse with. Rapiers and fencing foils sprouted out of round bins like umbrellas in a stand. Masks and witches' hats hung from tall poles, and stage furniture was stacked everywhere. Charlene placed her canisters on the floor beside two covered urn-like vessels that gleamed dully like gold, and motioned Jeremy to do likewise. Each vessel had a spout and as he bent over, Jeremy saw that dragons spitting fire had been etched on their sides.

"Would you mind telling me what's going to happen?" he said as he straightened up. "So I can get out of harm's way, you know."

"There won't be any danger. It will just *look* like there is."

"Uh, huh," said Jeremy dubiously, eyeing the two identical containers on the storeroom floor. "What are these cans for?"

"They're not cans, they're urns. Sacred urns."

Jeremy nodded gravely. He could image the obscene rites that would have sanctified the urns.

"Aren't you worried someone will smell the kerosene?" he asked.

Charlene shook her head. "Nobody will come in here until just before the performance. This place is just for storage. Here take this." She handed him one of the urns and picked up the other herself. "Come on, or I'll be late for rehearsal." Taking Jeremy by the arm, she propelled him out of the storeroom, locking it behind them.

"Don't worry about me," said Jeremy casually. "I'll go down to the work shop and touch up a few things."

But Jeremy didn't go to the workshop. Instead, he made his way backstage and watched the rehearsal that was underway. The performance was only one day away and John Smith was still improvising, but the main structure was in place. If nothing else, it was going to be a long drawn-out affair, Jeremy discovered, as he shifted uncomfortably on his hard backed chair. John Smith finally called a break for lunch, warning everyone to be back on stage in half an hour.

When the rehearsal resumed, Desiré began to dance, this time holding one of the urns over her head. This was more like it. Jeremy's flagging interest picked up as he watched the leotard-clad dancer leaping lightly about the stage. When her performance was over, Jeremy slipped away to the workshop where he spent an hour working on the props. Another hour in the morning and everything would be finished in plenty of time for the performance. Jeremy smiled with satisfaction as he put away his tools; working in a theatre once again was turning out to be a very enjoyable experience.

On his way to the lounge for a beer, he saw Kevin escorting a middle-aged couple. From the obsequious way Kevin was behaving, they could only be the Bensons. Benson was the chairman of some foundation that was going to donate a pisspot full of money to the Centre. The story was that Alec Fraser had been courting him for months. Kevin would be giving them a royal tour of the campus. But he would undoubtedly bypass one of the most interesting exhibits. With a gleeful grin, Jeremy changed course to intercept them.

Kevin eyed him warily as he came up, but introduced him effusively as a playwright who was working on a new play. The Bensons seemed agreeably impressed, and smiled politely as he fell into step with them. Kevin began to relax as Jeremy chatted away, extolling the unique virtues of the Centre. But he stiffened with alarm when Jeremy began to talk about the "fascinating" exhibit in the Walter Phillips Gallery, calling it a "must see" display.

"I'm sure they wouldn't be interested," Kevin protested.

Mrs. Benson shot him a glance. She obviously was not accustomed to being told what would or would not interest her.

Jeremy looked surprised. "But Kevin," he said in a sweetly reasonable tone, "this is the Banff Centre for the Arts and that's the only major art exhibit on display. I think they have to see it."

"Mrs. Benson and I are very fond of art," Harvey Benson said. "We'd like to see it."

Kevin cast a despairing glance heavenward and followed in their wake as Jeremy, chatting away to the increasingly charmed Bensons, led them over to the gallery.

"Interesting. And quite attractive," Mrs. Benson paused in the doorway to survey the gleaming white plastic shapes on the floor. "What are they, do you suppose? Some type of fungus, possibly?"

"You're very close," Jeremy complimented her. "This sign explains it all."

He led her over to the sign that was headed *Urinary Garden*. There was a sharp intake of her breath as she read. Pointing to his name in the list of contributors, he said, "I was happy to do my bit for the cause."

Mrs. Benson sniffed and turned away. "Come, Harvey. I think we have seen enough."

"Thanks a bunch," Kevin muttered as he followed them out of the gallery.

"I thought it would broaden their horizons," Jeremy said, adding sanctimoniously, "After all, isn't it that what the Centre's for?"

As she was doing more frequently now that the weather was deliciously spring like, Laura was taking the long way back from the colony. Her pace slowed as she thought about her relationship — if that's what it was — with Richard. He was undeniably attractive, wonderful company, and he was more than satisfactory as a lover. But did she love him? No. Not yet certainly, and probably never. But that didn't mean they couldn't have a mutually rewarding relationship.

Having reached this decision, Laura paused on the footbridge and let her thoughts roam back over the events of the past two and a half weeks. Were the killings behind them, or was there more to come? Were they purely random with no linkage between them? It certainly seemed that way. Maybe somebody with a grudge against the Centre, somebody who had been rejected or was jealous of the artistic success of the colonists. Like the student who had accused Montrose of plagiarism. Or like the frustrated composer Carl Eckart. If that was the case, she could be at risk herself. On the assumption that there was a rational motive behind the killings, Laura had not felt threatened because, try as she might, she couldn't think of a single reason why anyone would want to murder her. The divorce had been years ago, and her ex had remarried and had two young daughters. The few affairs she had allowed herself since then had ended amicably and she was on good terms with all her ex-lovers.

But what if the killings were motiveless, and were the work of a homicidal maniac? Laura shivered and hurried toward Lloyd Hall. Not that there was any safety there. The reality was that there was no safety anywhere.

Richard knocked on her door just as Laura was about to go down for dinner. His expression was easygoing as usual as he told her he had to drive down to Calgary to meet some people who were flying in with a proposal to purchase an office tower in Seattle. They were going to meet at the Calgary airport. "I almost feel like a traitor to this place," he added with a grin, "to be talking crass commercial deals, but it looks like an excellent opportunity and it won't be on the market for long."

He said that since it was only eighty miles he would drive back up after the meeting, but that it would be very late and he would see her tomorrow. "But not too early. I'll probably be bushed."

"Make a million, darling," Laura murmured as she kissed him.

He grinned. "I just might at that."

He was plainly excited at the prospect of doing a deal. If you had the knack, as he obviously did, it must be a great way to make your living, Laura thought. You could earn a great deal of money without having to spend all your time at it, and without having to spend every day at the office.

After dinner, Laura retired to her room and read, this time making notes.

chapter nineteen

As Tuesday, the first of April, dawned, John Smith's performance loomed over the campus like a palpable, physical presence. Linked as it was to the mysterious deaths in the "campus in the clouds," it had received extensive coverage in the local media, not only in *The Crag & Canyon* but the Calgary papers as well. The news stories speculated about the possibility that the promised "revelation" might reveal the identity of the murderer. From all accounts, it appeared that many, possibly hundreds, would have to be turned away.

At seven-thirty that morning, a worried-looking Kevin Lavoie and Corporal Lindstrom were standing outside the theatre, conferring on what could be done to control the situation. The police had persuaded several Calgary radio stations to broadcast messages warning people that the capacity of the theatre was limited to 959 people, and that many of those who showed up were bound to be disappointed. Those from outside Banff were urged to think twice about coming.

"There will be closed circuit television screens and loud speakers outside the theatre," said Lavoie. "That may placate those who can't get in."

"It will help," Karen agreed, but she was still frowning. "I don't like it. It could so easily get out of hand and turn into a major disaster."

She bit her lip and looked uncertainly at the coordinator. "I don't suppose the Centre could be persuaded to cancel the performance? On the grounds that the theatre can't accommodate the crowd?"

Kevin shook his head. "There's nothing I would like better. For more reasons than one. But to cancel the show would violate everything the Banff Centre stands for. It would be seen as a form of censorship and, worse, would tell the world that we are not capable of providing an adequate showcase for the artists under our wing. Whether we like it or not, John Smith's performance is art and we have a responsibility to uphold and nourish art in all its forms."

"I knew that's what you would say." Karen sighed and gazed unhappily up at the immaculate Alberta blue sky. "What I wouldn't give for a good spring blizzard to keep people away. It's calving time and the ranchers are always complaining about there being a blizzard when their cows start to calve. So why isn't there a blizzard?"

"Now that's more like it!" Harvey Benson boomed as he and his wife stood in the middle of Laura's studio gazing at the vibrant paintings. Kevin, desperate to repair the damage done by the *Urinary Garden* — last night Benson had harrumphed that so far he hadn't seen anything remotely resembling art — had asked

Laura for permission to bring the philanthropist and his wife to her studio. Knowing how vitally important it was to her beloved Centre, she had agreed at once.

The visit went swimmingly. The Bensons were openly delighted with the still lifes and tolerant of the abstracts. Mrs. Benson's gaze kept returning to a small painting of a vase with a bouquet of flowers and three pears arranged in front of it. Finally, she ventured to ask if they could possibly purchase it.

Laura replied that it had to go to New York as part of her show, but if they really wanted it, she would make sure the gallery reserved it for them. The Bensons beamed at each other. Its being exhibited in New York would give their painting a special cachet.

"You've saved the day!" Kevin whispered gratefully as he ushered his charmed charges out the door.

As always, entertaining guests in her studio drained Laura's creative energy. Leaving the studio, she followed one of the animal trails that meandered through the woods up to the top of a ridge. Here in the woods, patches of snow still lingered, but most of it had melted, uncovering the elk and deer droppings that carpeted the ground so thickly it was impossible to walk without stepping on them. Scattered among the droppings was the twisted black scat of coyotes. A pair of mule deer eyed her warily, then lowered their heads and resumed grazing.

On her way to the studio that morning she had paused for a few minutes to listen to Isabelle practicing Marek's concerto. Artists were different from other people, Laura mused. They had totally different priorities. The average woman on finding out that she had been callously used by her lover would fling her hurt and fury in his face. But Isabelle was clearly determined to keep her emotions in check for fear of losing the concerto. Marek was equally determined that she should be the one to introduce his masterpiece to the world. It would be interesting to see how those two would act toward each other during the rest of their stay. Isabelle might not be able to keep up the pretense that she knew nothing about Marek's womanizing. Laura knew that if it had been her, she would have confronted the deceiving bastard with icy disdain and sent him packing. But she could understand Isabelle's decision. Old Eckart would be disappointed, though, to see his spiteful act of revenge falling flat.

Laura's thoughts veered to John Smith's upcoming performance. Now that he had succeeded in creating all this interest, what was he going to do to live up to people's expectations? What if he had nothing to reveal? Or what if his great revelation was that he, John Smith, was the murderer? That would be a performance to end all performances. Laura tried to dismiss the idea as impossible, but it wouldn't go away. Not completely. Shaking her head, she began to retrace her steps down the trail.

Richard had spotted her and was waiting for her on the path. "How did the meeting go?" she asked, kissing him lightly on the lips. Drawing back to look at him, she said, "You don't have to tell me. I can see you're excited."

He laughed. "Am I that transparent? You're right, it did go well. I'll have the lawyers check out a couple of things and then I'll probably sign on. I've got to admit," he added, "it felt good to be back in that other world for a while. It's so fast moving and challenging. It's totally different from writing where you live with a novel for months or even years."

"Yet you inhabit both worlds with great success."

"I'm not complaining. Not at all. I enjoy the business world. Always have. But my books are more important to me. Much more."

"We'll have to line up early for the performance tonight," Laura said as they walked along the path. "I want to have seats right next to an emergency exit."

"It's all arranged," he told her. "Jeremy is going to let us in a side door just before they open the floodgates at seven-thirty."

Alec Fraser took a deep breath as coffee was served. He and his guests were finishing dinner in a private dining room. Joseph Moore, the provincial minister of culture, had arrived that afternoon, and the Bensons were there, as was Kevin Lavoie. Kevin had suggested inviting Henry Norrington and that had worked out well. Both the Bensons and the cabinet minister were clearly impressed by the internationally known philosopher and comfortable with the views he expressed.

The Bensons had positively glowed when they spoke of their visit to Laura's studio and the painting they had acquired. "It's going to be shown in New York first," Mildred Benson informed them happily. Her husband smiled benignly at her. He had discreetly inquired of Kevin what price range Laura's paintings usually sold for and was well content when he was told that since it was fairly small he could probably expect to get it for around four thousand.

That had been a brilliant move on Kevin's part, thought Fraser. If things would only stay the way they were right now! But they wouldn't. He took another deep breath and coughed gently to get their attention.

"I feel I should warn you that what we are about to see tonight might turn out to be somewhat upsetting," he said. "Performance artists are notorious for pushing the envelope — if I may borrow a term — and the one who's recital we are to attend is probably the most extreme of the lot." He paused, then added hopefully, "It's not really necessary for us to attend, you know."

"After what Mildred and I were exposed to yesterday, we're ready for anything," Harvey Benson replied.

That's where you're wrong, thought the president as he resignedly rose from the table and told them there was time to freshen up before going to the theatre.

A double line of people snaked its way from the main entrance to the jammed parking lot where they stood packed between the cars. "How many do you think there are?" Laura looked back over her shoulder as she and Richard headed for the steps that led to the rear of the building.

"There must be damn close to two thousand."

"That's double the capacity of the theatre. There's going to be a lot of disappointed people."

The air buzzed with excitement as people talked about the deadly events in the colony and speculated about what they might learn tonight. As they waited for the doors to open and the outdoor screens to light up, they were entertained by members of the opera program who had decided to take advantage of the captive audience. Costumed singers sang familiar arias and were warmly applauded. Before descending the steps, Laura turned to look back at the crowd. She spotted Marek and Isabelle near the head of the queue, clapping enthusiastically as the singers took a bow. Veronica was standing a few rows behind them, chatting animatedly with a charmed Carl Eckart.

Jeremy opened the outside door as soon as Richard knocked. Cautioning them to be quiet, he led the way to the main floor just below the stage, and they slipped into the three seats in the front row nearest an exit.

Then the president's party came in. Escorted by two young female ushers, they were seated four rows up on the centre aisle. Turning around in his seat, Jeremy caught Kevin's eye and blew him a kiss. Kevin turned away and Norrington, who was sitting next to him looked affronted.

"You're bad, Jeremy," Laura whispered. Jeremy merely grinned in reply.

"I thought you'd be helping out backstage," she said.

He shook his head. "Nope. My usefulness came to an end when the props were finished. John Smith may not want to admit it, but he's damn lucky I was around to lend a hand."

The theatre rapidly filled as the main doors were opened and people streamed in and took their seats. The house lights dimmed and a spotlight picked up John Smith alone on the stage. The right side of his face was covered with white greasepaint, and he was wearing a baggy black suit that might have been meant to represent a clown costume—one of the lachrymose, mournful school of clowns. Bathed in a blue spotlight, he launched into a long monologue in a flat, uninflected voice. Some members of the audience began to stir restlessly as he droned on. As is not unusual with performance artists, much of what he was saying was incomprehensible — to make sense would be showing disrespect to the words themselves. At some point, however, a garbled social comment began to emerge for those who listened carefully. It had something to do with slavery; of men and women being enslaved by an uncaring, monolithic society.

As he spoke, the spotlight was switched off to be replaced with a pale, diffuse light that slowly expanded to fill the entire stage area. On the catwalk high up in the flies, stagehands lifted counterweights from the arbours and a cage began its smooth descent. In the cage were five half- naked mannequins, shackled and bound the same way they were that afternoon in John Smith's studio. Jeremy leaned forward. "Charlene has an interesting bod. Too bad it's going to waste."

"I doubt if Charlene thinks it's going to waste," replied Laura.

A stagehand crossed to centre stage carrying a chair and a naked mannequin. He arranged the mannequin on the chair, spreading its legs suggestively apart, and walked off. Clever, thought Laura. That will reinforce the impression that all the figures are lifeless mannequins. John Smith's monologue was turning into an incantatory rant as he denounced society's debasement of women. The mannequins were unmoved. Some people in the audience exchanged glances, not knowing whether to go or stay. At the end of his lengthy harangue, John Smith produced a huge wooden key and pretended to unlock the door of the cage. He made a magician-like gesture and the shackles dropped from Charlene. She stepped out of the cage and beckoned the others to follow her, but they remained frozen in place. Hands clenched at her sides, she gazed upwards to follow the ascending cage as it disappeared from sight and the lights dimmed.

"They were going to do a voodoo show at this point, but John Smith cancelled it," whispered Jeremy. "He said he wanted more time for his revelation, but the real reason is that Desiré was upstaging him."

After a few moments of almost total darkness, a spotlight picked up Desiré standing in the wings. A curious, almost animal-like sound went up from the audience. Hands on hips she stood before them, magnificently imperious. Her head was crowned with a tiara, loops of gold hung from her ears and her defiant stance thrust her cape apart, exposing perfect, widely spaced breasts. A golden belt encircled her dancer's waist just below the navel, and skin-tight leotards, the same tan colour as her skin, encased her lower body. She was womanhood at its most magnificent.

"She's a living work of art," murmured Laura.

Desiré stared haughtily down at the audience and slowly removed her gold-collared cape. Handing it to an unseen someone behind the curtain, she began to dance.

John Smith entered wearing a dark business suit. As Desiré flashed by, he reached into a pail and flung something at her. It might have been red dye or it might have been blood. Desiré stumbled as if wounded, then recovered and went on dancing, her naked back streaked with red. On her next pass, John Smith lobbed a plastic bag at her. It struck her on the chest and broke apart, sending up a cloud of pink powder. Desiré pretended to stagger, then danced more slowly, trailing one arm like a wounded bird. John Smith gave a cry of triumph and stepped in front of her, smearing her body with white chocolate, screaming a polemic on society's institutionalized debasement of women.

Listening to his harangue, Richard muttered in an aside to Laura, "Is there a point to all this?"

"It's meant to be a catharsis, not a solution," she whispered back.

Desiré was now standing motionless on the stage, arms pressed to her sides while John Smith continued to slather her with white chocolate that stood out against her brown skin. Then he began to lick it, bringing a hiss of indrawn breath from the audience.

There was a rustle in the audience as Mildred Benson, her husband and Alec Fraser trailing in her wake, marched up the aisle and out the door.

"That tears it," said Laura. "Damn."

On stage, John Smith flung Desiré contemptuously aside and she collapsed in a crumpled heap. Electric lights flashed on, outlining a crucifix at the rear of the stage. Two men, both wearing business suits, marched over to the fallen Desiré and dragged her inert form over to the electric crucifix. She offered no resistance as they strapped her to it. There was a flash, accompanied by a crackling, sizzling sound, and the crucifix was obscured with a dense cloud of blue smoke. The curtain came down and the house lights came on for intermission. There was no applause, just an excited buzz of conversation.

"That last stunt was more like a magician's trick than performance art," remarked Richard. He and Laura had decided there was no point in leaving their seats and fighting the crush of people. Jeremy had gone off in search of a washroom.

"The two have a lot in common," agreed Laura, absently, her mind on the way Mrs. Benson had stalked out of the theatre. "Performance art is a pretty elastic concept. And getting more so all the time. It's changed a lot since the '70s when it seemed to be mostly people hitting themselves with raw meat."

She paused, then said with a frown, "I'm worried, Richard. The Centre may have lost that grant. The Bensons are nice but they're very conventional and straight-laced. I can't bear the thought of this place having to close."

"It won't come to that. The Centre is too important. The government couldn't afford the political backlash if they let it go under." He twisted around in his seat. "The cabinet minister is still here. He and Henry seem to be really hitting it off."

"Do you know Mr. Moore?"

"Not really. Alec introduced me when I ran into them on their way to dinner."

A recorded announcement warned the audience that the play would resume in three minutes. Then John Smith's voice testily announced a correction, saying it was a "revelation", not a "play".

"There was a hell of a line-up, but I made it." Jeremy said, sliding into his seat beside Laura. "I wonder what surprises John Smith has for us now?"

The curtain rose on a stage that was completely dark. Then a soft spotlight picked out a life-size, fibreglass horse painted a light beige.

"'Behold a pale horse, and its rider's name was Death'," Laura said, remembering the famous passage from the Book of Revelation.

"'... and Hades followed him'," Richard surprised her by finishing the quote.

A trumpet sounded off stage and a star fell out of the darkness.

"'The name of the star is Wormwood,'" murmured Laura and this time Richard merely nodded.

A gasp went up when a shower of stars, almost blinding in their light, cascaded down from the flies.

"It won't be long now," whispered Laura. "The dragon's tail has swept down the stars of heaven."

A tongue of flame shot out from centre left stage and was quickly extinguished, to be followed by another and another. The smell of kerosene began to permeate the air.

"Reminds me of the fire-eaters of Jamaica," Richard whispered.

The shape of a dragon slowly materialized out of the gloom. With a sudden roar, a flame shot out of its mouth, bringing another gasp from the now rapt audience.

"Jesus," mutter Richard. "Do you suppose there's anybody inside that contraption?"

"It's bound to be John Smith," Laura whispered back.

"It is," Jeremy told them. "He's wearing an asbestos mask."

There was movement on the stage and the light gradually intensified to reveal a tableau with a half-naked Charlene kneeling and holding one of the sacred urns over her head, while four male dancers, also bare from the waist up, stood motionless on the stage. They sprang to life when drums began to roll. Their bare feet slapped the floor as they circled around the kneeling Charlene. Bowing reverently, the first dancer removed the cover from the urn, dipped his torch in the kerosene and lit it from the flame shooting out of the dragon's mouth. In turn, each of the others did the same. Torches held high, they paraded around the dragon as the drums faded into the background to be superseded by a high-pitched wailing of human voices. "Voices of the damned," Laura muttered to herself as the eerie wailing rose and fell.

Another trumpet sounded, and Desiré stood before the red dragon. In the dim, smoky light it was impossible to be sure, but she seemed to be totally naked. Eyeing the taut lines of her body, Laura whispered, "He's departing from the biblical script. She's supposed to be about to bear a child."

"Not with that figure," murmured Richard appreciatively.

The mounting sexual tension in the theatre had become palpable, a tangible thing that seemed to be an integral part of the performance itself. John Smith had certainly succeeded in capturing the attention of the audience, but maybe not in the way he intended. Or wanted. With a clash of wooden swords, the dancers began an elaborately choreographed battle. Their torches were beginning to smoke as the kerosene burned off. Desiré danced among them while they fought their ritualistic duels. For the first time, the dragon moved. Lumbering ponderously across the stage like a reptilian flamethrower, he pointed his flame at each of the duelling dancers in turn. They threw up their arms in pretended agony, fell writhing to the floor, and lay still. The flame from the dragon's mouth was beginning to subside.

Desiré fluttered her hands in the dragon's direction, as if to reassure it, then deftly took the urn from Charlene's outstretched hands and danced away with it. She teased the dragon, first holding the urn out to him, then drawing it back. The stage reeked of kerosene and in the front rows members of the audience shifted in their seats and looked at each other nervously. The dragon seemed to be collapsing into itself as the flame flickered and nearly went out. Desiré made a spectacular leaping circle around the stage, brushing close to the darkened wings. The dragon held out his arms imploringly and she rushed toward him, holding out the urn. He seized it from her and held it up, tilting it as if to drink from the spout.

Horrified cries of "No!", "No!", "Oh, my God!" rang out. The dragon, flame trickling from its mouth, turned to took down at the audience as if pondering their advice. Women shrieked and others covered their eyes as he tilted the urn and a stream of liquid arced out from the spout. With an explosive whoosh, the paper-mâché costume ignited and John Smith was enveloped in flames. The flames reached out for Desiré, but she was saved by not having a costume to catch on fire, and jumped back out of the way.

After a moment of stunned silence, someone screamed and the theatre erupted in a cacophony of terror. The fire alarm went off, galvanizing the audience into a stampede for the exits. Richard grabbed Laura's arms and pulled her toward the door that was only a few steps away. She hung back for a moment staring up at the horror on the stage. John Smith was a blackened skeleton in the midst of the flames, his arms slowly rising as if conferring an unholy benediction on the fleeing crowd. The skeleton broke apart and fell to the floor as a stream of foam hit it. Justin, who was prepared to give the fire extinguisher one chance before fleeing, took heart as the flames flickered and died out. Moving forward, he quickly snuffed out a puddle of burning kerosene on the stage. Charlene was on her feet, staring out at the panicking mob that had once been an audience. She was screaming over and over again, "It was supposed to be water! Don't you understand? It was supposed to be water in that urn!"

"Attention everyone. There is no danger. The fire has been extinguished. I repeat, the fire is out. Stay where you are." Karen was up on the stage yelling through her cupped hands. The strident ringing of the alarm abruptly ceased, and she shouted out again that the fire was over. This time she was heard, and the mad scramble for the exits slowed. As they dared to stop and look around, the terror-stricken people saw that what the Mountie said was true. There was no fire. The grisly remains of the performance artist were covered under a blanket of foam.

There were moans and cries for help from a few, mostly elderly, people who had been knocked down in the rush. Some members of the audience remained behind to comfort them as they waited for the ambulances and paramedics to arrive. The rest filed out through the exits and the main entrance in a hurried but reasonably orderly fashion.

Kevin had leaped to his feet, as soon as he saw John Smith engulfed in flames. Grabbing the cabinet minister and Norrington by their elbows, he propelled them toward the same exit Laura and her two companions were slipping through. Shaking him off, Norrington used his swimmer's shoulders to bull a path for them through the crush of people.

Safely outside, Joseph Moore shook his head and stared grimly at the colony coordinator. "What's happening here, Kevin? This place is turning into a slaughter house."

"I have an idea that after tonight, it's all behind us, Sir."

"What do you mean?"

"I don't know what the police think, but my own theory is that John Smith was behind the terrible things that have been happening here."

"You think the man killed himself?"

"He's a performance artist," Kevin replied as if that explained everything. "I'm hoping he will have left a note confessing to the murders."

"You're wrong, Kevin," Norrington interjected. "John Smith would never kill himself. Never. He had too high a regard for his own importance."

"As you well know, Kevin," said Moore as they threaded their way through the shocked and murmuring crowd heading for their cars," some of my cabinet colleagues would like nothing better than to cut the Centre's funding to the bone. You people here at the Centre are doing a good job of building a case for them."

"But you are sticking up for us, sir?"

"I am. But recently I've begun to wonder why," the minister of culture sighed. "I suppose I better find Alec and see if I can help him with the Bensons. Unless I'm very much mistaken, we can kiss that three million good-bye."

chapter twenty

The sensational, and highly suspicious, immolation of the performance artist brought reinforcements in the form of a task force of detectives from the RCMP headquarters in Calgary. Karen conducted a briefing session for them in the Banff detachment office. She was the only uniformed officer in the room.

When it was over, shrugs and questioning looks were exchanged among the detectives. One of them spoke up. "If it wasn't for that woman writer being dead before she was torched, we could be looking at suicide and accidental deaths. Right?"

"The death of the performance artist could have been a suicide," volunteered another.

"There are easier ways to kill yourself than that," rejoined a detective sergeant. His remark was greeted with nods of approval.

The men closed their notebooks and the detective sergeant assigned each squad its area of investigation.

When he finished without mentioning Karen, she glanced questioningly at Inspector Gratton, the officer in charge. "I want you to be a floater, Karen," he said. "You know these people and you're familiar with the campus. You can poke around wherever you think it will do the most good. But I suggest you start with the team that will be questioning the people connected with last night's performance."

With Constable Peplinski at the wheel, Karen led the way to the Banff Centre with the Calgary detectives following in an unmarked sedan. They were met by a haggard looking Kevin. He assigned them a suite of offices, promised every cooperation, and implored them to find out who was behind the terrible events. "If this keeps up," he told them, "it could bring this wonderful institution down with it."

Inspector Gratton assured him that they wouldn't rest until the perpetrator was brought to justice, and asked who would have been the lead stagehand at last night's performances.

"Len Gerlitz. Would you like me to get him for you?"

"That would be very helpful."

"That urn was filled with water. I'm positive of that," Len Gerlitz, seated across the desk form the inspector, declared. "I filled it myself."

"The idea was to switch the urn containing kerosene for the one filled with water?" asked the inspector.

"Right. The audience saw torches being lit from the urn so they would figure it was kerosene that John Smith was going to pour over himself."

"Which, as it turns out, he did," interjected Karen quietly.

The inspector gave her a look, then turned his attention back to the stagehand. "How was the switch carried out?"

"Two of us were standing in the wings, out of the audience's line of sight. When Desiré danced by, she handed her urn to Bill Williams and took the second one, the one that was supposed to contain water, from me."

"How many people knew about the switch?"

Len shrugged. "I guess just about everyone in the show. There was no particular reason to keep it secret. Once the trick was over, the audience would realize what had happened. It was the shock of what they *thought* was going to happen that John Smith was after. It's the same idea as clowns dousing each other with pails of water, then one of them grabs a pail and runs toward the audience. Except when he throws it at them, it turns out to be shredded paper."

Karen, feeling a bit like she was back in school, raised her hand and the inspector nodded. "What about the revelation?" she asked. "Do you have any idea of what it was going to be?"

"None whatsoever. Some of the cast tried to pry it out of him, but they got nowhere. That didn't stop them from speculating though."

"Oh? And what did they speculate?"

"Everything from him naming the murderer, confessing to the murders himself, all the way down to him spouting some nonsense about world peace or something like that."

They continued taking statements for the rest of the morning without learning anything more than Len had already told them. At one point, Peplinski came in to report on the fingerprints found on the fatal urn. There were two sets, one was definitely Len's and the second set was presumed to be Desiré's, although that couldn't be verified since she had received burns to her hands and the doctor refused to let her be fingerprinted.

This was borne out when Desiré appeared for her interview. Her hands were loosely bandaged with gauze. For the first time that morning, the inspector rose to his feet. She accepted his concern for her burns with a gracious smile and said that she considered herself lucky to have gotten off so lightly.

Desiré confirmed in her melodious voice how the trick was supposed to work. Holding up her bandaged hands, she added, "It was a good thing for me my costume was so scanty."

"Or non-existent," murmured Karen.

"You have good eyesight," Desiré told her. "Originally, I was supposed to wear a body stocking, but John Smith thought it would be more effective for me to be naked. That undoubtedly saved my life."

"Apart from your hands, were you injured at all?" asked Karen.

"My eyebrows are a little singed and I can still feel the heat in my face, but I am told that will pass."

Karen had told the inspector that Desiré, as the highest-ranking member of the cast, would be the most likely to know about the revelation. But she claimed to know nothing. "That was John Smith's secret."

"Do you have any questions you wish to ask, Corporal? the inspector asked Karen.

"Just one. Do you think that John Smith might have left something that would tell us what his revelation was? In case something like this happened before he could announce it to the world."

"It's possible. It's just the sort of thing he might do. But it won't be obvious, you can count on that." She favoured Peplinski who was standing outside the door with a dazzling smile as she swept out of the room.

"I think I'll take a look around the theatre." Karen got to her feet.

"Good idea," said the inspector. "Al's in charge over there, but he and his men don't know what they're looking for."

"Neither do I, but I know someone who might."

"John Smith's dressing room is the logical place to start," Laura told Karen as they walked across the empty stage, still reeking of kerosene and smoke, and another sickish, sweet smell that Laura recognized only too well.

The dressing room door, decorated with a cardboard skeleton instead of the traditional star, stood open. The sight of the skeleton, so reminiscent of John Smith's last appearance on earth, almost unnerved Laura. Had he predicted his own fate? Had he even arranged it? A beefy detective, with his hands on his ample hips and an incredulous, baffled expression of his face, stood in the middle of the room. He had been told to expect Karen and her companion, and waved them in.

"Maybe you can make some sense out of the junk in here," he said, "but it sure as hell beats me." Giving the cluttered room a final disgusted look, he left, saying, "I'll leave you with it. If you find anything, I'll be up on the stage."

The dressing room was just what Laura would have expected from John Smith. It was filled with the paraphernalia of his art, including many items that were not needed for last night's performance. Those grotesque masks, for example. Probably he just liked to be surrounded with this kind of stuff. Laura picked up a black crucifix with a voluptuous female Christ nailed to it. The nails were in the correct position, driven through the wrists and ankles rather than the hands and feet as commonly shown. Nails in the latter positions could not support the weight of a human being. Trust John Smith to know that. She put the crucifix down beside an open Bible. There were a number of other books lying on the counter. Laura was not surprised to see one of both Richard's and Norrington's among them. John Smith liked to get inside the minds of people, and he obviously believed that possessing something personal gave him some sort of power over that person. Witness the lock of her hair he had snipped off, and the things he had stolen from Marek, Richard and Eckart. God only knew what rites he had intended to perform with them. Laura shivered. The spirit of John Smith, which she had finally come to acknowledge was truly sinister, seemed to pervade the room and its bizarre contents.

She picked up Richard's book *The Blue Agenda* and saw that some of the pages had been paper clipped. So had some pages in Norrington's book. Knowing what she was going to find, she turned to the paper clipped pages and read the paragraphs that had been highlighted. With a grim smile she put the books back on the table. So John Smith had figured it out, too.

She debated with herself as to whether or not she should tell Karen. But it had nothing to do with the murders, and would do a great deal of harm if word ever got out. Feeling slightly guilty, Laura pretended to carry on with the search, knowing there was nothing more to be found. Finally, she turned to Karen and said, "It looks as if John Smith's revelation, whatever it was, died with him."

Kevin looked up as the president walked into his office. Alec Fraser didn't take a seat, instead he went over to the window and looked out at the campus.

"I've just had a long talk with Benson," he said without turning around.

"And?"

Alec turned away from the window and seated himself across the desk from Kevin before replying. "Benson held a conference call with his fellow directors. The Chinook Foundation is prepared to give us not three million dollars, but seven-and-a-half million."

"What?"

"That's right. Seven-and-one-half million dollars."

'My God! I don't believe it. That's wonderful!"

"Not as wonderful as you might think. They want representation on the board of governors and a say over what artistic projects the Centre supports."

"That's censorship."

"Of the worst kind. I told him it was unacceptable."

"You couldn't have done anything else. But, Jesus, Alec, how we could have used that money!"

Fraser leaned forward in his chair; the look of ennui which Kevin had sometimes observed with concern in recent months, was gone and his eyes shone with excitement. "We've got to make this place more self-sufficient, Kevin. Much more. What makes money for us?"

"The executive management courses. They're a licence to print money."

"Exactly! And they're what we are going to concentrate on. Develop new courses, advertise around the world, maybe increase the fees. I bet if we approached some of the major corporations that send their executives here, we could raise the funds to construct a new management building." He broke off, seeing the look on Kevin's face. "I know what you're thinking. You're worried that it will overwhelm the arts side of our operation. But that won't happen. We won't let it. They are two separate streams and we'll keep them that way. Except that the revenues from the training programs will subsidize the arts. Now here's what I have in mind ..."

"I've got to get away from the smell of death. Let's just get in your car and drive, Richard."

Richard gave Laura a dubious look. "It is okay? I mean will the police let us?"

"You've given them your statement, haven't you?"

"Yes. Right after lunch."

"Then it's okay. I cleared it with Karen. She understands how I feel." Her voice quickened as she said, "I know what. Let's go to the Upper Hot Springs. Maybe the stink of sulphur will purge my system of that other smell."

The fog began as they started up Sulphur Mountain. It was patchy at first, then thickened into a solid grey blanket. As they approached the place where the earthmovers crossed the road, the fluorescent strips on the flagmen's jackets seemed to burn through the fog. Lights on dim, Richard slowed to a crawl, peering through the windshield. He was waved on with sweeping motions of the flagman's illuminated baton.

"That's a man. Your girlfriend isn't here," Laura said as they drove past.

"Yes she is." Richard leaned forward to peer through the windshield. "Look up ahead. She's just changed places. She's waving us on."

Recognizing the car, the blond flag girl smiled and gave a little wave with her free hand.

"Between the fog and the steam we aren't going to see a thing once we're in the pool," Richard said as he cautiously inched the Ford into the parking lot.

"That suits me just fine," replied Laura, picking up her bag from the rear seat. "I find the idea of being invisible very appealing just now.

"Are we the only ones here?" she asked the ticket seller.

"No. There's one other couple in the pool," she said as she gave them keys to their lockers. "A fog like this always keep people away."

The steps from the changing rooms led directly into the pool. Laura clung to the railing until she could feel the water rising around her ankles. "Is that you, Richard?" she said to the dim shape standing a few feet away. Something about the stillness and the grey opacity of the fog mixed with sulphurous steam made her keep her voice low, barely above a whisper.

The figure reached out and took her hand. "Let's go across to the other side," said Richard, also in a low voice. He led the way, his free hand outstretched to feel for the concrete island in the middle of the pool. His fingers touched its smooth top and he carefully felt his way around it, finally fetching up at the far side of the pool.

Laura opened her mouth as if to gulp the sulphur-laden air, and willed her pores to open so she could be saturated with it. With its pungent odour stinging her nostrils, she could no longer smell, even in her imagination, the sickening stench of burnt flesh. A low laugh and an indistinct murmur of voices, placed the invisible other couple at the far end of the pool.

An alarm began to beep and was quickly shut off. "The guy must have set his wristwatch alarm to tell them when they've been in the pool long enough," said Richard. As he spoke, they heard, rather than saw, the other twosome splashing their way across the pool and up the stairs to the changing rooms.

Laura took a deep breath and cleared her throat. "Richard," she began, "if we're going to have a lasting relationship, I don't want there to be any secrets between us."

"I like the sound of that 'lasting relationship' part, and whatever deep dark secrets you may have, I already forgive,"

"It's not me, Richard. It's you."

She felt him suddenly stiffen. "Oh? And what might that be?"

It was not too late. She could still back off. But she knew their relationship would never work while she still carried with her the secret burden of what she knew. It would be all right once she had shared it with him and he acknowledged it. That way, they would at least start out by being honest with each other.

"Henry Norrington doesn't only read your books, Richard, he *writes* them," she said quietly, her voice sounding disembodied in the enveloping greyness.

The silence lay between them, as thick as the fog. Then Richard gave a harsh bark of laughter. "That's crazy! What drugs are you on? For God's sake!"

Laura shook her head, the motion invisible in the fog. "I wish it were crazy. But there are too many similarities for it to be mere coincidence. You have to be around Henry and listen to him talk to spot it. There are some unusual phrases, like 'erotic allure' and 'dangerously possible' for example, that don't appear in his books, but crop up in his conversation. *And* in your books. You claim not to have met Henry before coming here. Yet you two must have known each other for a long time. For example, you knew that it was his papers on deconstructionism that got him tenure at the university. John Smith had figured it out, too. That was going to be his great revelation."

"That's not true. We knew he was going to name ..." Richard's lips abruptly clamped shut.

"Who's we, Richard?

"Never mind. It doesn't matter."

"Erika knew too, didn't she? That's why she was making notes during the TV talk show." Laura's eyes widened in horror. "Oh, my God, that's why she was killed," she whispered.

She heard him groan, then his hands closed around her ankles and she was on her back under water. She was paralysed with shock for a few seconds, then tried to kick out and free her legs. But he was holding them high in the air, rendering her helpless. Absurdly, she wanted to warn him that a laser scan would reveal the subcutaneous bruises on her ankles. As it had with Montrose. Her hands scrabbled frantically on the smooth bottom of the pool, but there was no purchase, nothing to hold onto. Wasn't this how husbands drowned their wives in the bathtub? She was going to die. And soon. His murderous attack had been so sudden and unexpected that she hadn't had time to draw a breath. But that would only have prolonged her agony.

It must have been Richard who had grabbed Montrose by the ankles and pitched him over the stairwell railing. But why? Oh, God! Of course. Her lungs were on fire. She had to draw a breath, she couldn't fight it any longer. Even though that breath would fill her lungs and extinguish her life.

Then the deadly grip on her ankles was suddenly released, and Richard reached down to grab her under the shoulders and lift her up. Laura spat out a mouthful of water and sucked in a great lung full of precious, life-giving air.

"I'm sorry, Laura. Terribly sorry."

"At least you couldn't go through with it. I'll remember that."

A capricious mountain breeze tugged at the fog, allowing them to see each other. Richard's face was sick with self-loathing and dread. The sound of voices made them both look up. A small group of sightseers stood on the platform above the pool, peering down into the mist and dissipating fog.

"You and Jeremy were in this together, weren't you?" Laura asked in a low voice between racking coughs. "He needed to get rid of Montrose and you needed to have Erika silenced."

Holding onto the tiled edge of the pool for support, she followed Richard as he moved farther away from the observation platform. When he reached the far end of the pool, he turned to face her.

"It started one night when we were having a few drinks and he was talking about a play he was thinking about writing." Richard's voice was uncannily matter-of-fact, as if he were relating something that no longer mattered. "The plot involved two men who each wanted to get rid of their wives. They agreed to kill each other's wives and the husband of the victim, who would be the prime subject, would arrange to have an unshakable alibi for the time of the killing. When he mentioned how convenient it would be for him if Montrose were to die, it began to dawn on me that it might be the way to solve my problem with Erika. The television show that Henry and I were to appear on would provide a watertight alibi."

"How did you know that Erika had discovered Henry wrote your books?"

Richard almost smiled. "Your little friend Erika was very intelligent. She was also very transparent; her eyes kept darting from Henry to me. Henry was the first to suspect it."

In a voice as matter-of-fact as his own, Laura asked, "You killed Montrose. Jeremy killed Erika. And he killed John Smith."

"Yes."

Up on the viewing platform, one of the sightseers sniffed the sulphur laden air, and announced in a loud voice, "It smells like somebody just let a fart," and turned to leave. The rest of the little group trooped after him.

"I'm not going to do anything to you," Richard said when he saw the fleeting look of alarm on Laura's face as they were once more alone in the pool. "It's all over for me."

"I'm not afraid," she said as she began to wade across the pool. She had to smile at the irony when they parted at the stairs that led to the separate changing rooms. The proprieties still had to be observed, even under these bizarre circumstances. It became even more bizarre when he politely asked if she would like to drive back with him. Equally politely, she told him that she would call a taxi.

Half fearful that Richard would have a change of heart and come looking for her, Laura hurriedly stripped off her bathing suit and began to dress. As she stepped into her panties, reaction set in and a sudden wave of dizziness swept over her, making her lean against a locker for support. The room tilted and swayed as she cautiously inched her way to a bench and sat down with her head between her knees. After a few minutes, she started to get up, but quickly sat down again as the room rocked around her. She had never experienced an attack like this before, but reassured herself with the thought that it wasn't surprising after what she had just been through. Fearing another onslaught of dizziness, she waited until she was sure it had passed before trying to stand up again. This time the room behaved itself and stayed in place. She glanced up at a wall clock and was somewhat shocked to see that her spell must have lasted for at least twenty minutes.

Richard would be long gone by now. Where would he go? What would he do? His situation was desperate. These thoughts ran through Laura's mind as she finished dressing. When she looked in the mirror to apply her lipstick she was startled to see how pale her face was, but the defiant slash of red helped to lift her spirits. Squaring her shoulders, she opened the changing room door, climbed the stairs, and walked across the deserted lobby to the outside. Knowing it was highly unlikely, she walked down the road to the parking lot to see if Richard's car was still there. The fog had been largely blown away; just a few cottony wisps clung to the tops of the pines lining the road. There was only one car in the parking lot, and it was not the silver Ford.

The public phone was outside the building, beside the entrance. Laura got change from the ticket seller and went back outside. Someone had made off with the telephone directory so she had to climb back up the stairs and go back inside to look up the number of the RCMP. She would try the detachment office first, even though Karen would likely still be somewhere on the campus. She was in luck. The switchboard operator told her that Corporal Lindstrom was in the office, but was in conference. When Laura gave her name and said it was urgent, she was told to hang on, a message would be sent in to the corporal. "She and the Calgary detectives are comparing notes," the operator added, knowing that Laura was helping Karen with the case.

"I'm at the Upper Hot Springs, Karen." Laura immediately felt safer with the police knowing where she was. Without giving Karen a chance to say anything, she went on. "Richard Madrin just tried to kill me. He was going to drown me in the pool, but relented at the last minute. Jeremy Switzer is his accomplice. They're both murderers."

"Where is Madrin now? Is he still with you?"

"No. He's taken off in his car. He may be on his way to turn himself in."

Karen must have placed her hand over the receiver because Laura could faintly hear her speaking to someone. Then she said, "As I remember, he drives a silver Ford Taurus?"

"That's right. It was a rental. I don't know the license plate numbers, but it had a Hertz sticker on the rear bumper. Are you going to put out an all points bulletin?"

"What's your number there?" Laura read it off, and was told to stay where she was and to answer the phone when it rang. Less than two minutes later Karen called back.

"Richard Madrin is dead, Laura. His car was run over by one of those huge earthmoving machines. One of our cruisers is at the scene." She paused as if interrupted, then came back on the line, saying with a touch of impatience, "A purist on our staff tells me the correct name for those brutes is wheel tractor-scraper, but the name doesn't matter. The car was badly crushed and they haven't been able to remove his body, but the paramedics have confirmed that he's dead. Stay where you are, Laura. I'm coming to pick you up."

"You've got the con, Corporal," Inspector Gratton said, borrowing a phrase from the days when he served aboard a RCMP patrol boat.

"Thank you, sir." Karen detailed two officers to go to the Centre and arrest Jeremy Switzer, reminding them to read him his rights. One of the constables tapped his breast pocket to indicate he had a copy of the printed statement to read out to the accused.

Karen, with the inspector and one of his detectives, piled into a cruiser. Peplinski was at the wheel and used lights and siren as they sped through the town, across the bridge, and up the mountain road. A police cruiser parked across the road, its lights flashing, moved out of the way to let them past.

"Holy Jesus!" Peplinski whispered as they pulled up at the accident scene. A giant tractor-scraper, with tandem engines fore and aft, straddled the road, the flattened remains of what had once been an automobile crushed beneath its scraper bowl.

"Those big wheels rolled right over the sucker," Peplinski muttered in awe, pulling on the handbrake with unnecessary force.

A Mountie and four firefighters, two of the latter holding crowbars, were talking to the operator of the machine. An ambulance, its lights flashing red and blue, was pulled off on a shoulder of the road behind the fire department's emergency response unit.

"Ain't no way you can lift that thing, man," the bearded operator was saying as Karen and her fellow police officers walked up. "That mother weighs 45 tons empty and she's carrying 22 yards of earth. The only way to get her off that car is for me to put her in reverse. It won't make no difference to whoever's inside." Seeing the stripes on Karen's sleeve, he broke off and said, "I didn't have a chance, officer. The guy drove right under my wheels. He went right past the flagman like she wasn't there."

"The victim was involved in your homicide case, wasn't he, Karen?" asked the Mountie who had been first on the scene, eyeing her companions. They were in plainclothes, but he recognized brass when he saw it. Karen introduced them, and he immediately asked the inspector if he had any instructions.

"Doesn't your machine have built-in jacks or something like that for when it gets stuck?" Gratton asked the operator.

"Them mothers don't get stuck, man."

"I see. Well, I guess there's nothing else for it."

The operator climbed into the cab, the idling engines thundered to life and the monster machine began to move slowly in reverse. There was a shriek of metal from the Ford's twisted frame as it dug into the asphalt until the front tires of the scraper found a purchase and climbed over the crumpled heap of steel.

"It looks like it's been through an auto-wrecking yard," muttered the inspector. A bulldozer roared up and pushed the wreck off to one side. The firefighters quickly arranged a canvas screen around it and then came the whoosh of an acetylene torch being lit.

"I think you should talk to the flag girl," the Mountie said to Karen. "She's pretty shook up." He beckoned to the young woman with the long blond ponytail. She wiped the sleeve of her jacket across her face and came over to join them.

"I tried to stop him," she said earnestly. "I almost jumped out in front of the car, but he just kept on coming."

"Maybe he didn't see you in the fog."

The flag person shook her head. "The fog had gone by then. And he saw me all right. He was staring right at me." She paused uncertainly. "I'll never forget the look in his eyes."

"Is there anything else you can tell us?" asked Karen gently.

"It's just that as he approached the crossing, he slowed right down as if he was going to stop. Then as soon as I held out the stop sign, he speeded up again. It was almost as if..." she let the sentence trail off.

"Almost as if he wanted to be run over," Karen finished the thought for her. "Anyway, you have nothing to blame yourself for. You did everything you could."

"I seen him before, driving up and down this road. It was kinda like I knew him. He was real good-looking."

Karen took the constable off to one side and instructed him to make sure the woman was taken to the hospital and treated for shock trauma. "She'll probably need counselling as well," she added .

The acetylene torch was still hissing away behind the canvas screen. "I'm going up to the Upper Hot Springs to pick someone up," she said to the constable. "But I don't want her to see them removing the body. Give me a 10-4 on the radio when they've finished cutting him out."

"Scraping him out would be more like it. But, sure, I'll give you the all clear when it's done."

Laura was having a hard time accepting that Richard was dead. The whole thing had happened so suddenly. Less than an hour ago he was trying to kill her, and now his own life had been snuffed out. But he hadn't killed her. He could have, but he didn't. Even though the fog had disappeared, no would-be bathers trudged up the road from the parking lot. All traffic was being held up at the accident scene. Absorbed in her own painful thoughts, Laura climbed the few steps to the viewing platform and stared down through the swirling steam to the pool where she had come so close to death.

What had brought Richard to this pass? She asked herself the question, but she already knew the answer. An obsession to be something he could not be. Accustomed to the power of money, it must have seemed totally logical to him to simply go out and buy the talent that would give him the recognition he craved. As a writer, he would have access to the world of press interviews, TV talk shows, lecture circuits, and bestseller lists — much more exciting than simply being known as a flipper of office buildings. How he must have panicked when he realized Erika was about to bring everything crashing down! To someone like Richard, nothing could be more humiliating than to be exposed as a cheat who had to pay someone else to write the books he passed off as his own.

Karen was alone in the cruiser. She lowered the window and called out to Laura who was still standing on the platform, wreathed in mist rising from the water. "Laura, over here. Are you all right?"

"I guess so," Laura mumbled as she collapsed into the passenger seat. "Richard killed himself, didn't he?"

"Everything points in that direction. You don't seem surprised."

"I don't think he had any other option. He said himself it was all over for him."

"Suicide by automobile. It's more common than people realize. I don't believe those who take that way out have any idea of the damage it does to other people. They aim at something big and heavy, like a train, or one of those transcontinental rigs, and figure it's okay because no one else will get hurt. But they forget about the trauma it inflicts." Karen had been going to say something about the flag girl being haunted by the look in Richard's eyes, but decided not to. Laura didn't need that.

The radio crackled into life, calling car 437. Karen acknowledged and got a 10-4. She put the cruiser in gear and drove slowly down the mountain. There was still a lot of activity at the accident site, but the ambulance had left. Mercifully, the canvas screen still hid the mangled remains of Richard's car. Further down the road, a Mountie moved a barrier to one side and waved the waiting cars through. As the cars streamed past them in the opposite direction, Karen called the detachment office and was informed that Jeremy had been arrested.

"He's one cool dude," the arresting officer said. "I read him his rights, and when I got to the part about him having the right to retain and instruct counsel, he said that his L.A. attorneys would make sure he got the best criminal lawyer in Calgary."

chapter twenty-one

"It was a pact. An unholy pact," Laura told her listeners. They were in the Centre's main boardroom in the Donald Cameron Hall. Besides the police, the group included Alec Fraser and Kevin Lavoie. Kevin looked drawn and miserable. It must be devastating for him to realize how he had been used and that he had been seduced merely to provide Jeremy with an ironclad alibi for the night Montrose had been killed.

"It all started," Laura continued, "when Jeremy told Richard about a play he was intending to write, involving two men who agreed to murder each other's wives. At some point, he confided in Richard how convenient it would be if Montrose were to die."

"He knew about the law that you can't libel a dead person?" asked Inspector Gratton.

"Yes. I'm sure that Jeremy had made up his mind that, one way or another, Montrose would die before his case ever got to trial. It was that which led to everything else."

"It doesn't make sense that Madrin would tell him what Erika had found out," Karen interjected.

"You're right. We know only too well the lengths Richard was prepared to go to protect that secret. But it would be easy to invent another reason. Erika was an investigative reporter, she could have come up with some information about Richard's business dealings that could ruin him, maybe send him to jail. That would be why it was necessary to burn her studio to the ground. To destroy everything stored in her computer, the discs, her files, everything."

"That still leaves her room," the detective sergeant remarked.

"Richard would have searched that. Erika spent most of her time in the studio, so there would have been plenty of opportunity." She glanced at Karen. "You and I searched her room. There was no place to hide anything."

Karen nodded agreement. "And everything was stored so neatly, it would be easy to replace things exactly as they were and leave no trace."

"How did he get in?" asked the inspector. "Slip the lock with a credit card?"

"Possibly. But it was likely even easier than that." Laura looked at Lavoie. "I don't know whether you're aware of this, Kevin, but every key seems to fit most of the doors on the sixth floor."

"Trust you to know that, Laura. It's because the locks are getting old and worn out. And they were cheap to begin with. I'll make sure they're replaced."

"It doesn't really matter how he got in, but you can be sure he did." Laura paused to collect her thoughts, then continued. "They did their best to make the deaths look like accidents but if the truth came out, they had their alibis to fall back on. Jeremy was visiting with Kevin when Montrose was killed, and Richard was up in Edmonton doing that television show with Henry when Erika's studio was burned. Even if their motives were discovered, they each would have a perfect alibi."

"The arson was bound to be discovered," the detective sergeant pointed out.

"Jeremy may not have realized that. He wasn't a professional arsonist. He wouldn't have known that a fire sometimes leaves tell-tale hot spots."

"A lot of them don't," another detective put in. "The arson squad says that from the way the wood — what little was left of it — was charred, he must have used solvent. The kind you can buy in gas stations. If he had used something less volatile, he might have gotten away with it."

"I gather Switzer wouldn't have any trouble gaining access to Ms. Dekter's studio even in the early hours of the morning?" asked the inspector doubtfully.

"That's right. Erika would have let him in regardless of the hour. He was very gregarious and, unlike that rest of us who respect each other's privacy, he would drop in for a visit at any time of the day or night. She had no reason to suspect him of anything. He always came across as a fun-loving, easy going sort of guy."

"She would find out otherwise as soon as she let him in." The inspector's face was grim.

Laura's stomach tightened. The image of Jeremy, likeable, fun-loving Jeremy, cold-bloodedly killing Erika in her studio would remain with her for a long time. Probably forever.

"So Switzer torched the studio, and it was Madrin who pitched the professor down the stairs," said the inspector with the air of someone who wants to put things in order.

"Yes. He did the same thing when he tried to drown me in the pool. Grabbed me by the ankles."

"But he didn't drown you," Karen said softly.

"Thank God for that!" Alec Fraser breathed.

"Do you have any idea why he didn't?" asked the inspector.

"I think it was because," Laura replied slowly, "he realized it was all over for him. Regardless of whether he killed me or not. In fact, he said as much. That's why he told me everything. He knew he would have to kill himself."

"He certainly chose a dramatic way to do it," Alec Fraser murmured.

"That must have been a spur of the moment decision," said Laura, thinking of Richard's offer to drive her back to the Centre. "But one way or another, he would have committed suicide."

"What bothers me a little," said the inspector, "is how did Madrin persuade Montrose to come out of his room so late at night?"

"Easiest thing in the world," Laura assured him. "Montrose fawned on Richard. Richard had money, lots of it, and Alan hoped to persuade him to finance his new play. If Richard had knocked on his door and said something about wanting to discuss a deal, Montrose would have joined him like a shot. The time of day or night wouldn't have mattered."

"I assume it was Switzer who replaced the water in the container with kerosene," said the inspector. "Or solvent, since that seems to be his accelerant of choice."

"Almost certainly. I'm sure he buttered up Charlene and got taken on to help with the performance so he could find some way of stopping John

Smith before he came out with his revelation. Most likely he did it during the intermission. He was away from his seat the entire time."

"And to think they were prepared to burn the theatre down and possibly kill God knows how many innocent people," interjected the president.

"The stakes were pretty high," replied Laura. "They thought John Smith intended to expose them as the murderers. But it wasn't that at all. He was going to reveal Richard's secret. Which, when you come to think about it, would have been even worse as far as Richard was concerned."

"Well, there you have it, Sir," the inspector said to Alec Fraser. "From here on it will be strictly police business, so you and Mr. Lavoie could be excused."

"Of course." The president immediately got to his feet. "Kevin and I very much appreciate the way in which we have been taken into your confidence. Is it safe to assume that this dreadful affair has finally come to an end?"

"It's over." Gratton assured him.

"Then Kevin and I will start the rebuilding process. Beginning right now."

When Inspector Gratton had politely but firmly invited the two men to leave, Laura wondered if she should leave with them. She glanced at Karen, who gestured that she should remain.

On the way out, the president paused at Laura's chair. Looking down at her, he murmured, "You've been through a frightful ordeal, Laura. We're very grateful for everything you've done. If there's anything we can do to help, counselling, anything at all, we're here for you."

"Thank you, Alec. I'm sure I'll be okay. I was sorry to hear about the Chinook grant falling through."

Turning in her seat to look up at Kevin, she said, "We artists are counting on you to stand up for us."

"You can count on me, Laura," Kevin looked the president in the eye as he spoke.

As soon as the door closed behind the two Centre representatives, Gratton called the police station on his cellular phone. The conversation was brief and his end consisted mostly of grunts and "damns." When it was over, he said, "Switzer's not talking, and Hubert Nasmith is on his way up from Calgary."

The detectives exchanged glances. The flamboyant Nasmith was Calgary's leading criminal lawyer.

"It ain't gonna be all that easy to convict the son of a bitch." Al, the overweight detective who had met Laura and Karen in John Smith's dressing room, mopped his face with a grungy-looking handkerchief.

Gratton nodded. "About the only real evidence we have against him is what Madrin told Laura in the pool. And that's probably not admissible."

"Why on earth not?" demanded Laura. "He *said* it."

"The rule against hearsay evidence," the inspector said with a grimace.

"I can almost guess what it means from its name," said Laura. "But maybe one of you experts could spell it out for me."

Both Karen and the inspector started to speak at once. Gratton waved his had to indicate Karen should carry on.

"Madrin is dead, so he can't testify or be cross-examined in court. The hearsay rule says that statements made by a person otherwise than in testimony on which he can be cross-examined are inadmissible." Karen paused. "There are a number of exceptions, however."

"What about a dying declaration?" suggested Al. "Madrin is sure as hell dead."

"Won't work." Karen told him. "For two reasons. One, the person making the statement must have a hopeless expectation of death while making the declaration. The fact that Madrin may have been contemplating suicide isn't good enough, even if we could prove that he was, which we can't. Second, the dying declaration exception only applies when the death of the deceased is the subject of the charge. In other words, the statement has to come from the deceased victim."

Gratton listened to Karen's dissertation with growing wonder. Then his face cleared. "The Jepson case. You were on Jepson."

"That's right. Everything turned on the hearsay rule. The only way we could get a conviction was if a statement that deceased had made to an associate could be admitted. And how we wanted a conviction! We knew the accused was a violent serial rapist who beat up on the women he raped, but we couldn't pin anything on him. Then he finally killed one of his victims. We had evidence that placed him near the scene of the crime at the right time and there was blood on the site, but there was no body. No *corpus delecti*, as the lawyers say. The body was never found. But we were sure the victim was a real estate agent who had unexpectedly gone missing. She had told one of her fellow agents that she was going to meet someone that night up in Green Hills Estates to sign a listing. That's where Jepson was seen and where the blood was found. The Crown prosecutors worked like mad trying to fit the statement into one of the exceptions to the hearsay rule. I found the whole thing so fascinating I nearly resigned from the Force to go to law school."

"You've got us all on tenterhooks," said Laura. "Did the statement get in?"

"Oh, yes. Jepson got life with no parole for twenty-five years."

"It was a landmark case," added the inspector. "Do you think it might work here, Karen?"

She looked dubious. "I don't think so. In the Jepson case, the court held that the statement was part of the *res gestae*." She looked a little embarrassed at using the Latin phrase, and hastened to explain, "That means it was so closely connected to the act being done that it was part of the act, or *res gestae*. But in our case, what Madrin said to Laura wasn't so closely connected to the murders as to form part of the act of murder itself. It was related to the murders, but it wasn't part of them, if you see what I mean."

The inspector nodded. He was looking at Karen with obvious respect. She's found a mentor, thought Laura. It'll be the fast track for her from now on. "There's *got* to be a way to get Laura's statement in," the inspector was saying. "It's absolutely damning to Switzer. Well, I guess we can let the Crowns worry about it, although you seem to know as much about the rule as they do."

"Spontaneous declaration, or spontaneous exclamations," Karén murmured, a slight frown creasing her forehead as she thought it through. "Statements made under pressure or emotional intensity when there's no incentive for the person making them to lie are allowed in." Her voice took on an edge of excitement. "God knows Madrin was under pressure and was in a state of emotional intensity. And he had no reason to lie, his statement implicated himself as well as Switzer."

The inspector was leaning forward in his chair. "Keep going. Are there any court decisions on this spontaneous exclamations exception?"

"Yes." Karen hesitated, then said, again almost apologetically, "I've followed these cases because I find the subject fascinating and I think I understand it."

"She has a textbook on evidence in her office," Laura smiled. "I've seen it."

"*Phipson on Evidence*," Karen acknowledged.

The inspector gave a pleased nod, and Karen continued. "The leading case on spontaneous declarations or exclamations — the terms are interchangeable — is one involving a sexual assault charge against a doctor. He was alone in an examination room with a young girl three and a half years old. Afterwards, she and her mother stopped at a Dairy Queen for an ice cream and the mother asked about a wet spot on the child's sleeve. The little girl told her mother what the doctor had done to her. How he asked her if she liked candy and told her to open her mouth, and, well, you can guess the rest. The wet spot was semen."

"Hey, is that the case where the doc promised her a candy and the kid said, 'You know what, Mom, he never did give me my candy'?" chuckled the fat detective.

"That's the one," Karen confirmed.

"Do you know what the case stands for, Al?" asked the inspector in some surprise.

The detective looked deflated. "No. I just remember hearing that line and thinking it was a hoot. That's all."

"In the sexual assault case against the doctor," Karen went on, "the court held that the child couldn't testify because she was too young to take the oath, or to appreciate the difference between telling the truth and lying. Without her testimony there was no evidence of the offence except for what she had told her mother. The doctor sure as hell wasn't going to testify."

"What happened?" demanded Laura when Karen paused.

"They let the mother testify as to what her daughter had told her. The court ruled that it was a spontaneous exclamation made by the daughter when she was under emotional stress and had no incentive to lie."

Inspector Gratton turned to Laura. "Could you repeat once more what Madrin said to you."

Without hesitation, Laura recounted every word of the exchange that had taken place between herself and Richard in the pool.

"That does it. We've got the murdering bastard!" the exultant inspector exclaimed. "I think we can consider the case of the Banff murders closed." As if to emphasize the point he shut his notebook with a decisive snap.

"You think you know someone, and then you find you don't know them at all," mused Laura.

"Were you in love with Richard?" asked Karen. She and Laura were standing beside Karen's cruiser outside the administration building. The inspector and his detectives had gone back to the detachment office, where Jeremy was lodged in a holding cell.

"No, I wasn't. I was attracted to him, and I liked him a lot. He was wonderful company. But I was not in love with him. Thank God."

"Excuse me, Karen." It was Constable Peplinski, who Laura would always think of as having just left the farm. "Professor Norrington's prints are all over the manuscript we found in Madrin's studio."

Karen glanced at Laura. "That confirms your theory. Not that it needed any more confirmation."

"I remember once telling Richard that he was a writer because he wrote," said Laura. "And he didn't write one word! How's that for irony?" She managed a rueful little smile and said, "I'd like to see a copy of the manuscript."

When the constable confirmed that the fingerprint people were finished with it, Karen told him to make a copy for Laura. "I'm sure someone on the Centre's office staff will make you a copy," she said.

"I know just the person," he replied with a grin. "She works in the president's office."

"It would seem the gallant constable has made a conquest," smiled Laura as he hurried off.

"He usually does. I'll have the manuscript delivered to your studio if you like. It shouldn't take long."

The press was in a feeding frenzy on the day following Richard's grisly death and Jeremy's arrest. But it wasn't the multiple murders that excited their interest; it was the literary hoax. People love to see reputations shredded, to see the successful and famous brought down, thought Laura as she watched Norrington holding forth outside the Valentine Studio. The "No Trespassing" signs meant nothing to the voracious reporters. Laura had been on her way to her studio when she saw them, and she immediately melted into the shelter of the pines. From her place of concealment she heard Henry say into a forest of tape machines and microphones that the ghostwriter's trade was an ancient and honourable one.

Knowing that she would be a prime target for the media, Laura quietly retreated. She would thwart them by borrowing Kevin's car and driving aimlessly along the highway.

It was late afternoon when she returned, and when she gave the keys back to Kevin he told her that the horde of reporters had departed. "They really wanted to interview you," he added, "but they couldn't wait. They had to file their stories."

"Good. Then I guess it's safe for me to go to my room."

As she stepped out of the elevator on the sixth floor of the residence she saw Norrington, wearing a bathrobe, coming down the corridor on his way to his daily session in the pool.

" 'Fearful symmetry', indeed," she said as he stopped in front of her.

"William Blake. English poet. 1757 to 1827." replied Norrington. "From his poem *The Tiger.*"

"And also from page 91 of Richard's manuscript. Somehow I doubt that Richard was all that well acquainted with Blake's poetry. But you are. You've written a paper about William Blake."

Norrington merely smiled.

"Your fingerprints are all over the manuscript."

"They would be, wouldn't they?" he replied blandly. "Where are you going with this, Laura? By now the whole world knows I wrote those books of Richard's. For my sins," he added with mock piety.

"For a great deal of money, you mean. But I think there's more to it than that."

Hands stuffed into the pockets of his robe, Norrington peered expectantly at Laura through his thick eyeglasses. "Pray continue," he murmured in his best professorial tone.

"I spent two hours with that manuscript last night. It's first class, as I'm sure you know. Somewhere along the line, Henry, you lost your contempt for thrillers and began to really write."

"As always, you are very astute, Laura. I finally realized that there was nothing to be ashamed of in writing thrillers. Quite the contrary. And, as Richard never tired of pointing out, they outsold my other books by a wide margin. A very wide margin. This revelation, if you will forgive my using the term, occurred about midway through *The Blue Agenda.* The way in which sales are taking off is very flattering as well. I like to think the new book, of which you speak so kindly, shows me at the height of my powers. I am quite proud of it, in fact."

"So proud you decided to claim authorship."

"You continue to impress me, Laura. Might I ask what led you to the remarkable conclusion?"

"You were preparing the ground by leaving a trail of literary clues. Like the quote from Blake. There are a number of other expressions that, if they were put under a microscope, as in a court case for example, could be identified only as yours."

"Such as?"

"In the manuscript you describe a character as, 'Measuring his words like medicine from an eye-dropper.' A memorable description; it's also used in your essay on the reclusive Israeli philosopher, Eli Kaplan. It's in the library."

"All my writings are, I'm pleased to say." Norrington gave a gleeful little chuckle. "If my claim of authorship had ended up in court, I would have called you as a witness."

"It never would have gotten that far, Henry."

"What do you mean?"

"Have you forgotten what happened to Erika?"

For once, Norrington was speechless. He stared at Laura in mounting horror as the realization struck home.

"You tipped her off, didn't you?" asked Laura. "Erika I mean."

Norrington shook his head. His expression was returning to normal as he realized the danger was safely behind him. "No. Not directly, that is. I might have been a little careless, leaving manuscript pages lying around, and so on. But that's all."

"What will this do to your career as tenured professor, much-quoted philosopher, and literary guru?"

Norrington smiled complacently. "I have lived that life for many years. Now I find myself rather looking forward to my role as the creator of the best selling fictional hero, James Hunt, who is surely destined for a long and successful career in bookstores and on television screens."

The message light on Laura's telephone was blinking when she entered her room. The switchboard told her there was a message to call Geoff Hamilton in New York. He had left the number of both his hotel and his office. Since New York was two hours ahead, Laura tried the hotel first, but Geoff wasn't in his room. She reached him at his office.

"My God, Laura, what's been going on up there?"

"How much do you know?"

"Only what I can glean from the press reports. It's had a fair bit of coverage here, because so many of the players are American. Including yourself. And that business of Norrington writing Madrin's books is a hell of a story. I gather you were the one who solved the case?"

"I think I was more a catalyst than anything else. Does it help now that you know the identity of Erika's killer?"

"Yes. It does. I can begin to come to terms with what's happened." He paused and Laura could picture him shaking his head. "I can see that Switzer character doing what he did, but Richard Madrin! To think the guy had Erika killed just so people wouldn't find out he didn't write those books of his."

"I know. I didn't tumble on to that until the very end. Just before he tried to kill me. He must have been in an absolute state knowing that Erika was going to expose his secret to the world. Knowing Erika as he did, he would have realized that he couldn't buy her silence. That book and her scholastic reputation were much more important to her than money."

"You're absolutely right. Erika liked nice things, particularly clothes, but money never was a high priority for her. Just so she had enough to live on, buy a new outfit every so often, and do her research and writing."

"Exposure would make Richard a laughing stock. Not a criminal. Just a vain, foolish cheat. The very opposite of the image he portrayed to the world. He must have seen Jeremy's plan as the only way out of an intolerable situation."

"The poor man," muttered Geoff with bitter irony. After another pause, he continued, this time with a hint of excitement in his voice. "I had a phone call earlier today. From a professor of zoology at Columbia University. He and Erika were close. In fact, they had been lovers, but that was over sometime before I met her. They remained friends, and he and I get along just fine. He's spent the past month or so in the wilds of Brunei researching something — orangutans probably. Zoologists will never leave those poor animals in peace. Anyway, he's been completely out of touch, didn't know anything about what happened to Erika until he got back to the university and a colleague told him that she had been killed in a fire 'somewhere up in Canada.' It seems that before she left, the professor installed a remote access application on her computer which gave her the ability to logon to his local network server. By using his user ID and password, she could upload her material to his secure drive as back-up files."

"Are you telling me Erika's book is in this professor's computer in New York?"

"That's exactly what I'm telling you. When Ed — his name's Ed Godwin — booted his computer and called up the directory, he found twenty-four of her files. So she must have uploaded the chapters she had written before going up there, as well as what she wrote at the Centre. If there are twenty-four chapters the book must be pretty complete, don't you think?"

"I know she was awfully close. She was really driving herself the last couple of weeks."

"The last file was time stamped 1:26 a.m. on the morning of the fire. I asked Ed to read it. Apparently it's very long, so he skimmed through it and gave me the gist of it. It's the chapter that has all that business about Norrington writing Richard's books. According to Ed, her analysis is very convincing."

"So Erika's book survived. Will it be published?"

"Without question. It's the last and best thing I can do for her. One of New York's leading literary agencies is a client of my law firm, and I will put them on it. If it needs some editing, we'll hire an editor. With all the publicity about the murders, and that business about the professor being a ghostwriter, I expect publishers will be clamouring for it."

"Having her book published would have thrilled Erika. It's what she wanted more than anything else."

"I know. It'll be her dream come true."

And Richard's worst nightmare, thought Laura as she rang off. The humiliating tale of how he had bought the fame he couldn't achieve on his own would live on between the covers of a book.

Unable to sleep, Laura got out of bed and dressed in her painting clothes. Using her flashlight, she walked through the darkness to her studio. Her paintings sprang to vivid life when she switched on the lights. They were good. The best she had ever done. Pure and luminous, they stood apart from the human condition, with its greed and deadly vanity. Looking at them brought Laura a measure of serenity and peace. Placing a blank canvas on an easel, she picked up her palette and brush and began to paint.